AFTER THE WEDDING CAME THE MARRIAGE

P.S. I Love And Forgive You

STELLA LOUISE

This is a work of fiction. All of the characters, names, incidents, organizations, and dialogue in this novel are either the products of the author's imagination or are used fictitiously.

WestBow Press books may be ordered through booksellers or by contacting:

WestBow Press
A Division of Thomas Nelson & Zondervan
1663 Liberty Drive
Bloomington, IN 47403
www.westbowpress.com
1 (866) 928-1240

ISBN: 978-1-5127-3073-9 (sc)
ISBN: 978-1-5127-3074-6 (hc)
ISBN: 978-1-5127-3072-2 (e)

Library of Congress Control Number: 2016902248

Print information available on the last page.

WestBow Press rev. date: 1/13/2017

CONTENTS

CHAPTER 1

WHO DID IT?

This was a day most people dreaded. After receiving an emergency phone call on her cell phone, April rushed to the hospital to learn the fate of her husband. It was Friday evening, and April was in the middle of rush-hour traffic when she received the call. While she was on the way to the hospital, there was an accident a few miles ahead of her. A car ran into the back of a truck loaded with watermelons. The impact caused the melons to spill out onto the freeway, which brought traffic to a snail's pace. April's mind switched into panic mode.

Thinking to herself out loud, she said, "Paul is in the hospital. Paul is in the hospital. Why! Why would he be in the hospital?"

Quickly she tried to form a mental picture of a map of all the streets that would provide the quickest route to the hospital. When she passed the accident, she became even more panicky. Talking to herself was helping to calm her down. "You can do this, April. Just breathe. There is a good chance it is not serious."

She took the first exit off the freeway, which allowed her mental GPS to take over; however, she didn't know how many traffic lights and stops signs she would have to go through to get to her destination. Then she thought the freeway may have been better.

She told herself, "Do not second-guess yourself. I thought things like this only happened in the movies. God, this cannot be happening to me."

Each time she stopped at a traffic light, it felt like an eternity. While she waited at each light, she fought the temptation to visualize different possibilities for why her husband would be in the hospital. Each light lasted at least two minutes, but it felt like an hour before the light would change. She finally arrived."Oh, God, please help me find a parking place."

After spotting a family of four walking to their car, April followed them and waited for their parking space. Once the children were safely secured in their car seats, the family drove off, leaving the parking space for April.

She walked as fast as her feet could take her. Once she was inside, there was a large sign that gave directions to the emergency room, which she quickly followed. Once there, she joined the line. She was the tenth person just waiting for her turn to be helped.

Please, Lord, how much longer will I have to wait? she thought. Please let Paul be all right. Just let him be alive. What am I saying? Of course he is alive! I think I would have been told if he is dead. Just let him be all right, and please make sure that there is nothing seriously wrong with him.

Finally, it was her turn to receive help. The clerk looked at her and asked her how she could help her. Trying to keep her composure, she managed to say, "I am April Parker, and I was told my husband, Paul Parker, was brought here. Do you have any information on his condition and where he is?"

"I need to see your ID, and I need you to fill out this form. When you have finished, return it to me." April took the form and looked for a chair where she could sit to fill it out. As she surveyed the room for a chair, she saw there was one in the far corner waiting for her. As she walked to the chair, she softly said under her voice, "Thank You, Lord." Once seated, she carefully looked over the form.

There were two things April disliked doing—filling out forms and getting gas. These were her pet peeves. She would rather pick weeds than fill out forms. Nevertheless, this was for Paul.

After she had answered all the questions, April returned the form to the attending clerk. The clerk looked over the form and told her to take a seat. She said someone would be out to speak with her soon. Once again, she found herself waiting for answers, but she remembered the message from her daily devotional reading that gave her comfort:

God was the only one who had all the answers to her questions, and He would not forsake her. She sat back in her chair, but getting comfortable was impossible. She was too tense to do so. Only focusing on how God would not forsake her was helping her to relax. Before she realized it, the ER nurse came over to April and informed her of Paul's condition and what floor he was on.

"Mrs. Parker, I am Georgia, the ER nurse. Your husband is in surgery—"

"Surgery? My husband is having surgery? For what? Why is he having surgery?"

"Your husband is in surgery right now and will be transported to ICU once he is out of surgery. Apparently, your husband was shot."

"Shot! My husband has been shot! What do you mean shot? Shot with a gun? Why? Why would someone want to shoot Paul? How! How was he shot? Who did this? I do not understand." April could feel herself going into shock. She knew that she needed to listen, to receive and understand the information the nurse was giving her about what had happened to Paul.

"Mrs. Parker, your husband was shot twice, once in the stomach and once in the back. When you get to ICU, read this message to the nurse, and she will admit you in."

April read the message. "I do not understand this message. Why do I have to read this to the nurse before she will allow me to go in to see my husband?"

"This is a secured area, so this is a coded message that only you and the nurse will know. That is all the information I have about your husband. I hope he will recover from his injuries. Just take the elevator down the hall to the third floor. Once you are on the third floor, turn right. There will be double doors and a button on the right. Press the button, tell them your name, and then read the message. They will open the doors for you. I will let them know that you are on your way there. Someone will be waiting for you."

April took the card and thanked the nurse as she went to the elevator. She pressed the button that pointed up and waited for it to open to take her to the third floor. She was the only one on the elevator, and it took her directly to the third floor. She walked toward the double doors, pressed the button, read the message, and told the nurse she was Paul's wife. She could see a camera pointing in her direction. When the doors opened, she walked through. The ICU nurse, Nurse Williams, met April and showed her a place where she could put her things. She told April that Paul was still in surgery for two gunshot wounds and would be coming to the ICU when the surgery was completed.

"Who did this to my husband? Why was he shot?"

"Mrs. Parker, I'm sorry, but I won't be able to answer any of your questions related to the shooting. The police are the only ones who can answer those questions. I am sure they will be happy to help you learn the facts surrounding your husband's shooting, so you will need to contact them. The surgeon will be able to give you any information about the condition of your husband. I will keep you updated on your husband's progress once he is out of surgery."

April went to the seat where she had put her things. She buried her face in her hands as she thought about the events that had brought her to the hospital. As she raised her head, she thought about how she could do all things through Christ, who strengthened her. Then she noticed the area where she was in the ICU. From her view she could see rows of beds with patients in each one. Monitors made beeping sounds, and the beds were partitioned from the ceiling to the floor by curtains for privacy. The nurses were seated in the center of the room, and a system console gave them a view of all the patients and their monitors. The scenery was more depressing than comforting.

Paul was brought to the ICU. He had been heavily sedated, and IV tubes were connected to different parts of his body. Lying there, he looked more dead than alive. When he was brought to his area in ICU, he was connected to machines that would monitor his body's functions. Finally, April was able to see her beloved.

She bent down to kiss his face and whispered, "I love you."

A tall, olive-complexioned man covered head to toe with surgical clothing walked toward her. He introduced himself as Dr. Benjamin, the surgeon who had operated on Paul. She was expecting to see Paul's blood covering the doctor's clothing. It was a comfort when she did not see that.

"Mrs. Parker, I am Dr. Benjamin. I operated on your husband. We removed two bullets from your husband's stomach and chest."

"I thought he was shot in the stomach and back."

"No, we removed a bullet from his stomach and one from his chest. He will be heavily sedated for the rest of the evening, which will help him rest. This will be a good time for you to get some rest yourself. I will be in tomorrow to check his progress and to let you know when he will be able to leave ICU."

"Thank you, Dr. Benjamin. About what time will you be here to see Paul tomorrow?"

"I usually make my rounds between ten and eleven a.m."

"I will be here waiting to see you. There is so much I want and need to know. Right now I just cannot think. So much has happened. I still do not know who did this and why. Thank you, Doctor, for all you have done to save Paul's life. Thank you."

April took a seat by Paul's bed, held his hand, and prayed. Her praying was so intense that she was unaware when the nurse came in several times to check on Paul's vitals. As she sat holding Paul's hand, she looked out the window that was near Paul's bed. Even though it was late, there were several couples sitting in the patio area. One was an elderly couple eating. The way they ate and looked at each other, she knew they had been together for a long time. They tended to eat in rhythm, and they handed each other things without the other asking for them. They just knew what the other needed. There was another couple sitting across from the elderly couple. They seemed to have unresolved issues. It looked as if they were having a conversation while trying not to let others know they were in the middle of a disagreement. Then there was the couple who got April's attention. They seemed to be about the age that she and Paul were when they first met. Paul was tall and handsome with an athletic build. He looked as if he could pose as a model for a fashion magazine. But besides his good looks, he was a man of integrity. He was everything she wanted in a man. Because April was a petite woman, Paul always made her feel safe and secure, and he always let her know that she was beautiful and how much he wanted to share his life with her, which was very important to her. As she sat there, her mind went down memory lane to when she first met

Paul. That day would always be etched in her memory. She took her eyes off the couple and looked at Paul. He was truly the love of her life. She told herself to keep her thoughts focused on life, love, and doing things with Paul again.

When April passed out from exhaustion while sitting in the chair next to Paul, Nurse Williams came in, gently tapped her on the shoulder, and told her to go home to get some rest. If there was any change in his condition, she would be notified immediately. April made sure the hospital had both her cell and home phone numbers. She gently kissed him on the forehead and on the lips and whispered, "I will come to see you tomorrow. Please get better. I want to take you home."

Early the next morning, while lethargic and drowsy, April was awakened by a knock at the door. She grabbed a robe, a handful of breath mints, and a rubber band to put her hair up before she answered the door. She looked out the peephole and saw two men standing in view of the peephole. Even with the obscured view through the peephole, she gathered the two men were dressed in suits, waiting for someone to respond to their knocking. She was sure they were no one she knew personally. For her safety and precaution, she answered without opening the door. "Yes, who is there?"

"It is the Redlands Police. We are looking for Mrs. Parker, April Parker."

Still a little drowsy, April partly opened the door to get a better look at the men. When she did, one of the officers placed his badge out in front underneath his face so she would have an easy and clear view and could verify him as an officer.

"Good morning. Are you Mrs. Parker, April Parker?"

"Good morning. Yes, I am Mrs. Parker. Yes, yes, please come in."

She knew they had to be there about Paul being shot. She was glad they had come. Even so, she would have liked her appearance to look a little more put together, and she would have preferred to have a written list of questions ready for them to answer. When she opened the door, Detective Wilson and his partner introduced themselves. Now she actually got a better look at the two men. She wanted to make sure to have a mental image of the men and their names for future reference. She was little more alert, but was her attention enough for the information they were going to give her about the shooting? She thought to herself whether or not she should take the time to make coffee, and then she asked the officers if they would like coffee. "I am glad you are here," she said.

"Mrs. Parker, I am Detective Wilson, and this is my partner, Detective Miller. Is Paul Parker your husband?"

"Yes, he is."

"We are here, Mrs. Parker, to ask you some questions about the shooting that took place yesterday at the Chic Boutique."

"As I said before, I am glad you are here. I have questions myself that I want to ask you about the shooting. You said you have questions to ask me? I thought you would be here to give me information of what happened yesterday. What questions do you have to ask me? I don't know anything about what happened. I believe it was the police who called me."

"Mrs. Parker, how long have you and your husband been married?"

"For thirteen years."

"Does your husband work at the Chic Boutique?"

"Yes."

"How long has he worked at the boutique?"

"He has worked there for about fifteen years."

"What does your husband do at the boutique?"

"He is a manager."

"How long has he been a manager?"

"I believe he's been a manager for about five years. I do not understand why you are you asking me these kind of questions. How will this tell me who shot my husband and why? I want to know who did this to him and why!"

"Do you know if your husband has any enemies?" one asked.

"Do you know of anyone who would want your husband dead?" then the other asked. "Mrs. Parker, has your husband been arrested before? Does he have a criminal record?"

"No! No! My husband does not have any enemies. My husband is not that kind of a person. I do not understand! Are you telling me that my husband has enemies who want him dead? I thought I would be the one asking the questions. Why are you not giving me information about this shooting? You are making my innocent husband sound like a criminal. Your questioning insinuates he has committed some kind of crime."

Before April could finish answering the questions, the phone rang. "Please excuse me." Once her conversation on the phone was over, she informed the police that the hospital has just called and that she needed to leave. She could not continue their conversation, but she felt like she was being interrogated. She told them that they would have to return at a later date. Detective Wilson reached inside his suit jacket. He took out a business card from the inside pocket and gave it to April. He explained to her that they wanted to return to continue the questioning. If her husband remembered anything that happened to him, they wanted her to call the number on the card. She looked at the men to let them know she understood what they expected of her. She took the card and thanked them. They thanked her for her cooperation and left. She was glad she did not have to continue this interrogation. She'd learned nothing about the shooting, and she did not want to be alone when she answered their questions without Paul being there with her. All the same, if the hospital was calling, that meant Paul's condition had changed. Was it for the better, or had his condition worsened?

Because of the chaos that was happening in their lives, April had completely forgotten to return May and June's calls. It had been a year since April had seen them. Years ago after their college graduation, they made a pact to meet every year at Camp Pendleton Marine Base in Oceanside, California. This year she was determined not to let another year pass without them keeping their pact.

When June's father retired from the US Marines, her family went camping on the marine base to end their summer vacation every year since junior high. While she was in college, the year she met June and April, she invited them for a weekend excursion on the beach at the base. They split the cost to rent a bungalow for a few days. It was a great time for them to just relax from the stress of their hectic schedule. After the first experience as a group, they knew this was something they wanted to continue to enjoy together. After the third time, they made a decision to get together once a year to see each other. This has helped them keep in touch over the years. There had been many challenges that almost prevented them from meeting, but somehow they still managed to get together, even though they lived in different parts of California.

May traveled out of the state for her job as a consultant for a pharmaceutical company. She had worked as a consultant for about eight years. She enjoyed the traveling and the different people she would meet, especially the guys. There was never a boring moment for her when she went out of town.

There was always someone waiting for her to come into town, looking her up to socialize. There was a time when it was unimaginable that she would give this life up. In spite of that, it was beginning to become tiresome. She was the only one of the three who was not married. She'd had countless offers, but no one gave her the feeling of butterflies in her stomach, letting her know intuitively she had found the right one. One would think that with her looks and beauty, which many compared to superstar Beyoncé's, she could have any man she wanted. However, her taste in men had always been problematic. After years of dating different men, she knew she wanted someone in her life like the men April and June had in theirs. But that perfect man would give her a relationship more like April had with Paul. In short, she found herself wanting a husband, one who would want to have that same kind of relationship.

Whenever she was in town, she would let them know. She had made a very important decision, a decision that they needed to know about. She e-mailed June two weeks ago to let her know she had arranged her schedule so that she would be in town for their retreat.

June was the one who would organize the yearly retreat. She would make sure when and where they would meet her so that they could get on base. She enjoyed doing this. Organizing and planning was her expertise. After helping her husband start their own business designing websites, she had learned a great deal in how to research by surfing the Web. Having the looks of a fashion model, she went to college to study fashion design. Always knowing what was in style and what the latest fashion was. She knew what to wear and what not to wear, what colors went together during what season. As the campus fashion police, June knew her stuff. She was always right. When someone needed help with what to wear on a date or what to wear to a job interview, depending on the type of interview, the person would consult her. She had mastered the skill of fashion. Getting married changed her proficiency in fashion to being an expert in website designing. She was so looking forward to seeing the girls again and sharing all the latest news with them about becoming an aunt.

June wanted to get an early start on her day. She always started her day by checking her e-mails. She had gotten an e-mail from May letting her know when she would be in town, and she put the retreat date on her calendar. After she finished reading the e-mail, she noticed that she had not received an e-mail from April. She e-mailed May back to let her know how good it would be to see her and show her pictures of her new niece. It turned out that she had not heard from April either, but she would try to call April later in the week.

When June had not heard from April, she called May to let her know.

"Hello, May."

"Hello, June, what's up?"

"I wanted to let you know I still have not heard from April." May could hear the concern in June's voice. "She still has not e-mailed or called me. I think I will try again today to call her on both her cell and home number. This is so not like her. I will call you later today and let you know what happens." Later that evening June called May to let her know what happened when she tried to contact April. "Hello, May."

"Hello, June. Were you able to reach April today?"

"Yes."

"You heard from April? Is she all right? Is there something wrong?"

"Paul is in the hospital," May told her.

"Paul is in the hospital? For what? What happened? How is April?"

"May, I am sorry, but I do not have much information to give to you," May interrupted.

"When did you speak to her?"

"This morning when I called, she was at the hospital. She could not talk then, because she was with the doctor or doctors. I did not understand that part. Just the same, she told me she would try to call me later. The call was very short, so I did not get much information from her. That must be why I have not received an e-mail from her. Plus she doesn't have my new cell number."

"When she does call, please let me know. Better still, see if we could have a conference call. I want to know everything."

June reassured her that she would do just that.

* * *

April was so relieved to get to the hospital to see Paul. She prayed the whole way there that Paul's condition had improved. Her timing was perfect. Dr. Benjamin was doing his rounds. When she came into Paul's room, she found Dr. Benjamin standing at his bedside while Paul was asleep.

"Good morning, Mrs. Parker. It is good to see you."

"Good morning, Dr. Benjamin. How is Paul's condition? When will he be able to leave the hospital?"

"Paul's condition is improving, but he is still not out of the woods. We think all the precancerous lesions were removed when we were in surgery removing the bullets."

"What do you mean? Paul had cancer? What kind of cancer did you remove?"

"When we removed the bullet from his stomach, we found your husband had several premalignant carcinoma lesions, small growths on his stomach. We got it just in time before it became malignant. Your husband is a very brave and lucky man. I do not meet many people like your husband. We will keep a close watch over him. We're giving him the best medical care."

April told the doctor how grateful she was. "Thank you so very much doctor. I know I speak for Paul in expressing our gratitude for all you have done." April found some comfort from talking with the doctor. Now she had a better understanding of Paul's condition. She did not want to think about all the doctor had said. *To think that he had cancer and two bullets inside of him.* This was just too much for her to think about now. Despite that, was this shooting a blessing? If Paul had not gotten shot, the doctor's would not have found the precancerous lesions and stopped them from metastasizing. This was too much to think about and understand. Knowing God was in control gave her some comfort and eased her mind. Now she could focus her attention on other things, like how to be more cooperative with the police. She needed to remember that their purpose was to learn who committed this crime against Paul. She just wanted to see Paul and tell him how much she loved him. She stayed by his bedside, waiting for him to open his eyes. She wanted to be the first person he saw when he opened them.

It had been about a couple of days since the shooting, and Paul's condition was improving each day. Even so, his strength was not completely there. His body had been through a great deal of trauma, and April was hoping today would be a good day to learn more about the shooting. She noticed that right after breakfast was a good time for Paul. His first meal of the day seemed to energize him. After their morning hug and kiss, April stood at the side of Paul's bed, put her hands into his, looked him in his eyes, and gently said to him, "Paul, I did not want to bother. Well, I mean badger you with questions about what happened. You have been so weak. I know this will not be easy for you, but what happened? Do you remember what happened? Who did this to you? Who shot you? Why would someone want to do this to you?"

Paul carefully raised his bed to better position himself to talk with April. While still in much pain, he took his time to speak. As he thought about the questions, his memory of the shooting was slowly coming back to him. "I was not the intended person. I think it was a mistake of identity. After I got my things together, I started turning off the lights to leave. Then two men came in. Well, I think they did not come completely in, but they were standing in the hallway under the security light or night light. And one of them spoke, simply saying, 'Eric, this is for you.' The next things I heard were two shots. Then I felt pain in my chest. Becky came in and called the police. I do not think I was the intended victim. I think Eric was. They were looking for Eric."

"Eric? Eric Bishop? You mean your boss? Why would someone want to kill Eric?" she said. "Have you seen them before?"

"Yes, well, one of them. The other man I don't think I have ever seen before. Or maybe I did and do not remember. Maybe I didn't get a good look. I can't remember. I do not know. It was dark. Well, I think it was dark. It all happened so fast. Someone spoke. Then there was a flash of light. The next thing I know, I am on the floor in a lot of pain and trying to breathe."

Holding Paul's hands more tightly, she softly said, "That's okay, my love. Just take your time. Take it slow."

"But the other man, yes, I think I do remember. Yes, I have seen him before. I believe I saw him several times at the boutique talking to Eric."

April moved from Paul's bed and sat in the recliner a few feet from his bed. Then she asked,"Where is Eric? You know, he has not been here to visit you. I know the police will be here any day now. I have tried to keep them away from you. Well, until you were stronger. A Detective Wilson came to see me right after the shooting and was questioning me. Or should I say, he was interrogating me. I did not like the sort of questions he was asking and the way he was questioning me. I felt he was insinuating that you were a criminal. You know he will be here to continue the interrogation, don't you?"

"Yes, I know. Who else knows about the shooting? So you have not heard from Eric?

"No. You would think he would have been here by now."

"Was it in the papers?"

"I do not know. I have not had the time to read the papers. May and June have been trying to call me. I totally forgot that it is time for our annual retreat at Camp Pendleton. With so much going on, I'm not sure I want to go. I'm not sure I need to go either."

"You and the ladies met last year, right?"

"Yes, that's right, but we can meet later. I can call and ask them to do that. This will not be the first time we have not been able to meet."

"So what is keeping you from meeting this year?"

"As if I need to explain why. Do you think I am going to leave you here alone while I go on a retreat? Not on your life! I want to make sure you are getting the best medical care while you are here. I want to take you home ASAP. Paul, your body has been through a great deal of trauma. Remember: the doctors took not only two bullets out of your body but precancerous lesions as well. So you need to take it slow. Recovery will take time."

As Paul reached out to her, he said, "Yes, I know, my love. I am in no rush to say the least, although I do think that you should go on the retreat with June and May. You yourself have been through so much as well. Coming out here every day to visit with me and talking to the police—this has been as stressful for you as it has been for me. Now, Nurse Williams will make sure I get all my meds, therapy, and anything else I am in need of. You have your cell phone, and we can still call each other. It is not like you will be gone a month or more. It will only be for a few days for you to relax and rest. Do it for me, okay?"

April walked over to Paul, cupped his face in her hands, and softly said, "Okay, my love."

When June and May finally reached April, they wanted to know everything that had happen to Paul. June thought that seeing one another would be the best thing to do. So they all decided to keep their date at the beach. Everyone would meet June in Old Town at the coffee shop. They would wait until after rush-hour traffic and leave their cars at the plaza. Then they could carpool in June's SUV. Before they reached the marine base, they stopped to get dinner. Dinner consisted of a couple of sandwiches, some hot chocolate, Hershey's chocolate bars, graham crackers, and marshmallows to make some s'mores.

When they were taking their luggage out of the SUV, a man drove up and sold them some firewood. They all thought a fire in the fire pit on the beach would be great. Once everyone was settled, they made their fire, made the hot chocolate to have with the sandwiches and s'mores for dessert, and then sat around the fire to talk. Catching up with one another was short-lived. They all wanted to hear April's story about what had happen to Paul.

May told April that nothing much was happening in their lives that needed to be discussed in detail, nothing that was a life-and-death situation. June agreed. Since they did not have any details about what had happened to Paul, they wanted to learn, so they were all ears. May started the conversation when she politely said, "April, tell us everything that happened to Paul."

June added, "And we mean everything. Don't leave anything out."

April had prepared herself for this moment, not for herself but for them. She had prayed to God for wisdom about what to say to them, so hopefully they would see how He was working through the situation.

"Well, Paul was working late. He was getting his things together to leave, and he was turning off the lights. Then two men came into the room and said, 'Eric this is for you.' They shot Paul twice. Paul does not remember much after that, except the receptionist, Becky, calling the ambulance and the police. I am just grateful God was with him and was watching over him." June wanted to know if the police had any information on the identity of the two men. May asked if they knew why the men wanted to kill Paul.

April now was in her own thoughts. She walked toward the ocean while tears started to fall down her cheeks. It was the first time she was able to cry about the situation. June and May followed her. As May walked beside her, she handed her a napkin to wipe the tears from her face. April took the napkin and said, "Yes, I want to know what happened. I am grateful that he is alive. I know I needed to be strong for him as he tries to get well and learn who and why someone wanted to do this. I am grateful God is with us. I need to know how God wants us to handle this and what He wants us to learn from this. I know that there is a purpose for this, even though we do not know it now. Right now this is so much to take in. I need to prepare myself to be there for Paul and learn why all this has happened."

"Who shot him, and why?" June asked. "Do you have an idea who this Eric is?" April wanted to speak in a soft voice, but the waves of the ocean were making it difficult to do so. The sound of the waves was relaxing her, but speaking over them was burdensome. She thought to herself about how God was comforting her in so many ways. He wanted her to know that His presence was always with her. He was not going to leave her. June continued in her line of questioning. "What did you tell them?"

"I only told them that I was Paul's wife. I did not say much, because the hospital called to let me know Paul's condition had changed. I really do not know much, but Paul and I do know that those men were not trying to kill Paul. They wanted to kill Eric."

June asked again, "Who is this Eric?"

"He is Paul's boss. He is one of the owners of the boutique. I do not know the answers to most of your questions. I just know Paul is improving with time, thank God."

Then May said, "Why do you have to bring God into everything? If God was there, maybe Paul would not have gotten shot."

June was beginning to feel somewhat uncomfortable with where this was going and decided to change the subject. "Well, the most important thing is that Paul is doing better. Isn't that right, April? Paul is doing better?"

"Yes, he is. The doctor who did the surgery, Dr. Benjamin, informed me that they not only removed the bullets, but they also took out precancerous lesions."

May said, "Paul had cancer."

June repeated the question, "Paul has cancer?"

April corrected them. "No, Paul had precancerous lesions. He does not have them now. The doctors were able to remove all of them when they removed the bullets. You can say that if Paul had not been shot, we would not have known he had precancerous lesions. Now, while Paul is recovering from the shooting, our concern is the police's interrogation. When they questioned me, I felt they are insinuating Paul had something to do with the shooting. I just do not want this to get in the way of Paul getting better and cause him to have a setback."

June encouraged April to keep the faith. When June said this, May looked away with a sarcastic expression that suggested the statement was ridiculous. The gesture made June feel uncomfortable. They stayed on the beach until curfew. On the way back to the cottage, May remembered she had to make a phone call. She told the girls that she would meet them at the cottage. June told April that she was not a religious person, but she would pray for her and Paul. She felt somewhat obligated to apologized for May's behavior. "You know how May is about religion and God. She seems to hate any and everything that has to do with God, and she does not like or want the name of Jesus mentioned around her at all. Sometimes I cannot figure her out. Anyway, I do hope Paul will get better. Just keep us up to date."

After her excursion April arrived at the hospital to visit with Paul. She wanted to let him know that the police had called and wanted to know if his condition had improved. To her surprise, the police were there visiting with Paul.

"Hello, Mrs. Parker. It is good to see you again. I was—"

April interrupted the detective, "Detective Wilson, when I spoke with you the other day on the phone, I told you what Paul remembered. I thought you wanted me to call you if my husband remembered anything else. I did inform you that my husband is not strong enough to be questioned. So why are you here? I did informed you that he is fighting for his life and was not in any condition to be interrogated."

"Yes, ma'am, I know. I called before I came. The hospital told me that you were out of town and did not give me a number to reach you. So I left a message for Mr. Parker and a number where he could reach me once he felt better and wanted to talk." April turned around and looked at Paul with a wife's look that said more than words could.

"You called him to talk?"

Paul gives his wife a look that told her everything would be all right.

"Yes, dear, I wanted to. No, I needed to get this over with and hopefully learn why this has happened." April's response cleared the air of any hostile feelings.

"All right, dear, if this is what you want."

Detective Wilson was ready to make progress on the case and proceed with his questions. "Mr. Parker, may I call you Paul?"

"Yes, please do."

"Do you know Eric Bishop?" Paul learned to only answer the questions that they asked and not to give any more information no matter how much he thought he knew.

"Yes, I know Eric Bishop."

"What is your association with Mr. Bishop?"

"He is my boss."

"Where do you work for Mr. Bishop?"

"I work at the Chic Boutique."

"How long have you worked for Mr. Bishop?"

"I have worked there for about fifteen years."

"How did you come to work for him?"

Paul paused. He knew that just answering this question would take more than a simple response. He was sure that if the detective already knew the answer to the question. He was sure the questions were meant only to confirm what they did know, and he was getting the feeling that they knew everything about him.

"Several years ago I worked for a jewelry store while I was going to college," he started. "It was supposed to help me pay my tuition. But somehow I accumulated a gambling debt, and my creditors were ready for me to pay up. Some of my associates knew about my dilemma and were more than willing to help me out. What I did not know was how long and how they had planned to do this. Unbeknownst to me, they were planning to rob the jewelry store where I worked. I was working the holidays when the store stayed open late and we made large amounts of cash during the week. Well, this weekend it had snowed, and we left the cash and receipts in the vault at the store until Monday. To this day, I do not know how they knew when the owner, Mr. Ruben, would go to the bank to make the deposits. I did not know this myself. There were certain things only Mr. Ruben did himself. Anyway, one of my partners …I mean associates, Billy, better known as Bird-eye, came in that week to look at a ring for his girlfriend. At the time only Mr. Ruben and I were left at the store. His wife had left earlier that day to do some last-minute shopping, and she would return later to pick him up and help him close the store. While Mr. Ruben was assisting Bird-eye, I was gathering the day's receipts together when a car horn started going off. I went outside to see what was wrong. The noise stopped, so I went to the coffee shop next door to get some coffee. As I was returning, I notice the door was locked and the blinds were closed. I shook the doorknob, and then I heard a gunshot. I ran to the back and saw a car drive off. When I went in, I saw Mr. Ruben lying on the floor in a puddle of blood. I called the ambulance and the police. Mr. Ruben survived the shooting. I was left to help Mrs. Ruben to manage the store while Mr. Ruben recuperated.

"In the meanwhile, my gambling debt was paid anonymously. By the time I had learned the debt was paid, the police were at my dorm, letting me know I was under arrest and reading me my rights. I was totally in shock. I didn't know why I was being arrested. When you looked at the evidence, which was very incriminating, it was difficult for me to explain how my friend Bird-eye could rob the jewelry store without my knowledge. But the most damaging evidence against me was that my gambling debt was paid off anonymously. When the case went to court, the jury ruled that I was an accessory to the crime. I pled innocent, but it did not matter. I was not a part of the crime no matter what the evidence was or tried to prove, but the police thought I was in on the robbery.

"Nevertheless, Mr. Ruben came to see me while I was in prison and told me he believed that I was innocent. He counseled me about the friends I had, letting me know that I needed to change my life. He shared Christ with me, and I accepted Him into my life. What did I have left? I lost my scholarship for school and my job. Living in a small community, I lost my integrity.

"After I did my time, I returned to the neighborhood and looked for work. My parents told me about a job fair at the community center. I went, and that was when I met Eric. He saw me and called me over. He seemed to know who I was. Later he reminded me that we had once been classmates. We had taken several classes together. He told me he had heard about what happened and wanted to know if I was looking for a job. I told him that I was. He informed me that his father needed someone to help in one of his stores. He let me know that it was an entry-level position with some benefits, but he said there would be an opportunity for me to work my way up. I had been looking for months for a job, and no one was willing to give me one, especially after I had done time in prison. I took it and was grateful."

"Did his father know about your criminal record?" Paul was beginning to feel weak. He lay back in his bed, and April held his hand. Detective Wilson could see that Paul was getting weak, and he let him know that he only had a few more questions.

Paul told him that he was not sure whether Eric's father knew about his imprisonment. "It never came up. Mr. Bishop liked my work and made me manager of several of his stores. Not having finished college, I thought I had a good future working for the Bishops. I felt that I had my integrity, and that was more valuable than money.

"What did Eric do?" Paul took a minute to collect his breath. April was getting concerned and held his hand tighter.

"Detective, I would appreciate it if you would come back another time. Paul needs his rest." Detective Wilson agreed. He thanked Paul and April. He and the other officer left. Paul lay back in his bed, and April told him to rest and said she would return tomorrow.

The next day April came to visit Paul and found him looking and feeling much better. She wanted to know how he rested last night, and if he had talked with his doctor. After lunch Detective Wilson returned and told the Parkers that his visit would be short. He wanted to know how much of Eric's personal life Paul knew about. Paul explained that since Eric was a buyer for his father's clothing stores, they did not see much of each other.

"Eric is a buyer for his father, who had a line of ladies clothing stores that were upscale boutiques. He spent most of the time out of town, looking for new clients and merchandise. We went out once or twice for beers after work. That was about it. We did not socialize. I must say I was somewhat surprised when he invited me to his wedding."

"Why is that?"

"Well, Eric did not seem like the marrying kind, but he not only invited me. He also wanted to know if I would be in the wedding. He said one of the escorts had to drop out at the last minute and wanted to know if I could take his place. I must admit that I felt somewhat obligated. He did help me get a job, and it was the opportunity of a lifetime. Besides, I was happy to do it. It was a way to say thank you."

"Did your friendship grow after that?"

"No, it did not. Well, not socially."

"Did you know his fiancé?"

"No, not personally. I only saw and met her at the wedding rehearsal and at the wedding. There were a few times she came to the boutique to see Eric, and there were times when she came to some of the office parties. She seemed to be a very nice person. They both seemed to be very much in love."

"How did his father feel about Eric?"

"I do not know."

"Is the main store where you work?"

"Yes."

"How many people are employed there?"

"Four cashiers, three stock persons, one driver, and a receptionist."

"Who was working on the day of the shooting?"

"I don't know. I mean, I don't remember. Wait. Becky did. She came to work. She is the only one I can remember who came to work that day. She was the one who called the police and an ambulance."

"How long has she worked for you?"

"I cannot remember."

"How often did Eric work at the main boutique?"

"He was here about three to five days a week."

"Did he ever discuss his personal life with you?"

"No, like I said before, our relationship was strictly business."

"What kind of boss was Eric?"

"He was okay. There have been times when his wife would call, and he wanted me to tell her that he was at work when he wasn't."

"So how did you handle that?"

"I let him know that I didn't lie for anyone."

"What did he do?"

"He said fine and left it at that."

"Did he ask you again after that?"

"No."

"Who is Nicole Warner?"

"Nicole Warner, she is one of the buyers for the stores in Orange County. Eric mentioned to me that she was going to assist him in opening several stores in New York."

"Do you have any idea where Eric was on the night of the shooting?"

"He went to New York on business. He went to look at two buildings for two stores he was planning on opening this year."

"When was he due to return?"

"He was only going to be there for a few days. He had shown me pictures from an e-mail that he had gotten from the person who wanted to sell him the buildings. I am sure Eric could answer your questions better than I could. I mean, I don't know all that Eric was involved in. He should be back by now or any day."

"I want to thank you for taking the time to answer my questions. I will not trouble you anymore. However, I received information earlier today that Eric was killed in a car accident two days ago. His body was identified this morning."

"Eric is dead?"

"I am sorry to have to tell you this, but I needed to know what you knew about him. I hope I did not upset you, but I wanted to let you know what happened to him."

April asked, "What about the shooting? Does this mean the case is closed, Detective?"

"No, ma'am. Someone tried to kill your husband, thinking it was Eric. I still need to know what else Eric was involved in and who would want him dead. Are you sure that there is nothing else you would like to tell us that will help in this case?"

"Like what? I think I told you all I know."

"Did Eric have any money problems?"

Paul looked at the floor to think, and then he looked up. "Well, one day a man came to see Eric. I think his name was Bruce. I saw from a distance that they were having an argument. When the man was leaving, he turned around and looked back at Eric. Then he said in a loud voice that he wanted his money and he wanted it now. Then he left."

Detective Wilson told Paul that he had been very helpful and that he should please call him if he recalled anything that would help in the case. He gave him one of his business cards and thanked them both again and left.

CHAPTER 2

THE PACKAGE

Denise was trying not to lose hope in her marriage. She really wanted to make the marriage work. She was trying everything she could to make Eric happy—everything from breakfast in bed to short excursions to going to sporting events to seeing his favorite team play at the sports bar, which was her least favorite thing to do. Being in an environment completely dominated by males made her feel invisible. Still, she wanted to understand the sports of his interest desperately. She wanted him to know that she truly wanted to be a part of his world. There were times when she found herself at these events, hoping to make a favorable impression in order to please him. Nothing seemed to work. There were times when Eric would seem so distant from her. She started going to a marriage counselor. She thought maybe she was the problem. One day she thought she would surprise him by taking him out to lunch at his favorite restaurant, Mamma's Handmade Delights. She put on his favorite dress and got her hair done. She wanted everything to be perfect, just the way Eric would want it. She really wanted this to be special. When she came to his office, she was told that he was out on a business call. She waited in his office for several hours, hoping he would return soon to experience her informal date. She tried calling him several times on his cell, but it would go to the voice mail. So she decided to go to Mamma's Handmade Delights and bring dinner home. She thought that maybe he would be tired and would prefer to have a nice relaxing dinner at home together. She got his favorite dish with dessert and wine. When Eric got home, he was somewhat surprised. She gave him all of her attention. He seemed to enjoy all she had done to make the evening special. She asked about his day. He just said he was in a long, boring meeting all day. It gave her hope to see him enjoying the evening. She hoped this would be an evening that would bring the two of them closer together, though it would be short-lived.

One day while doing their bills, Denise noticed a bank statement that said there had been a withdrawal of five thousand dollars from their savings. It was a special account that they were using to save money to build their dream home. When she went to Eric and inquired about the withdrawal, he became very angry and irritated. Then they started to argue. Denise was angry and hurt because they had an agreement not to use the money for anything else. They had also agreed that if there was a need to make a withdrawal from the account, they both had to agree about it. Eric never mentioned the withdrawal to her or told her what the money was for. He did not answer any of her questions. He just got his coat and told her that he needed to get some air and left. Denise was hurt, angry, and confused. Why would he do something like that and not talk to her about it? He made her feel as if she had done something wrong, as if the argument was her fault. When he returned later that night, Denise apologized for upsetting him. She did not want to do anything to upset him. She just wanted to work things out. Eric told her that he needed the money for business and that he was going to replace it. He told her it would be better for him if they discussed this at another time. He had had a long day, and he wanted to get some sleep because he had an early flight in the morning.

It was getting late, and Eric did not want to miss his flight. He wanted to know if Denise would take him to the airport. Then he wouldn't have to waste time looking for a parking place to leave the car at the airport. He misplaced his flight itinerary, so he said he would call her once he got to New York to let her know when he would be returning. As he was getting out of the car, Denise told him that she was sorry for their argument last night. She loved him and wanted him to be safe, and they kissed each other and said good-bye.

When Denise got home, she cleaned the house, did some shopping, had a light dinner, and went to bed. The next day she started her day by listening to her phone messages. Eric called while she was out shopping, and he gave her his flight information and when he would be returning home.

After she came home from work, Denise decided to go to the movies and have dinner with her girlfriends. A girl's night out was something she really needed. It wasn't until the next day that she learned she had a message from the New York Police Department. She called right away. They informed her that there had been a car accident and that Eric had been killed.

Nothing could have prepared her for this. She felt like dying. She was glad that there hadn't been any angry feelings between them the last time they saw each other. They had reconciled. She had dreamt of a life with Eric. They would have children, build their dream house, and grow old together. Now all of that would never happen. How could she live without Eric? She did not want to.

Before the funeral Denise had to go to New York alone to identify Eric's remains. There was not much left to identify, only what Eric was carrying on him. His wallet had been thrown out of the car from the impact. Apparently, it was not on him. The police thought it may have been lying on the seat during the accident. How else could it have been thrown out of the car? It was just too overwhelming for Eric's parents to go with her. She thought it may have been a good idea that they did not accompany her to New York. Seeing Eric's remains would have been devastating for them. After the funeral Denise took some time off from work to grieve Eric's death. She spent most of her time looking at pictures of the different places that they visited and the souvenirs they had collected together—moments that she would always treasure in her heart. She could not stop herself from watching their favorite videos and listening to their favorite music. Grieving was very difficult and emotionally painful.

One day after Denise returned home from getting something to eat, she found a package that the UPS person had left by the door. She picked up the package, the mail, and the mail from Eric's post office box. Once she was inside, she put everything on the kitchen bar. She poured a glass of wine to have with her dinner. She turned on some jazz and dimmed the lights. She would read her mail and open the package later. When she had finished part of her meal, she decided to open the package. She knew the mail was mostly bills and advertisements, so she would open them last. She looked to see who had sent the package. It was from the Trump International Hotel in Las Vegas, and they had sent it to Eric. She took the package and held it close to her chest. She closed her eyes as she held the package. It was as if she was holding Eric in her arms. Tears started to come down her cheeks. She moved the package from her chest and looked at it. She wondered, *What could possibly be inside?* She slowly tore the wrapping away. Once the wrapping had been removed, she opened the package. She could see it was a gift. She removed the tissue paper that concealed the gift. She lifted the article from the box. She was completely speechless. It was the most beautiful negligee she had ever seen. The dim lighting made the garment glow. She held it tightly to her chest. It was as if she had a piece of Eric with her, and he was pressed to her heart now. Also she found a bottle of For Her Scent Only, a $685 bottle of perfume. She opened it. She let her body, soul, and mind take it all in. The scent had full control of her. She was making memories of the moment. She never wanted to forget this moment in her life. She felt as if she was being hypnotized. These were articles of love from Eric. She tried on the negligee and scented her body with the perfume. She told herself that these were things Eric had brought for her. Now his presence had filled the room. She looked in the mirror and softly said, "How do you like it, Eric? Thank you. I will cherish it always." She lay down on his side of the bed, scenting his pillow with the fragrance of the perfume, and she went to sleep. The next day when she woke up, the perfume scent still filled the room. It was the best sleep she had had since his death. She felt good for a short time. She looked in the mirror again at the negligee. It was even more beautiful than she had remembered it was last night.

While she was enjoying the gifts, she decided to read yesterday's mail. There were several bank statements. She opened each one while humming to herself. She noticed that one of the statements was from a bank where they did not bank. She took a glance at the name on the statement and knew right away that she had someone else's mail. She went through the other mail and told herself she would return it to the post office later. As she was picking up the wrappings from the negligee and perfume, she noticed that a card had come with the gifts.

She smiled as she bent down to pick it up. It said, "For you, my sweet, with all my heart. Let's build a life together in love. From Eric to the one I deeply cherish, Nicole." It was in Eric's handwriting. Denise went into shock. All she could focus on was one word—*Nicole*. She said out loud, "Nicole! Who is Nicole? No! No! Eric, you were not having an affair on me! This cannot be true. No, no, this cannot be happening!" She simply went crazy. She ripped the negligee off. Then she picked up the perfume bottle and threw it against the wall. She screamed, "No, no, no!" She threw anything and everything she got her hands on. After the trauma of learning what Eric had done and the tantrum that followed, she fell to the floor, completely exhausted, crying uncontrollably. Her pain quickly became rage. Words she would not normally use entered her thoughts. She calmed herself down and started to think out loud, "You can do this. You can do this. You will get through this." She got up from the floor and started to straighten up the room. As she was picking up the mail, she stopped and looked at the name on the bank statement again, the one she thought had been sent to the wrong address. It was addressed to Nicole Warner and Eric Bishop. She could not believe what she was looking at. She had not seen Eric's name the first time she had looked at the statement. She opened it and read the information on the statement. It was a joint checking account with a deposit of $5,000.. In fact, the money had been deposited around the time she had questioned Eric about the withdrawal from their joint account a few weeks ago. From the statement she could see trips to Las Vegas, Florida, clothing stores, and restaurants. She knew this was the business he was talking about. This was the money they had been saving for their dream house. She thought out loud, "Who was this Nicole, Nicole Warner?" She spoke to the statement as if it was a person. "Nicole Warner, I am going to find out who you are, and I will get you for this." She started to cry again and said, "My husband is dead. My marriage was dead, and now I am dying."

Later that day Denise managed to listen to her calls. One call was from the Trump International Hotel in Las Vegas. The hotel called to informed Eric that he did not put an address on the card, so they didn't know where to mail his gift. The cashier called the contact number he had left with the hotel to get his home address. The hotel also wanted him to know how much they enjoyed serving him and that they mailed his order from the hotel's boutique as he had requested. They hoped he enjoyed his stay in the penthouse, and the hotel was looking forward to having the pleasure of serving him again, hopefully in the near future. Eric had purchased the negligee for $85 and the perfume for $685 in Las Vegas for his mistress while they stayed in a penthouse. "Who does he think he is, J. D. Rockefeller or Donald Trump?" She went through the mail again to get a better look at the bank statement and see what purchases he had made and where. The Bank of America statement showed the time when Eric went to the Trump International Luxury Hotel in Las Vegas, which was a charge of more than two thousand dollars. As she continued to look at the statement, she saw other charges made within that same week for restaurants and shows. It looked like a weekend of fun at upscale shops, restaurants, and casinos—approximately five thousand dollars of fun spent with his mistress, Nicole. Denise sat for a long time, wondering why Eric would want to have an affair. What was wrong with her? Was she not pretty enough, small enough? What did this woman have that she did not? Denise said her thoughts out loud, "My husband, that's what." The second call got her attention and left her wondering.

"Hello, Mrs. Bishop, this is Detective Wilson at the Redlands Police Department, the homicide division. Please give me a call after you received this message. My number is—" Before she could write the number down, a call came in. She answered the call.

"Hello," the voice on the other end of the phone said, "may I please speak with Mrs. Bishop?"

"Yes, this is she."

"This is Detective Wilson."

Denise interrupted him, "I just got the message you left earlier. What do you want, Detective? Why are you calling me?" She realized the detective had called right in the middle of a traumatic moment, but she found it very difficult to control her emotions. The angry tone of her voice glared through, and there was little she could do to be pleasant.

"Mrs. Bishop, I would like for you to come down to the station to answer some questions about the shooting at your husband's boutique."

"Shooting? I do not know anything about a shooting. I think you have the wrong number."

She was about to hang up when the Detective said, "Your husband is Eric Bishop, the proprietor of the Chic Boutique?"

Still irritated by the call, Denise just simply said, "Yes."

"Mrs. Bishop, I would like for you to come down town to the police department. Just ask for Detective Wilson."

"Detective, can you please tell me what this is about?"

"Mrs. Bishop, we believe there was an attempted murder made on your husband's life."

"What! Someone tried to murder Eric? I do not understand. Can you—"

"Mrs. Bishop, I think it will be better if you come to the station." He did not answer her question. Instead he gave her the address and the time he wanted to see her.

Denise wrote the information down, and after she hung up the phone, she said, "Lord, what will be next? Eric had an affair, or maybe he has had several affairs. He died, and now I am learning someone wanted to kill him. What will be next?"

When Denise arrived at the police station, she went to the information desk and got the information she needed to find Detective Wilson's office. She knocked on the door, and a voice behind the door told her to come in. When she entered the office, it was neat and tidy. Pictures of the president, governor, mayor, and other prominent social elites were hanging on the wall. Well-kept potted plants were on the windowsill and in the bookcase. The man who was sitting at the desk stood up and extended his hand. After they shook hands, he asked her to sit down.

"I wanted to thank you for coming down, Mrs. Bishop. I know this is a very difficult time for you. I need to get some information from you about the attempt made to murder your husband."

Denise immediately wanted the detective to explain what he meant by someone wanting to murder Eric.

"Detective Wilson, you said someone wanted to or tried to murder Eric?"

Detective Wilson took his time. "Yes, ma'am. There was a shooting at your husband's office the week of his death. Did you know anything about that?"

"No, I did not. I was out of town, identifying Eric's body, making funeral arrangements, and burying him. I have not heard anything in reference to a shooting at the boutique. Eric was his parents' only child, and they have been so distraught and traumatized by his death. If they knew anything about a shooting at the boutique, I am sure they are in no condition to discuss that with me."

He continued with his questions for her.

"Where were you on March 10?" Before he could finish asking the question, Denise answered with irritation in her voice. "I was home."

"Does your husband travel for business?"

"Yes, there are times. Maybe I need a lawyer here with me. I know nothing about a shooting at the boutique."

"Do you know Paul Parker?"

"Yes, he works for my husband."

"What does he do for your husband?"

"He manages the clothing stores. Detective, please get to the point of these questions. I thought you had information for me. I didn't know I would be giving you information. Please tell me who was trying or who wanted to kill my husband."

"Mrs. Bishop, or may I call you Denise?"

"Mrs. Bishop would be fine. You were saying."

"Mrs. Bishop, two men entered your husband's office. They were looking for him. Two shots were fired. They thought they hit your husband, but they hit Paul Parker."

"When did this happen?" He told her it was the week Eric was killed in the car accident.

"Why did you ask me if I knew Paul Parker? Is he the man who was trying to kill Eric?"

"No, Mrs. Bishop, as I told you before, Paul Parker was the man who was shot. They shot him, thinking they were shooting Eric."

"How do you know they were trying to shoot Eric?"

The detective explained to her that the men told Paul that they were there to kill Eric. "Their words were, 'Eric this is for you.'" Denise sat back in her seat. It felt as if the life was being drained out of her, and she looked out the window. She did not say anything after that. The detective waited for her to respond, but she did not.

"Mrs. Bishop, do you know of anyone who would want to murder your husband?"

She thought about his question and thought to herself, *Yes, I would.* She knew why she would want to kill him, but why would someone else want to. She turned to look in the detective's direction. "No, I do not. How is Paul? Was he killed?"

"No, he was shot twice and left for dead. He is in the Methodist Hospital, recovering from the shooting. Do you know much about your husband's business dealings, Mrs. Bishop?"

She told him that she did not. She wanted to tell him about the affair, but she could not bring herself to do that. That would only make it look like she had a reason to make an attempt on his life. She felt she needed to go home and think about all of this. She needed to understand how the man she was learning about was not the man she loved and had married. It was as if two different men had been living with her. She wanted to know if there were any more questions. The detective told her no. He handed her his business card and told her to give him a call if she learned anything more. He thanked her for coming and showed her to the door.

Before she would go home, she decided to go to the hospital to see Paul. Maybe he knew something. After all, he had worked for Eric for a long time. But this was the man who had taken the bullets for Eric. She wanted to see how he was doing. When Denise got to the floor, she asked where Paul's room was and if she would be able to see him. The nurse told her a short visit would be great. After she told her his room number and pointed in the direction of his room, she left. When Denise entered his room, she found April was there with him. She was sitting at his bedside with her back to the door. Denise introduced herself and went over to shake their hands. Paul lay back in his bed and recalled who she was.

"Denise, it has been a while since we last saw each other. This is my wife, April."

"We are sorry to hear about your husband," April said.

"I am sorry we were not able to go to the funeral," Paul mentioned.

Denise asked how he was doing. Paul told her he was doing fine. Paul and April looked at each other, and April said, "We are hoping and looking forward to him going home." Denise could see the love that they had for each other. She told him that she was sorry that this had happened to him. Paul asked how she knew where he was. Denise explained that she had just left Detective Wilson's office. He wanted to see if she knew anything about the attempt made on Eric's life.

"I could not tell him anything. The truth is that I didn't know that an attempt was made on his life. I thought maybe you would tell me what this is all about."

"What did the police tell you? Did they tell you why someone had made an attempt on Eric's life?" Paul asked.

"Nothing. Only that the men who shot you said, 'Eric this is for you.' I really do not know anything. Can you please tell me what this is all about?"

"I will tell you what I told Detective Wilson. Several months ago a man whose name I think was Bruce was leaving one day, and he told Eric in an angry tone that he wanted his money and wanted it now. Then the night of the shooting, two men came into his office and said, 'Eric, this is for you,' and shot me."

"Who is Nicole Warner? Do you know her?" Paul thought very carefully and prayed before he would answer. He had some idea why Denise would want to know about her. He said, "She is a buyer for the stores in Orange County. I believe Eric was going to make her the buyer for the new stores he was planning to open."

"Did she come here often?"

Once again, Paul paused and thought before he answered. "I did not always know Eric's schedule, especially when he would meet with the different buyers." He knew that he did not have all the facts, so he thought it would be best to say nothing. Denise thanked him for his time and hoped he would recuperate enough to go home soon. Then she left. Before she returned home, she stopped at the liquor store to get something strong to drink. The store clerk offered to assist her. "May I help you find what you are looking for?" Denise was wearing her sunglasses inside the liquor store, where there is no need to block out the sun, but she was wearing them to conceal her teary red eyes.

"I am looking for something that will take away all my troubles and pain and will knock me out too."

She came home, got comfortable, and turned on some music. She then closed all the shutters and turned on the light near the living room window. She sat on the sofa, opened the bottle of NightTrain Wine, and started to go through the photo albums of their wedding pictures. Then she opened the small music box that her mother had given them a few days before their wedding. It was a special music box that had been handed down as a wedding gift for three generations. It was something to bless each generation with so that they would have a happy marriage. It was an heirloom, a priceless antique. It was about the size of a large jewelry box. Now who was she supposed to hand it down to? She felt like a failure. As she looked through the wedding pictures, she remembered something her nana had told her about marriage from the book of Proverbs. Nana told her she should guard her heart because the condition of it would affect everything she would do. She remembered her Nana telling her that she was spending too much time and money on the wedding without thinking about what it was going to take to have a good marriage. She would say, "After the wedding comes the marriage." She took all her pictures and started to tear them apart. When she could no longer tear the pictures, she began to cut them up. After she had consumed the whole bottle of wine, she passed out on the sofa, mumbling, "After the wedding comes the marriage."

CHAPTER 3

THE SESSION

Life had become unmanageable for Denise. She had to face the fact that life as she once had known it was no more. The life that she had now was not one of her choosing. This was not how her life was supposed to be. These were not the dreams she had imagined for her life. Her life had become a nightmare. Every night she found it hard to sleep. She could not get Eric's burnt body out of her mind. She could not stop thinking about the pain he must have felt dying alone in that burning car. She had often thought, *Why did God allow this to happen? Where was God?* She did not know what hurt her the most—learning about Eric's death or learning about his affair. It all had become too much. It was as if a war was going on in her head. She had begun to give some serious thought about taking her girlfriends Amy, Sam and Gwen's advice about getting counseling, although she did not know any counselors or anything about finding one. She called her mother and asked for her advice. She knew her mother had a friend who was a social worker. Maybe she could give her some idea where to go and what to do to finding a counselor. Her mother's friend found a grief counselor. Her mother called, gave her the information, and told her that she prayed that it could help her. Denise took the name and number and gave the counselor a call.

The counselor was named Irene Baker, and she wanted to know if Denise wanted to or was ready to make an appointment. Denise told her what a difficult time she was having with her life. Irene told her about the type of grief counseling she and her brother, Samuel, did, and she wanted to know if Denise was willing to come in to learn more. They made an appointment. Eventually Denise went to her grief counselor to have their first meeting.

Denise made the intake appointment for a Friday afternoon, and she would start her first counseling session the next morning at ten o'clock. The intake took some time because Denise was not sure how to answer the questions. Some of the questions were caused her to feel uncomfortable, and others questions let her know that counseling was going to give her the help that she needed.

Early Saturday morning, by eight thirty, Denise left for her first counseling session. She was not sure what to expect, but she wanted to be ready and on time. She was beginning to feel that maybe this would help her feel like living again. She stopped at a Starbucks for coffee and a blueberry muffin. It was not much of a breakfast, but she did not want a full breakfast, just something to get her through the day. She was getting a little nervous as the time of her appointment got closer.

It was nine forty-five. when she walked into the receptionist's office. A receptionist was at the desk and asked Denise her name and which group was she in. Denise told the receptionist her name and explained to her that this was her first session. She said she didn't know that she was in a group. She told the receptionist she was under the impression that she would meet only with Samuel. The receptionist took out a black notebook that listed all the patients and the different groups they were in. Some of the visitors were in two to three different groups, depending on the type of counseling they were receiving. The receptionist looked up from the notebook and told her which group she would be in. It was group A, and the woman gave her the room number where the group would meet. Denise asked the receptionist if she was sure about the information. The receptionist explained to Denise that all new counselees met with Samuel fifteen minutes before the scheduled appointment to explain more about the group they would be in. It was his way of helping patients through the first session. Then the receptionist reminded Denise of the directions and the room.

When she entered the room, Samuel was there waiting for her. He welcomed her in and told her to have a seat. He asked her how she was doing. She told him that she had not been aware that she would be in any group. Samuel explained that it was important for her to be in a group because it was not good for her to grieve alone. Being in a group with other people who are experiencing grief would be good for her. He explained how grief could take many forms with different stages, and she needed the help of others who had experienced her pain and who had made progress through the stage she was in. As he explained, she was going to receive Nouthetic Counseling, which would come straight from the Bible. He explained that using God's holy Word would give her comfort, love, and the truth in knowing how to face and deal with her grief. He reassured her that it would be the best thing to help her grieve her husband's death. Many people who received this type of counseling received complete healing and were able to have a closer and better relationship with God. Denise was not sure that she really needed a closer relationship with God. The truth was that she was not interested in having a relationship with God. What she really wanted was sleep and to get answers to her questions. *Why would Eric have an affair? How could she go on living? How could she live a life that had died? Why would someone want to kill him, and how could she live without Eric?*

Samuel looked at his watch and told her that it was time for group. As they walked down the hall to the room where they would hold the group session, he reassured her that it was a small group with people who were in different stages of grieving. This was a very compassionate group of people. He cautioned her not to feel uncomfortable if people felt the need to cry. They would do that, and he let her know it would be fine if she felt the need to let out her emotions too. They would find another way to come out, and they could have a negative effect on her after all.

It was a small room with no pictures on the walls. The room was painted a sage green to help everyone feel relaxed. There was a large picture window that was framed by two artificial floor plants on each side of the window. God wanted the patients to see His creation as simple as a flower or a bird flying over or even people taking in the sun. All these were miracles and gifts from God. He used these to show His love for them and how He wanted to bring healing to each one of them. There was a wall clock to remind them what time the session was over. That way they could talk about something if there was limited time left. Samuel led Denise to her seat as the others started to come in. It was indeed a small group.

Ron and Sarah Lowe were there. They were grieving their son, Harley, a ten-year-old who had been hit and killed by a drunk driver while he was walking home from school. Six weeks had passed since the accident. They had always taken the seat directly across from the window to see the flower bed of roses planted in the park across the street. The flower bed always reminded them of the time their son helped them plant a bed of roses when he was only six years old. They remembered how exciting it was watching him learn things for the first time. Now their hopes and dreams for their son were gone. They would never see him marry or raise a family of his own. The counseling was helping them with the whys. *Why was the drunk driver allowed to be in the streets and kill their son? Why would God allow this horrible thing to happen to them who loved him?*

Then there was Amy. She was coming to counseling with her aunt and uncle. Amy was the youngest in the group. She was grieving the death of her parents. Her father died a year ago from cancer, and her mother was killed in a drive-by shooting three months ago. Her uncle and aunt were not just bringing her to counseling. They needed it for themselves too. Counseling was helping each of them learn how the other one was feeling. They knew that if they did not have the counseling, communication between them and understanding would have been very difficult.

The last members included Mr. and Mrs. Grisham. They have been grieving the death of their granddaughter, Melinda, for three years. They raised her since she was three years old. She committed suicide. She was only seventeen years old. They still do not understand why she would want to take her own life. They thought that they were giving her a good life and showing her how much they loved her. They always wondered, *What did we do wrong? Why didn't we see that something was wrong?* Of course, they had always blamed themselves, however, since they started coming to counseling, they learned from God's Word that they were not to blame.

It was 10:05, and the group was ready to start. Samuel introduced Denise and let the group know that she would be joining them. In front of the group, he let everyone know that so many things were happening to Denise mentally, physically, and emotionally. "It's difficult for anyone to understand what is happening to us, and those who are our friends and family do not always understand," he said. "Sadly, they want you to hurry up and finish grieving and get on with life so that things will get back to normal for them. You will be in pain no matter how long it takes to grieve." He also reminded the group that his assistant, Irene, would be out for three weeks.

Each member introduced themselves and explained how the counseling had helped them. Denise introduced herself and shared her reasons for being there, but that was all she said. She did not give any details about Eric and the deep pain she was experiencing. She needed time to open up. She hoped that with time, her need to hold back would change.

Three months passed, and Denise had been coming to counseling every week. And she was doing her homework too. One day the receptionist called Denise and told her that Samuel and Irene wanted to see her. She gave Denise the day and time of the appointment. Denise came just as they asked. When she entered the room, Samuel was sitting at his desk, and Irene was sitting in the back of the room, holding a pen and a writing pad. Samuel told her to come inside, and she sat down. Irene and he indicated that they were thankful that she came. She turned and looked in Irene's direction to say hello.

Samuel said, "Within this time period, we usually do an evaluation to see how the counseling is helping the individual. We go over the homework and what happens at each session. We want you to know we commend you on doing your homework and coming to the sessions on time. Even so, I feel that there is still much ground we need to cover."

Irene was nodding her head in agreement, and she said, "We feel that there are things you have chosen not to talk about. We want to make sure that we are giving you all the help that you need in getting well."

Denise asked, "What do you mean I am not talking about everything? How do you know if I am and if I'm not? I was under the impression that I tell you what I want you to know. First, you tell me that I am doing good. Now you are telling me that I am not opening up. You called me away from the group to reprimand me? I do not like where this is going. Do you want me out of the group? Is this what you are trying to tell me?"

Samuel motioned to Irene to let her know that he would take charge of the session now. He wanted her to observe and take notes.

"Denise we do not want you to leave. You are doing fine just as we have told you before. However, I feel you are not telling us everything. I feel you are hindering your own progress. He took the folder that contained Denise's homework, which included Scriptures responding to questions she had to look up. He opened the folder and read to himself some of the things that she had written. He could also see from her journal that she was not allowing herself to feel, which meant she was keeping things inside, trying to control her feelings and behavior. He wanted her to know that this was not good for her.

"I have done everything you have said for me to do," she said.

"I know you have, Denise. Nevertheless, you have not done everything God has told you to do."

"What do you mean? What have I not done that God has told me to do, and how do you know if I have or haven't?"

"You did not answer any of the questions in the section that speaks about forgiveness. Who do you forgive, and why? How has forgiveness changed your life? Why do you need to forgive? These kinds of questions.»

"I am here to talk about my husband's death, not about forgiveness. This is something different.

"No, Denise, it is all the same. To have one, you must have the other. To have complete healing, you must forgive. You must have forgiveness to be able to move on with your life."

"Who says I must have forgiveness to move on? Who?"

"God tells us we must have forgiveness to receive His healing."

"God, you talk as if He is supposed to be in charge of my life. What does God know about my suffering? What does He know?! Everything for Him is rosy and perfect. He cannot see and feel my pain," she said.

"He does, and He will know if you tell Him. Irene and I thought that this type of session might be beneficial to you. We thought that there may be something you need to discuss, something you may not feel comfortable saying before the group. We want to see you get better."

"What makes you think that I am not getting better?" Samuel looked her straight in her eyes and let her know she was not fooling anyone. If she wanted to continue to receive counseling, she was going to have to face the truth, because if she did not, she would continue to grieve. Her grief would always be in control of her life, and he was not going to let her back into the group and let her inability to deal with her issues hurt the group. "So tell us. Who do you need to forgive who's related to your husband's death?" The conversation was becoming very unbearable for Denise. She had never experienced someone being so direct with her. She did not want to face the truth and the pain that came with it. She had had enough and was ready to leave, but for some reason she could not move. It was as if someone was holding her in her seat. She felt compelled to talk. She wanted to control what she was going to say, but it seemed once she had open her mouth to speak, the words just poured out of her. For a long time she wanted to talk; however, her anger was in control, and it kept her from opening up. Irene and Samuel had both prayed for her obedience to God's Word. It was the power of God that was helping her to open her wounded heart and receive His healing grace.

"Denise, did your husband do something that you do not want to forgive him for?"

Denise put her hands to her face and started to sob. Then she stared out the window. She just started to talk as if she was reliving the whole ordeal. "The New York Police Department informed me that Eric was in a car accident and had been killed. They needed me to come to claim the body, but first, they needed the body to be positively identified. I asked my mother to come with me. We could not get to New York, because of the attack on the World Trade Center. No flights were coming into or leaving New York. It was like this for several days. We were finally able to get a late flight from California to New York." She took a deep breath and continued, "It was a five-hour trip. For five hours I sat in that seat, thinking all kinds of thoughts, just hoping that maybe some mistake had been made. It could be someone else. Eric was really fine, and this was all a bad dream. But once we got into New York, things were even more difficult. After the Trade Center attack, New York was like a city that had been shut down. I do not remember everything. I just remembered going to the coroner's office and being asked to identify Eric's body."

Tears started to pour out of her. When she took a deep breath, Samuel gave her some tissues to dry her eyes. This gave her the strength to continue. "Eric's father was supposed to be there to help me identify his body and to tell us what he knew about the accident. He was supposed to meet Eric there for a business meeting they were going to have about buying or renting a building for their business. But he never made the trip. Even though my mother was there with me, I felt so alone." Denise's body language changed.

She pulled her arms around herself. It was as if she needed to be held in order to continue. As she told them about being in the morgue, it felt as if she was actually experiencing the coldness of that place again. "I walked into that cold, still, lifeless room, and the smell made me feel sick. They opened the door to the place where they held his body, and pulled his body out in this cold, steel drawer. It reminded me of something I had seen in the movies hundreds of times. I would always cover my face so I wouldn't see the person who was dead. I did not want to see the lifeless body lying in that drawer. Now I was about to experience the same thing, but this was real. They pulled back the sheet that covered his body. This body was lifeless just like the ones in the movies. I looked, and then … I passed out from the shock of seeing his body burnt beyond recognition. This could not be the man I had been married to. There was nothing there to identify. I was shown the things found on his body. I just told them that it was Eric. I became so sick." She fell back in her seat. Denise felt weaker emotionally and physically as she told the story. She was reliving the trauma she had experienced that day. "I couldn't touch his body, so I couldn't look at it for birthmarks. There was nothing there to identify. It was just a large mass of burnt flesh. I could not see his eyes or even his lips to kiss him good-bye. They gave me his belongings, and we left. I do not remember much more of the trip. After the funeral several days later, I learned Eric was having an affair."

Quickly her body language changed as she thought about the affair. "I was still grieving over his death, and then I learned our marriage was dead as well." Denise's face became tense, and then she formed fists in both hands and raised them in the air. She only brought them down midway, hitting the air. Then she let out a cry that was deep, long, and loud. People down the hall could hear her. The pain that she had felt for so long was coming out. It was an eerie scream that turned into a cry. Really it was a cry for help. "How can I grieve when I cannot tell him how I feel about what he has done to me? I have never felt so much anger before in my life. I wanted to kill him. He took our savings and spent it on this woman. Eric, why? Why would you do this to us, to me! I loved you."

With those words the tension she was feeling began to fade. Then her voice changed to rage and anger, and her body became tense again as she said, "You want me to forgive this monster? Forgive! How can I forgive when all I want to do is hate him? I want to make him feel the pain he has caused me. I want him to hurt. I want him to hurt, and I don't want anything to bring him relief from his pain."

With compassion in her voice, she expressed her love for him then. "One minute I am missing him, and I want to hold him and tell him how much I love him." Then her voice turned to rage. "Then another minute I want to kill him. I want to see the pain in his face as he looks at me and realizes that it's me who's giving him this pain, and I want to tell him why in that moment. I want him to experience a long, slow, painful death. How can I love him one minute and hate him the next? I think I am going crazy. I sound like a crazy person."

Her body shook as she spoke with intense emotion. She looked at Samuel and said, "Who could and will understand that? That is why I could not answer those questions. I cannot forgive him. I will never forgive him. My pain is so deep. I don't know what hurts me the most—learning about his death and identifying his body or learning about the affair. No, I cannot forgive! Not now, but maybe fifty years from now when I have no memory of him. Maybe when I have become senile from old age."

Samuel spoke softly to Denise. He wanted to get her attention and let her know that he understood her pain. "Denise, what your husband, Eric, did to you was terribly wrong. Few people can understand the pain you have experienced. I cannot imagine going to a morgue to identify someone I love. I have only seen things like that in the movies. Now you have to face forgiving him for the pain he has caused you by being unfaithful to you with an affair. We want to see you get through this, and you will. It will take time for the heart to heal. It always does. Denise, you can do this. God loves you, and He does not want to see you bound in a prison of your anger and unforgiveness."

"My nana has always told me that unforgiveness makes you a prisoner of hatred, and forgiveness will always set the prisoner free. You do not understand the pain I have been in. I have not slept in weeks, and when I do sleep, I have nightmares. I needed to talk and get these thoughts out of my head. That is why I came to see you. Right now I do not want to hear that things will be all right and that all I need to do is forgive. As I told you before, you do not understand my pain. You could not know what it is like to have someone you love betray you. As I told you, you do not know my pain. You know, I am not the only one who wants to kill him."

With an expression of disbelief, disgust, and anger, she continued, "Several weeks ago—and don't ask me how many, because I can't recall and I don't want to—I was called to the police station to answer questions about my knowledge of his business dealings, and they shared that someone had come into his office around the same time he was in New York and shot one of the managers, thinking it was Eric. We had vowed to love each other until death did us part! Well, it has!" With that, she looked at her watch and told Samuel it was time for her to leave.

As she went to her car, Irene called out to her and asked her to wait. "Denise, I would like to talk to you. Please can we go next door and have a cup of coffee?" Denise turned to her and shook her head no. She did not want to go for coffee, and she was through talking. Even so, Irene did not want to miss this opportunity to comfort Denise. She also wanted to help her realize that she did not have all the facts about the reason Samuel wanted to help her.

"Denise, I know this has not been easy for you. I just want you to know that Samuel cares very much, and he does understand your pain. Twenty years ago Samuel was married to Helen. He was so happy. He was married to the woman he had dreamed about for years. He loved loving her, and when he learned he was going to be a father, the love he felt could not have gotten better. After the birth of their son, Patrick, he wanted to build their dream house in a place where their son could experience the joy and freedom to roam and discover life. He only wants you to understand how important it is for you to know how and why you need to forgive."

"Irene, I really do not want to hear this," Denise replied curtly.

"Denise, you are not the only person who has been hurt in this world. Please just give me a few minutes of your time." Denise stood by her car and held her car keys in her hand as a sign she would give Irene the minute that she has asked for. Irene saw a park bench by a tree and suggested they sit. Then she continued on with her story.

* * *

"As I was saying, Samuel was very much in love. He enjoyed surprising Helen with little gifts—things like a T-shirt with her favorite cartoon character that he found at a garage sale or a toy to make her feel like a little girl when she was having a bad day. Just little things that might have been silly but still expressed his love for her. He was known for bringing her breakfast in bed, delicacies that could have cost anywhere from fifty to a hundred dollars. One day he was on his way to work when he stopped at the post office to mail a letter, and he noticed a collection of stamps of the Civil Rights Movement. He bought them, and since he was only a block from home, he decided to surprise her so she could add them to her stamp collection. Unexpectedly, he came through the front door and not the usual entrance from the garage. He saw their neighbor Mildred from across the street coming over to return the cookbook she had borrowed from Helen three weeks ago. When he walked in, he found Helen and his best friend, Mark, on the sofa, making out. He could not believe his eyes. He looked again, and yes, it was them, Mark and Helen lying on the sofa, their clothes on the floor. Who was this guy holding and kissing his wife? He dropped the stamps and ran up the stairs to get his gun, but luckily, he had an asthmatic attack and had to be rushed to the hospital. He almost died. If it hadn't been for that asthmatic attack, he would have killed them. He had been married for ten years, and he had been a friend to Mark for fifteen years. Mark had been the best man at Samuel and Helen's wedding. It goes without saying that he ended their friendship. His marriage to Helen was headed for destruction, but he could not bear to see their son grow up with divorced parents. So they committed to work on the marriage. They went to counseling and tried to understand what went wrong. It took about a good five years of hard work before things started to change. One afternoon Helen was preparing to pick up their son from school and take him to his soccer practice. She asked Samuel if they could talk after she had returned from Patrick's practice. There was something she wanted to talk to him about. Samuel had an evening counseling session, and he was running late too. He told her that it would work better for him if they talked later on that evening. She told him it was somewhat important, but she would wait. That night Samuel received a call while he was in counseling session to let him know that he needed to go to the emergency room at the hospital. His family had been in a car accident. A drunk driver had caused a head-on collision. When he got there, Helen was still conscious, but their son was badly injured. He was bleeding badly, and he needed blood. Helen still wanted to talk to Samuel, but there was so much confusion and chaos from the accident. So many people had been injured. He was trying to comfort Helen, but the doctors needed his permission to give Patrick some blood, as he had a rare blood type. They asked if he could give blood to their son, but he was not a compatible donor. He was not the right blood type. At first he did not think much about it—that is, until he overheard one of the nurses say that he probably wasn't Patrick's biological father. There was not much time, and Patrick would die in a couple of hours without the blood. He went to tell Helen, and she looked at him and told him that was what she wanted to talk about with him earlier that day. She wanted to tell him that Patrick was not his son but Mark's. He ran out of the room to call Mark, and he told him to rush to the hospital. The doctors explained to Mark that they needed to test him to see if he was a compatible donor. Samuel reassured them that he knew he would be. Samuel did not want to see his son die. No matter what Helen had done, he did not want his son to die. He stayed by his son's bedside until he was out of danger. He did not think Mark would ever be back in his life. He told Mark that if he tried to take Patrick from him, he was going to kill him. Mark told him that he had caused him enough pain and that he had no intention of hurting him further. He knew that telling him how sorry he was would not be enough.

The conversation continued. "Samuel returned to Helen's room. Now he wanted answers. He wanted to know why she had never told him that Patrick was not his son. For more than ten years, he had raised

Patrick as his son. He wanted to know why. There Helen lay in bed, barely able to move, but she was going to answer all his questions that day.

"She explained to him that she did not know that Patrick was not his son until she took him in for his recent physical to play soccer. After Patrick had the physical, the doctor's behavior gave her reason for concern. She told him that she lied to the doctor and told him that Samuel had adopted Patrick. But she wanted to be honest with her husband now. She did not want to hurt him again as she had done with the affair. During the years they had worked on their marriage, she learned how love and honesty went hand in hand together for a healthy relationship. She lay in the bed, pleading and begging for forgiveness. The problems that they had suffered in their marriage were because of her. She was the guilty one. She pleaded with him to please believe her. He said no words could describe how he felt. Somehow—and he does not know how—he reached out to hold his wife. He held her in his arms for what felt like several hours, but it was not. She died in his arms that day. Her internal injuries were too severe for the doctors to do anything that could saved her. After her funeral Samuel was never the same. For the first time in my life, I was the one taking care of my big brother. He had always been the one taking care of me. Now I had to care for him and Patrick. Samuel was in no condition to take care of anyone. I thought he was dying from depression. He was dying a slow death. My father and I prayed. Our church prayed. We put Samuel in the circle of prayer with Patrick. God had mercy on him and gave him the strength he needed to find the desire to live again. I am telling you that Samuel knows your pain. That is why he does not want you to hold on to an unforgiving heart. Helen dying in his arms made him realize what unforgiveness will do to you. It will rob you of life and love."

Denise could not say anything. When Irene had finished telling her this story, Denise was no longer listening. Not another word was said. Denise went to her car and drove to the liquor store. She got a bottle of cheap wine, went home, and drank herself into a drunken stupor. As she was passing out, she said, "Forgiveness? How do you forgive?"

CHAPTER 4

NANA'S PAST

It was time for the yearly charity sale, the CWHS (Color Women's Home Sale). This was an organization of grandmothers who wanted to take back their community and teach the children in the different neighborhoods about their culture. Each year the charity yard sale raised money to take the kids on field trips and other activities, including day camp, where the children learned how to sew, quilting, arts and crafts, home economics, and the art of storytelling. The kids have an opportunity to share their family's history, listen, and learn stories about how the neighborhood has changed over the years and the different contributions made by citizens who once lived there. This yearly event brought the whole community together. Different businesses volunteered at the day camp to host workshops teaching the kids how to cut hair, how to grow a garden, among other things. This was a way to keep the kids off the streets, where many often got involved in criminal activities and often got killed. It also brought senior citizens and young kids together. The event enabled the two diverse groups to learn from each other and share life experiences.

Nana was one of the original organizers of CWHS. She wanted to give back to her neighborhood. She grew up in the neighborhood, and she saw how it had deteriorated over the years. But it was not until she saw her uncle Buddy get killed in a drive-by shooting that she knew something had to been done to bring a change in the neighborhood.

During this time of the year, Nana would do her spring cleaning. Throughout the year she would collect items from friends and family or anyone who wanted to make a contribution to this special event. She would put all of the collected items in her garage. She said it was a good way to help her keep her attic clean from clutter and get rid of things she would never use again.

Connie Lakeshur, one of the organizers, would not be able to assist with the event this year, because of an illness in her family. Nana would be shorthanded, and there was little time to find and train someone to fill Connie's place. So she decided to call Denise and ask her to come and help out. She would know what to do. After all, she had worked in the event before. She also thought it would be just what Denise needed to help get her mind off her grief. She could focus on living again. She knew grieving took time, and with what Denise was going through, she did not need to be alone. She needed to be in a place where people could love her. Maybe a change of scenery would do her some good and persuade her to continue going to her counseling sessions. So she e-mailed her and waited for a response.

Denise still cried at the very thought of her life. She cried herself to sleep every night and wondered how she would make it through the next day. The things she had learned in counseling helped, but she was not ready to surrender to God's will in forgiving Eric.

When she got her nana's e-mail, she thought to herself, *This is not a good time to be around so many people*. But she loved her nana and would do anything for her, but this was something she didn't want to do. Besides, she didn't feel that she just could not do either. This was just not a good time for her. She was still grieving Eric's death, his affair, and their marriage. When Nana did not hear from Denise after two days, she decided to call. Denise explained that it just wasn't a good time for her, but Nana was not going to take no for an answer.

It was only fifty miles to her nana's house, so she thought she could take the scenic route. Of course, it was the longest route, but she needed the time for some tranquility. Once she was at Nana's, there would be little time to relax and think. Since the sale would only last for a few days and work was slow, she took the time off.

She arrived in the late afternoon just before Nana was leaving for the charity meeting to make some last-minute changes. Nana hugged and kissed her and reminded her how happy she was to have her there.

She repeatedly told Denise how big of a help she would be. After Nana helped Denise bring in her luggage, she put her right to work. She told Denise to collect all the bags and boxes with the brown labels in the attic and put them by the garage door. "Someone will be there in the evening to pick them up," she said.

When Nana left, Denise made her way to the attic. Seeing all the old things up there brought back memories of her childhood. After she had taken some time to go through some of the old stuff, she collected all the bags and boxes and put them by the garage door just as her Nana had requested. Once the last box was put in place, she noticed a very beautiful box that she had never seen before. It was partially hidden under some old newspapers. She went over to examine it. It was about the size of a small jewel box. She tried to open it to see what kind of treasure was inside. From the tension, the lid seemed like it had been sealed for years. She looked around to find something to use to help her open the very appealing box. It made her feel like a little girl again on a treasure hunt. She knew without a doubt that something priceless was inside. When she finally got it open, she became excited, anticipating what waited inside.

There before her eyes was a box filled with letters. They were all addressed to Debbie Whitehead at 1555 Blair Drive, Riverside, California, her nana. What got her attention was the man who had written the first bundle of letters—Mr. George Wooden. Who was he? Curiosity got the best of her. She felt bit guilty about reading her grandmother's personal and private letters. *Well*, she thought to herself, *since they're old, it doesn't matter.* But the more she wondered, the more she wanted to know who this George Wooden was and who he had been to her grandmother.

She began to read the first letter right away. As she read, she knew that this was no ordinary letter. She quickly looked through the bundles of letters and saw that they all were written by the same person. The same name appeared on all the letters, George Wooden. Denise found an old chair and made herself comfortable so she read without interruption. As her eyes became fixated on every word, she no longer felt the guilt of reading the letters. Soon she read one letter after another. Before she realized it, she had spent several hours reading the letters. They were all love letters written to her grandmother when she was twenty-three years old. This was not her grandfather writing to her grandmother. It was another man, a married man. She could not believe what she was reading. Her grandmother had once had an affair with a married man. How could this be? This could not be the woman she had known all her life. It was hard to think of her grandparents as people who are intimate with others. This was very hard to take. The more she read, the angrier she became. How could she think of her grandmother, Nana, as the other woman? There had to be some mistake. She really wanted it to be a mistake, but the more she read, the more she realized that the man was indeed married and that he had a family too.

It was about seven thirty in the evening when Nana returned home. Denise was finishing the last letter of the third bundle when Nana came in.

"Denise, I tried to call you several times, and you did not answer. The men who were supposed to pick up the boxes told me they rang the doorbell several times, but no one answered. So they left, thinking no one was here. So I decided to come home to make sure you were all right."

Denise did not answer her grandmother. She just looked at her as if she was a ghost or someone she did not recognized. Then Nana looked at what Denise was holding. Her eyes went immediately to the box and the letters that were in Denise's hands. But Nana was not moved with emotions. She was not surprised. She just simply took the letters from Denise's hand and picked up the others that were on the floor and put them all back into the box. Denise was waiting for Nana to say something, but neither of them said a word.

It seems Gramps was the only one who was doing the talking in the Franklin house. Well, Denise was the only one who would not talk to Nana. Nana and Gramps did not have to talk among themselves about what was wrong. They knew why Denise was troubled, and they also knew she would need some serious time to think about what she had learned. They knew she would not understand, and only they could explain what she had learned.

Denise moved away from the stove and her gramps. She softly said to him, "I am sorry, Gramps. I should not have said those things to you … about Nana. They were not nice things to say about her. I am sorry. It's just … I never thought of her in this way. And now she tries to—" Before she could finish her thought, Gramps stopped her.

"Your grandmother is no longer that woman."

Denise quickly responded, "She had no right to wreck someone else's life. That was a terrible thing she did. Gramps, grandmothers do not do this kind of thing. Grandmothers are supposed to be sweet, little, old ladies who bake cookies and sing songs about Jesus. They sew mittens for presents, not have affairs with married men."

Gramps turned Denise around and said, "Denise, I love your grandmother, and what she did in the past has been left in the past. She has been forgiven, and if you are going to deal with this, then you need to do the same—forgive her!" With that, he left the room, leaving Denise with her thoughts about how to forgive her nana.

It had been a year since Denise had participated in the CWHS festivities, and it had been a year since she had had one of those heart-to-heart talks with Nana. Things had not been the same between Nana and Denise. Denise felt a great deal of pressure to continue her relationship with Nana after finding out about her past. Learning about Nana's affair made it that much more difficult to think about forgiving Eric. Two people who she loved dearly had betrayed her trust, and that fact was making it difficult for her to trust anyone again. Time wasn't healing her wounds like many assured her it would. There were times when she felt numb. Was her life only filled with people she loved who would eventually deceive her in some way?

Gramps called Denise and asked if she would do him a favor. He needed her to come down and helped Nana with the CWHS fundraiser. He would not be able to help her this year, because of an out-of-town business convention he needed to attend. It took some persuading—about an hour on the phone—to get her to come and help Nana. Reluctantly, she finally agreed to come.

Denise took her time driving to Nana and Gramps's. Even though she took the scenic route, her mind was not on the scenery. She was thinking about what she would say to Nana. How was she going to live with her while Gramps was away? She really wished her mother was here to do this. But she had given Gramps her word, and she had to keep her promise to him. She would do anything for him. But this situation really pushed how far she was willing to go to keep her word. She knew in her heart she still loved Nana, but she felt she was just not ready to forgive her. Nonetheless, she was beginning to realize that it took a lot of energy to feed that anger and unforgiveness.

It had been drizzling all day, and now it started to pour. Denise had passed several accidents along the freeway. Each accident made traffic move at a snail's pace. Finally, the pace of traffic picked up. She didn't want to stop, and she took the opportunity to make up for lost time. She was too tired to stop to get something to eat. She wanted to spend as little time on this freeway as possible. She was hoping Nana had prepared something to eat. On a day like today, Nana's chicken noodle soup would hit the spot. When she finally arrived, the rain had stop, and the temperature had dropped too. After several knocks on the door, she realized no one was home. Then she looked for her key to let herself in. It was not in its usual place. She went through every compartment in her purse, and still, she couldn't find the key. She tried to remember where she had put the key, but she couldn't. The cold wasn't helping. She decided to look one more time in the place where she usual kept the key. There, she found it. That made her day. She just hadn't reached deep enough before. Once inside, she went straight to the bathroom. She had been driving for more an hour without stopping.

It felt good to be at Nana's on a day like today. Nana's home always had a welcoming feel. She felt like a little girl. The smell of Nana's delicious chicken noodle soup led her to the kitchen. After a hearty bowl of soup, she found her favorite chocolate chip cookies. They were soft and warm, just the way she liked them, waiting for her. With a full stomach and a tired body, Denise thought that maybe she should take a nap. There was a nice warm bed waiting for her. Nana had done everything to make her feel welcome. It was like getting a much-needed hug. Once she was prepared for bed, she wanted to hear the news. She turned the TV on and surfed the stations. Then she saw Nana on the local news, talking about the CWHS. As she moved to get closer to the TV, she accidentally changed the station. But when she clicked over to a different station, she heard the whole story from the beginning. The news reporter was telling the audience about the influence of CWHS and how it was bringing positive and favorable changes to the community. The children's summers were no longer filled with violence, they no longer suffer the danger of becoming potential victims. They now enjoyed various activities. The station showed pictures of children taking a trip to the children's museum, which promoted a hands-on educational experience, enabling the children to learn through the arts. They interviewed some of the kids and got their reactions about the trip and the museum. All the kids who were interviewed thought the trip was great, and they all wanted to do it again. Then they showed girls and boys at the center, learning how to sew quilts. Each kid was working on his or her own quilt. The camera zoomed in on some of the quilts the kids had designed. They were great! They talked about how much they had learned from the women who were teaching them, and some of the children wanted to learn how to design their own clothes. The news included scenes in which the kids where fishing and learning how to use computers. They told the reporter about what a great time they were having and how they were looking forward to next year. At the end of the report, the reporter interviewed Nana as one of the organizers and recapped some comments from the mayor about the wonderful job the CWHS was doing by servicing the community for so many years.

Denise felt proud of her grandmother. She did not know how much work she had done for the community, but then she quickly reminded herself of the anger she had been harboring in her heart.

She turned the TV off and lay across the bed, thinking about her grandmother's affair. She thought about all the things her grandmother had done and all the people's lives she had touched. Then she thought about that much-needed hug. She knew that only Nana could give her that hug. She was beginning to feel tired, and her thoughts about Nana caused her to fall asleep.

When Denise woke from a restful night's sleep, she could hear the sound of bacon sizzling, and she could smell coffee and blueberry muffins cooking. It would be a breakfast fit for a queen. This is what Denise had always called a "grandma breakfast." No one could make blueberry muffins like Nana. Not even Costco. She got up and got dressed. She thought about what she would say to Nana. They had not seen or spoken to each other since she had learned of Nana's affair. Since she had come here, it was becoming more difficult for her *not* to forgive Nana. After she dressed, it was time to leave the bedroom and face Nana … and that delicious breakfast.

Before she entered the room, Nana spoke, "Good morning, Denise. I hope you slept well."

Denise took a seat at the breakfast nook, and then she softly told Nana, "Good morning." The kitchen looked different than it did last night. As her eyes surveyed the kitchen, she noticed new appliances, and she realized the patio door had been changed to French doors. The countertops had also been changed from white tiles to Baltic granite. She wondered why she hadn't noticed these changes last night. She must have been too tired and hungry. The table was set with matching placemats and napkins, and three white orchids sat in a square ceramic vase as a centerpiece. Nana had also changed her place setting to a more sophisticated look of vanilla white. The colors really made the placemats and napkins look great. The whole kitchen looked as if an interior decorator had designed it, and the scene helped Denise feel more relaxed.

When Nana took the last muffin out of the pan, she brought them over to the table along with the other food. Denise waited for Nana to sit, and as a family custom she had learned as a child, they said grace over their food, giving thanks to God in Jesus Christ's name. Nana looked toward Denise's direction and said, "I hope you enjoy your breakfast."

After the first bite of muffin, Denise was able to answer. "Yes, Nana, it is as good as always. Thank you very much for dinner last night. It was great after that long drive. I guess I was more tired than what I thought."

After a small sip of coffee, Nana said, "You are welcome. I figured you would be tired and hungry after the drive. I appreciate you coming out here to help. Gramps and I know it was not easy for you to come on such a short notice. We can use all the help we can get. Thank you."

"I see you have made a lot of changes in the kitchen. It looks great. Whose idea was it to make the changes?"

Nana looked up from her plate. "We both did. We thought it was time to update everything."

"What do you mean everything? There are more changes?"

"Oh, yes. When we finish having breakfast, I will show you—the family room, Gramps's study, and our bathroom."

Denise thought out loud, "I guess it has been a while." Nana was careful not to respond to the remark. Denise then said, "I saw you and the kids from the CWHS last night on the local news. I was impressed. I didn't know just how much the CWHS was having an impact in the neighborhood. The kids who were interviewed said they looked forward to returning to the workshops next year. I didn't know how much work it takes to do this and all the people who are benefiting from your organization. I mean, people's lives are being changed and touched by you, Nana. I know it has been a long time since we last talked. I guess that is because of me. I didn't know how to deal with your past. Knowing what you had done and what has happened to me, well, it just made me angry all over again."

Nana stopped eating her blueberry muffin and placed it on her plate. She cleaned her hands with her napkin and placed one on Denise's shoulder. Then she softly said, "I know, sweetheart. I can understand how all of this is difficult to accept and comprehend. I know it has not been easy for you. I'm sure you must have felt betrayed by my past. I can only ask you to forgive me."

Denise turned to Nana and started to cry. Nana and Denise stood up together, and Nana held her granddaughter close to her. She hugged her tight. Denise softly said, "I needed that so much. Thank you, Nana. I missed your hugs. Last night when I got here, the smell of the house and taste of the food was like a hug. I mean, it felt like I needed a hug from you. I have missed you, Nana, so much."

Nana pulled Denise away from her and gave her a napkin to clean her face and dry her eyes. "It will be okay. I didn't know that those letters were still in that box."

Denise took the napkin from her face and asked, "What do you mean? How long had those letters been there?" Nana looked away from Denise and sat down. She looked out the window into the backyard with her garden of roses and orchids. Nana had that look on her face. She was taking a trip down memory lane.

* * *

"Well, I guess those letters have been in that box since the night I went to the Billy Graham crusade with your Gramps, the night I accepted Christ into my life. I thought we had thrown them away. I wanted those letters to be far away from me and any thoughts of George with them. I wanted George and those letters completely out of my life. George was a professor at the college I attended. That was going to be his last semester teaching at the college. He had gotten a position at the University of Oregon as a dean of the department of art history and architecture. When I first met him, I did not know that he was a professor. He taught history. As you know, history is one of my favorite subjects to study. I met him at the museum. One day one of my classmates asked me to meet her at the museum to work on a project we had together. I waited for more than an hour for her. When she did not show up, I gathered my things to leave. I was upset that I had wasted my day waiting for her. As I was leaving, I was not paying attention to where I was going, and I bumped into him and caused him to spill his coffee all over his pants. I was very apologetic and offered to have the pants cleaned. He insisted that it would be okay. He thanked me and reassured me that it was all right. At the time he asked me my name, but I didn't think we would spend the rest of the afternoon together at a cozy little restaurant. No, no, it was a cozy café, and we were having coffee. He asked me if I was married. I told him I was not. I asked him if he was, and he said that he had been separated for three years. He told me that his wife had left him for another man. He wanted her to come back, but she was not ready to. But in reality, she was caring for her grandmother, who lived in Canada and was having heart surgery."

Nana paused and continued with her explanation. "That day we talked for about three hours. Then after that day, we met just about every day at the same little cozy café for coffee before he moved away to Oregon. He was all I could think about. We would call each other every day at the same time. We even wrote letters to each other. It was so very romantic. Every week I knew I was going to receive a letter from him. It truly made my day. After a stressful day, I would sit down and compose a letter to George. I would wish he was there with me, because I knew his presence would bring me such contentment and delight. Writing to him helped take my mind off the stress and focus on more pleasant thoughts, mostly about him. We planned for the times when we could get away and be with each other. When we could plan our excursions, we would take the train to the different museums and art exhibits. We would have lunch at exotic places. We would always do something new and different with our time together. It seemed wonderful. He always told me about not letting everyone know what we were doing or where we were going. The more secretive we were, the better it felt. We were in our own little world. It made me feel special. Other men would ask me out, but I would always refuse them. I felt no man could love me the way George did."

Denise was so deeply in engaged in what Nana was telling her that she lost track of time. She was telling herself "I am hearing Nana's life story. This is so amazing." As she was finishing that thought, she heard Nana say, "Nothing would keep us apart. One summer George came back to teach summer school classes at the college. One day George told me he would not be able to meet me for lunch because of a business meeting that he could not reschedule. It was the first time we did not meet. I felt terrible. Nonetheless, George had a gourmet meal sent to me with violin and a harp players and flowers. I was taken totally by surprise, and so was my roommate. After that, she just had to meet this magnificent man. We both felt he wrote the book on romance. After a year and a half of this affair, he would send me gifts for no special reason. I cherished them.

"Then one day George told me that his love for me would never die. He wanted to love me forever. Then he asked me if I felt the same about him. My heart knew what he was going to say, and I answered before he finished asking his question. That night I reassured him that I did love him. He told me that there was no one else who he wanted to be with.

"One day George told me he had to go out of town for a business trip in a week. He would be out of town for several days. He did call me once he was there, and he told me how much he missed me. I believed everything he said. I did not think to ever question anything he said.

So we decided to do something special before he left. Unfortunately, something unexpected came up for me. I cannot remember what it was. But anyway, we had to cancel our plans. But then later that day, things changed in our favor. I tried to call George, but I was not able to get through, so I decide to go to his office and tell him personally. When I got there, George was not there. So I decided to wait. As I was waiting, I decided to catch up on my studies. I started eating a sandwich when the phone rang. With a mouthful of sandwich, I could not answer it, so the answering machine picked up. Somehow I knew this call was bad. It was a woman caller. She said, 'I cannot wait to get my hands on you, because I am going ...' Whatever sandwich was left in my mouth fell on the desk. I could not believe what I was hearing. The last thing I remembered hearing was, 'I will see you next week, and don't forget: leave behind any clothes because you will not need them.' I do not know how I got out of there. I was in shock. All I knew was I wanted to die right there right then. I did not want to live. I wanted to kill myself."

Denise interrupted with the question, "Nana, you wanted to kill yourself?"

In a very calm and low voice, she answered, "Yes. In that moment I wanted to die. I wanted to commit suicide. The faster and sooner, the better. When I left the building, I looked down the street, and I saw a bus coming. I walked over to the bus stop, and as the bus came closer, I just stepped out in front of it. As I did, I felt someone or something push me very hard. I felt myself land on the hard ground, and then I was knocked unconscious. When I came to, I was in the mental ward in the hospital. Tubes were coming out of both ends. My hands were secured to the bed. I was hooked up to a monitor so that the staff could watch me. I cannot tell you how horrible I felt. I lay there, thinking, *Why am I here? Where am I?* I wanted to get out, but I could not. I could only lay there with my thoughts continuously going through my head. Here I am in a mental ward, and George is out of town, having fun with another woman. I was in that place for about a month. They would not let me leave until I could show them that I was not going to hurt myself. I lost my job, my home, and my self-respect. I was so hurt and angry. I have never felt this much anger before in my whole life. I wanted to hurt him. No, I wanted to kill him. How could he do this to me? With these thoughts, the hospital kept me another month."

Denise stopped her grandmother's story to ask one very important question. "Nana, who or what pushed you?"

Nana looked around and saw the clock, which reminded her that she had a doctor's appointment in twenty minutes. "Oh my, it is getting late. I almost forgot I have a doctor's appointment in twenty minutes. I am sorry, dear, but I do not want to be late for this appointment. It took me three weeks to get it. Why don't we talk later?" Denise did not want their conversation to end. She was learning things that would have been impossible for her to even imagine. She was in total shock. Nana got up, cleaned the table, and put their breakfast dishes in the sink. Denise tried to help, but it was so difficult to stay focused. She thought about going with Nana so that she could finish the rest of the story. She asked Nana if it would be okay if she went with her to her doctor's appointment, but Nana told her that the CWHS center would need her afterward. But they could talk later that evening. So Nana went to her doctor's appointment, and Denise went to the center.

When Denise arrived at the center, she was warmly greeted by some of the organizers and volunteers. They gave her an updated tour of the facility. After the tour she assisted in mailing some letters telling the community about the weekend workshops.

Denise felt like she had been in a history class all day. She had learned about Nana's history, and now she was receiving a history lesson about some of the people who had become involved in the CWHS. From people who were homeless to prostitutes to drug addicts, each had their own stories about how CWHS had helped give their lives back to them; however, all of them had one thing in common, and that was Nana. Nana entered their lives, and she became one of the reasons they wanted to give back to the community. That evening Denise left the center with a sense of pride that she was Nana's granddaughter. Denise thought about how Nana's life had had such a powerful influence on the lives of so many people.

When Denise returned to the house, Nana still had not returned from her doctor's appointment.

Denise went to her room to rest for a few minutes, but her thoughts were focused on Nana's return. Denise felt a little ashamed about how she had felt toward Nana. She had come to realize Nana was not the woman she once was. She wanted to finish their conversation. She wanted Nana to answer all of her questions. There were two questions she really wanted answered. Who pushed her out of the way of the bus, and whatever happened to George?

Denise heard the key turn in the lock. It was Nana returning home. Denise went to greet her. "Nana, where have you been? I thought you were coming to the center today. I tried calling you, but I did not get an answer."

Nana put her things down on the coffee table and responded, "Oh, I am sorry, honey. I went to see a friend of mine who was in the hospital."

Out of concern, Denise asked, "Are they all right?"

"Oh, yes, dear. Thank you for asking. Has anyone called?"

Denise turned to go to the refrigerator to get something to drink and said, "No." Nana wanted to know if there was any mail, but Denise told her that she hadn't checked. After all, she had just gotten in herself. Nana left to get the mail and had a brief conversation with one of her neighbors. When she returned, Nana asked Denise how her day at the center was.

"It was busy. I met and introduced myself to several people. That is a large place. It seems everyone I met knew you."

Nana went through her mail. When she was finished, she laid the mail on the coffee table and looked up. "What makes you say that?"

Denise held her head down, moved around in her seat, and quickly said, "Every person I spoke with today did." As they went into the kitchen, Denise thought about how to ask Nana to finish the conversation they had started this morning. She got distracted when Nana asked about dinner.

"What do you want for dinner? I have some meat loaf, soup from the other night, or takeout?" Denise decided on the meat loaf and soup. After they ate, there would be no more interruptions. They could continue their conversation at home. She wanted to know more about the men who had been in Nana's life. After dinner was prepared, Nana blessed the food. After the first bite of Nana's meat loaf, the phone rang. Denise thought to herself, *Not another interruption.* After the phone call, Nana turned on the TV for the evening news. Denise was still trying to think of a way to get Nana's attention, but once again the phone rang. It was a telemarketer wanting Nana to buy energy-saving windows. They did not want her to end the conversation, so Nana explained it was not a good time for the call. With that, the call ended. When the local evening news had finished, Nana turned the TV off and went to clean the kitchen. Denise went to help. While Nana washed, Denise dried the dishes. Finally, Denise thought the moment was right. "Nana, you didn't finish telling me about George. How did you get to the hospital? Who pushed you?"

Nana took her hands out of the dishwater. She squeezed water out of the dish towel, wiped the counter clean, and placed the towel on the faucet to dry. She turned to face Denise and said, "Gramps pushed me."

When Denise heard that, her mouth dropped open and repeated what Nana had said, but she did not believe what she heard. "Gramps pushed you?"

"That is right. He saved my life. He saw me coming out of the office building, and I guess I dropped something. I really do not remember. He said he called out to me. But I did not answer, and I just walked right by him. He said I was crying. Anyway, he watched me and knew something was wrong. I really do not remember anything else. I was instructed to get therapy. At the time I did not think I needed therapy, but the only way they would allow me to leave the hospital was to get some therapy. The first therapist I had was so far off in left field that I knew he needed therapy more than I did. I don't know why, but he never came back. My new therapist was Maureen. She was fantastic. She helped me realize that I was responsible for the choices I made. I should not blame or make someone else responsible for them. I thought that this was the hardest thing to do. But she said I needed to forgive anyone and everyone who had caused me pain. Then I thought that I couldn't do it. I did not know how to forgive, especially not George. I really did not want to forgive George. At the time it felt like they were telling me to tell George that what he did to me was okay. Now I had two people I wanted to hurt, George and this therapist."

Denise had to stop Nana so that she could explain what she meant. If this woman was so fantastic, why did she want to hurt her? Nana was hoping to explain it in a way that Denise would understand. Nana explained, "When I first went into therapy, my anger made me want to hate everyone. I found myself telling people that they did not know what they were talking about. I was hurting because someone who I really loved did not love me. I was sad because I did not want anyone to see me in that place. But most of all, I was scared because I did not know what was going to happen to me. Maureen was an experienced therapist, and she continued to tell me I needed to forgive not only George but myself."

Again Denise interrupted Nana to ask, "Nana, why did you need to forgive yourself?"

Nana knew her granddaughter would ask that question, and she was ready to give the answer. "Because of who I had hurt—George's wife, Maria, and their children. I was having a relationship with this man when I knew he was married. I knew it was wrong, but I wanted to believe his lies. And I did believe his lies about both his marriage to Maria and his love for me. What I gave to George belonged to the man I would marry. What he was giving me belonged to his wife, Maria. What George and I were doing was wrong, and we both knew it. I was hurting someone, and someone was hurting me. And we called it love. This was a lie from Satan. This was not what God calls love.

"Well, I thought for a long time after that therapy session. I realized I had no choice but to stop being angry and feeling sorry for myself. After a few more sessions, my behavior changed, and believe it or not, I started feeling better."

Denise wanted to know if George knew what had happened to her and where she was. Nana told her. "I'm not sure what he knew or how he found out, but he knew. He wanted to talk to me, but I did not want to talk to him or see him. I had made up my mind that this was not the kind of relationship I wanted or how I wanted to be loved. It was hard and painful, and I did not want to experience anything like that again, especially if I had choices.

"When my therapist told me I was learning how to make better choices for myself, I felt that I no longer needed to come to the sessions. I was offered an opportunity to earn my keep. Since I had lost my job and my apartment, I was allowed to stay in a small room with a tiny cot. You could say it was the bare minimum, just enough to get by. Nevertheless, it did have one luxury I was very grateful for, and that was a tiny bathroom with a shower. I quickly learned the true meaning of luxury—having a bathroom all to yourself. It did not matter if it was large or small. It was a bathroom that I could use by myself when I wanted to. I earned my keep by being a note taker in counseling sessions. I took it and did anything else that needed to be done. It was work, but I felt I was giving something back.

"I remembered one day while waiting between sessions, I went to have a cup of coffee at the café near the clinic. I think it was the Jazz Cafe. I just remembered the coffee was great and the music wasn't bad. As I was reading the latest fashion magazine, someone came up and asked if they could take the seat at my table. I didn't look up. I just said, 'Sure.' Then they asked how I was doing. I stopped reading my magazine and looked up and saw a man I didn't know. He repeated the question again. I asked him why he wanted to know. He made a funny joke that was only funny to him. He said he wanted to know how all the people he pushed out of the way from being hit by buses were doing. I looked him straight in his eyes and told him I was doing fine. He wanted to know if I still wanted to kill myself, and I told him no. He was sorry he had pushed me so hard, but he was glad that I survived it. I told him that I was glad too. We talked until it was time for me to go to my next note-taking session. He asked me out. I wasn't sure about accepting a date with this weird man, so I asked where he would take me. He said, 'I want you to hear a great speaker whose words will blow your mind. The music will be heavenly, and you'll want to be friends with the people for eternity.'

"I had not been out for a while, and I thought it would be good to have some fun. So I accepted the invitation. We were to meet in front of the clinic. He showed up on time like he said he would. I told him he never told me his name. He laughed and said that his name was Goffery Franklin but that all his friends called him Gramps. I had to ask why he would let someone call him Gramps, and he told me they called him that because he behaved like an old man. Well, that evening did not happen the way I thought."

"What do you mean Nana?"

"Well, I thought just the two of us were going out. He met me in front of the clinic. Then he walked me to his car. When we got to his car, two other people were in the backseat, waiting for us. I thought this would be the last time I would go out with this guy. Eventually we got to the fantastic event. There were lots of people everywhere.

"There was no alcohol of any kind, and there was no using profanity. People were well behaved. Posters about the speaker, singers, and musicians were everywhere. The music was good. I had never heard this type of music before. When it was time for the speaker to take the podium, the music had prepared my mind and heart to receive his message. His words were music to my ears. I felt as if he was just speaking to only me. I actually started crying. I felt like I was being cleansed from within. His words of love were something I needed from deep down in my soul. It was as if my soul was dry, and his words were what I needed to quenched my soul's thirst. It was a Billy Graham Crusade. I did not know who he was. All I knew was that I needed what he was saying. He asked those who wanted to ask Christ into their lives to come forward. I wanted to move, but I could not. Then I felt a gentle nudge, and suddenly I was standing at the front, praying with several other people. They needed the same thing I needed, and they were all doing the same thing with me, praying to receive Jesus Christ into our lives. Later I spoke with a counselor who gave me more important information. I never felt so good. That was the first date Gramps took me on, and there were more eventful outings that helped me grow in my knowledge of Jesus as my Savior. So there you have it—the events that changed my life. After I had accepted Jesus Christ, I prayed and asked the Lord to use me to help change other people's lives just as someone had helped changed mine."

"Is that how CWHS was started?"

"Yes. It has been wonderful to know how God loves me and wanted to use me to bring change to other people's lives. I am so grateful."

"Nana, what happened to George? Did you ever see him again?"

"Yes, I know what happened to him. Several years later after Gramps and I were married, I volunteered at the county hospital. I would read to some of the terminally ill patients. Well, one day there was a new patient on the floor who had AIDS. When I went into the room, the patient thought I was the nurse and wanted me to give him some pain medication. I went to get the nurse and told her what he wanted. As I was waiting outside for the nurse to finish administering the medication, I noticed the patients' names on the wall. There was only one name on the wall. At first I could not believe my eyes. It was George Warden. I did not recognize him. I guess George finally succumbed to his extramarital affairs. I was really his only visitor, except for one old friend who knew him in college. His name was John Ray. He told me that George's wife finally had enough of his extramarital activities and left. He was not sure if they were divorced, but he had two boys. I thought, *This could have been my life*. I came every day to read to him. He was in and out of consciousness. He did not recognize me. I prayed for strength, and then I asked for the opportunity to share Christ with him. I knew in my heart that I had forgiven George. I had forgiven him years ago. One day George was awake and very much alert. He told me about his life and some of the things he had done. I cannot tell you what it felt like sitting there, listening to him tell me about some of the things he had done. He talked about the time he stole his wife's inheritance. He took the money to pay off the creditors he owed from a business deal that went bad. He told me about the time he left his wife while she was in labor having their first son. He took her to the hospital. When the nurse told him it would be a while, he left to play golf with some friends. He felt a man had a right to be a man and to hang out with other men. He told me how he would leave her alone with the kids to go be with his friends and watch sporting events. I sat there, thinking about how I had once thought this man was everything to me. I had once thought of him as my world. I wondered where I fit in this twisted world of his. As I was thinking, he told how he once had an affair with another woman that he really thought about leaving his wife for. He said, 'This woman really wanted me and would do anything to get me. She was good, and she had a very giving heart. I think her name was Debbie, Debbie Whitehead. She really had the hots for me. Always wanted me to meet her at this coffee shop. No, it was a café. Yes, that's right. It was a café, and we always went to exotic places on the train and to museums.' Then he told me about how a previous lover wanted to come back into his life. That made him feel like a real stud. There were three women who wanted him at the same time—his wife, this other woman, and me. Now I was learning where I was in his life. I was that giving woman with no future with this man. I had wanted to kill myself over this man who did not think of me as a person but as a trophy to prove his manhood, a stud who thought he was making women happy. He thought he was God's gift to women. But then I heard him say, 'All those wasted years. I hurt so many people. I was so selfish. I thought of no one but myself. How I wish I could change things and be a better person. I was not a good husband to my wife, Maria, and I was not a good father to our sons. I did not set a good example for my sons as a man, a husband, and a father. I was not there for them. I think about all the women I have hurt by making them think that I loved them. I never loved anyone but myself, and I do not think I really even loved myself. I am sorry to say it, but I have wasted my life. I have nothing to show for it. I have lost everything that made life meaningful. I had the love of a good woman, and I threw it away.'

"I knew in my heart what George needed. He needed to repent and ask Christ into his life. I asked him if I could read from the Bible to him. He said yes. I read from the book of Luke. When I finished, I asked if he wanted to accept Christ into his life. He said that he did. I led him to the Lord. He said he was thankful that he had been forgiven for all the wrong he had done. When I returned the next day, the nurses told me that George had died in his sleep. I thought, *George took life from me, but God blessed me and used me to give life to him.*"

Nana and Denise stayed up talking until early into the morning. Denise told Nana she was glad she took this alone time with her. It felt like it did when she was a little girl. Nana was glad that they talked as well. Then Nana gave Denise a hug and a kiss on her forehead and told Denise how important it was to forgive Eric. "Denise, I know the pain Eric caused you, but the only way for you to go on with your life is to forgive him. As long as you don't, he is still in control of your life, even though he is dead. But most of all, you need to forgive yourself." Denise pulled back and looked Nana in the eyes.

"Forgive myself for what? I did not have the affair. He did. Why do I need to forgive myself?"

Nana sat Denise in a chair at the dinner table. She knew a fight was about to begin. Nana wanted to encourage Denise to change her old ways of thinking and to look at her situation differently. She knew Denise needed to understand how sin could cloud our thinking so that we didn't see how we were sinners.

"Because you are as much at fault as he is."

"How is that, Nana?" Denise asked.

"Because when you chose Eric, you knew he was a *worldly* man. He was a man of the world, not a Christian. Do you remember the day I came to visit you, and your friends were getting ready to go out for the evening after you had spent the entire day getting your hair, nails, and face done? You went shopping for the right outfit, and for what? To go to a dark nightclub where people are drinking, just looking for men or women. To do what with? To have *fun*. Now, let's think about that. You went to a place that was dark with people who were drinking something that would influence how they think. You went there with your friends to find someone to have fun with, maybe someone to have a future with and to be committed to for a lifetime. You were looking for Mr. Right. Is that not what you did? You found what you were looking for, right? And didn't your mother and I try to tell you not to do that? You invested a fortune in the wedding. How much did you invest into learning how to have a successful marriage? Did you get counseling to learn more about each other's moral values, your inner selves, and understanding what those vows really meant? Did your parents, Gramps, and I try to tell you to learn more about Eric, the man who vowed to love you? This is why you need to forgive yourself. Remember: love is from God. It is not from this world. You went outside of God's will and committed your life to someone who did not belong to God. Remember, Denise: after the wedding comes the marriage." This was too much for Denise to deal with, so she got up and left the room. Nana said a quick prayer and went to bed. The next day Denise came into Nana's bedroom and told her how sorry she was for her behavior last night.

"Nana, you were right. I had never thought about my marriage that way. I am sorry I left. It was painful having to face the truth about my life and the choices I have made." Then the phone rang. It was Gramps calling to see if Nana would pick him up from the airport. After Nana finished speaking to Gramps, she and Denise gave each other a hug and a kiss.

CHAPTER 5

DENISE'S DECISION

A week after Denise returned home from her grandparents', she went to Stella's Place to have coffee with her friends Sam, Amy, and Gwen. They meet once a month at Stella's Place to have coffee. It gave each of them an opportunity to see one another and catch up. They always planned to meet downtown at Stella's Place at nine o'clock on the first Saturday morning of each month.

Gwen was the first to come. The waitress, Louise, took Gwen to their usual table, a booth that faced a beautiful garden of assorted flowers. It was the perfect place to sit to have coffee. You could be alone in one's thoughts, or you could socialize with friends. Once the group met and became friends with the owner, Stella, she always made sure the table was reserved for them the first Saturday of each month.

After everyone had arrived and was greeted with hugs and kisses, they put in their usual orders for their favorite coffees along with Stella's delicious blueberry muffins and Spanish omelets for everyone. Before their meal came, they made small talk, but the girls were all thinking about Denise. She was emotional and depressed when she reluctantly left to help her grandmother. They knew she was still grieving Eric's death, his affair, and their marriage. So they were ready to hear and learn about what had happened. After the girls shared what was happening in their lives, their meals came, and it was Denise's turn to give them an update about her life. She told them about all the work Nana and CWHS were doing in the community. Gwen spoke for all the girls when she asked, "How is your relationship with your grandmother? Before you left to go help your grandmother, you did not really want to talk to her."

Sam agreed with Gwen. "Yeah, what happened? Did you learn any more about your Nana's past?"

Denise took a bite of her freshly baked blueberry muffin and a sip of Irish cream coffee. "Well, we had a chance to talk. She explained everything to me."

Gwen asked, "What do you mean everything?"

"Well, let's say that after talking with my grandmother, I can say now I know her for who she is. The day after I got there, we were having breakfast together, and she started to tell me things about her life I could not have imagined. She told me how she met the man with whom she had the affair. His name was George Warren, and he died. But she shared Christ with him before he died. She explained how she met Gramps and became a Christian. It was like meeting people for the first time. I also learned how CWHS was started. She was even on TV. The local news did a report about how the community was changing because of what CWHS was doing. Well, after seeing that, I knew for myself how much my grandmother's life had changed and how she was having an enormous effect in other people's lives. It made me want to be like her. She also helped me understand forgiveness. Learning how to forgive is not going to be easy. I will need time to understand how to forgive."

Sam said, "Wow! I am glad you and your Nana are talking again. That is so good to hear. I could not think or see myself not talking to my grandmother. I am sure that was a nightmare for you. You and your grandmother have always been close. Now does that means you will be participating in the fundraiser every year?"

"Right now I do not know. I know I am making some progress with life without Eric. On the other hand, it is not enough. I need something more. I wanted to tell you about a decision I have made that should help."

Gwen looked up from her partially eaten plate of Spanish omelet and toast and asked, "Denise, what decision? What are you planning on doing?" All the women looked up from their meals with concerned looks on their faces, all waiting to hear what she had to say.

Denise took a deep breath and said, "Well, my grandfather has found a job for me. I will be helping a friend of his who owns an art gallery. It will last for about a year, for sure."

Amy, who was the first one to finish her meal, wanted to understand. "Why?"

"Because Barbara Simon, the art museum curator, is due to have her baby any day now, and she wants to take a year of maternity leave. So at least I know I will have a job for a year after I have moved."

"After that?"

"Well, who knows what else can happen? I am in no rush. Nana told me to take it slow. She thinks I need to continue to go for counseling to help me understand why Eric had an affair. Of course, that will be difficult to understand fully because he is not here to speak for himself.

"Have you gone to see a counselor?"

"Yes, I have."

"Well, did it help?"

"Yes, it did. It was not easy being told what I did not want to hear and facing my fears ... and learning what my responsibility was in the relationship. I guess the hardest thing is being told to forgive Eric. Counselors and Nana have said the same thing. To move on with my life, I need to forgive Eric.

"Every day I am reminded of him. It seems no matter where I go or what I do, the thought of Eric floods my mind. I think moving into a new environment will help me deal with his death better. I want to have good thoughts about him, not ones that will remind me of the affair. I want you all to know that I have given this a lot of thought, and I know this is the best thing for me to do for now."

Gwen asked, "When are you planning on leaving?"

"I will be leaving in two weeks, and I will be staying with my grandparents." She wanted to answer all their questions and wanted them to know that this was not the end of their friendship. Their connection was a promise she was committed to keep.

After they finished with their meal and started waiting for the check, Gwen suggested that they meet next week at her house before

Denise left. Everyone thought that was a good idea. In the parking lot, they said their good-byes with hugs and kisses.

* * *

After Denise had finished packing the last box, she placed it with the others and thought out loud, "Lord, I hope I am doing the right thing. Please help me. Nana said that You always know what is best." Denise was afraid of the future, unsure about what it would bring. Living with her grandparents brought some comfort. She knew she would not be alone in facing her future.

Two weeks later Denise and her parents were on the road to Nana and Gramps's house. Once they arrived, they found Nana had something special prepared for them after the long drive. While Nana was setting the table, she had an opportunity to talk to Denise's mother, Irene. "How is Denise doing since Eric's death? How is our girl doing now?"

Denise's mother turned and said, "She seems to be getting better. Her wanting to do things that will take her focus off of Eric is a good sign of some healing. Nevertheless, I still think she should continue with counseling. I have tried to encourage her. What could it hurt?"

"I have to agree with you. It will do more good than harm."

"We will have to continue to encourage her."

"Of course, praying for her will always help. She also needs to be encouraged to seek God. Having a relationship with the Father is what she truly needs."

"Nana and Gramps, I wanted to know if my moving in will be a problem for the both of you. Are you sure it's all right for me to stay with you until I find a place?"

Gramps spoke for the both of them. "Sure you can. Your room is always waiting for you." Denise was so excited. That was comforting to hear.

Denise completed her move to the new house, and she was getting her routine together. She was getting organized at work and at her new home. All of the upstairs was hers, so she had all the privacy she needed.

It was two weeks before the CWHS annual sale. Each year two weeks before the annual sale, a thank-you dinner was orchestrated for all of the volunteers. It was the CWHS's way of showing their appreciation for all the hard work the volunteers did to make the sale a success. Nana felt that each day something new was added to her already busy schedule. Gramps and Denise were a big help to her as the CWHS days approached. On that Saturday morning, Denise and her grandparents were finishing their breakfast when Nana asked Denise if she would mail some letters for her at the post office. When Denise got to the post office, there was a line. She was third in line, so her wait would not be long. There were two ladies waiting before her. When it was her turn, Denise went up to the counter, requested stamps for the letters, and placed them on the letters to be mailed. The clerk read the name on the letters and asked Denise if she was Mrs. Franklin's granddaughter. After she placed a stamp on the last letter, Denise looked up and said that she was. The clerk told Denise, "Your grandmother said you are going to live with her and your grandfather for a while. I am surprised to see you are doing this. I am accustomed to seeing Mrs. Franklin doing the mailing for the CWHS. I know this is the time of year she is in here every day, doing something for the CWHS. Your grandmother is a great lady. She and your grandfather and the women of the CWHS have done a wonderful job in helping the kids in the neighborhood. Well, you have a nice day."

"Thank you, and you do the same."

After running the errand for Nana, Denise decided to go shopping at her favorite store. Chy's Place of Treasures where she could shop for books, makeup, and bath and body products, and sometimes she could find a movie. It was a store that catered to the working woman's needs. Denise knew if she needed or wanted a good love story, she could always find one in the store. She found a good mystery book to read, some bath salts, and a CD with nature sounds. This was just what she needed to call it a day.

CHAPTER 6

THANKSGIVING WITH AUNT ANNIE MAE

The holidays were the best time of the year for Denise because her family would come together to celebrate. Everyone would come to Nana and Gramps's for the holidays. Nana and Gramps would always make each holiday a special event. There were decorations with all kinds of food, and the festivities for each holiday would generally last for a month. At the end of October, Nana would put up decorations for Thanksgiving. Then she would start making pastries to give to her friends, neighbors, families, even strangers, whomever her heart desired. It would seem each week she looked forward to making something different. She would look for new recipes to introduce into her holiday specialties. She would give out some of the holiday favorites as gifts. So holidays with Nana were delightful.

But this year it would be different. Nana's sister, Annie Mae, was coming for Thanksgiving. Aunt Annie Mae was a missionary. She had traveled the world, spreading the gospel of Christ, and she could speak several languages. Denise could not wait to see her. She was someone very special to Denise, and she would always have a special place in Denise's heart. Whenever she could come to town to visit, she would always bring gifts from all the exotic places that she had traveled to. When Aunt Annie Mae would give a gift, you knew no one would have anything like it. That's what made her gifts so precious and special. You would have the only one of its kind. Denise remembered the time when she was in her late teens and needed a dress to wear to her prom. When her mother told Aunt Annie Mae, a special delivery came for her in the mail. She opened the package, and to her surprise, it was a beautiful pink dress, her favorite color. It was a pink chiffon, tulle dress that zipped up in the back with a silhouette line, a sweetheart neckline that was sleeveless, and it was embellished with rhinestones. The shoes were white lace stilettos also had rhinestones. The earrings were sterling silver with purple stone drops. She was so happy, and so were her parents. After all, they didn't have to spend hours and hours looking for a dress with the possibility of getting only what was left from the ones that had been picked over.

One time Aunt Annie Mae came home for a visit, she brought a surprise that everyone talked about for years. She only said she was coming home, and when she came, she shared the news. She had gotten married! She walked in the house and said, "Hello everyone, I want you to meet my husband, Joseph."

Nana and Denise didn't know what to say except, "It is nice to meet you." Joseph was not from United States. He was from Athens, Greece . They had met years ago in Italy, and they had kept in touch. While attending the 2004 Olympics in Greece, they decided to get married. It was the first marriage for the both of them.

When Denise learned that her aunt Annie Mae was coming, she wanted to get to Nana's early to see her before the crowd came. When word got around that Aunt Annie Mae was coming to town for Thanksgiving, they family knew that everyone would be there.

When Denise got to Nana's from work, Aunt Annie Mae was there with her husband, Joseph, and the Rev. Brown. She wanted Nana to meet the new minister she had worked with in Villahermosa, Mexico. They explained how they had worked together building houses in different countries for Habitat for Humanity. Aunt Annie Mae told them Rev. Brown was coming to work at Bishop Green's church as a counselor.

While Denise was listening to the conversation, she wondered if she should return to counseling. The more she listened, the more she knew God wanted to help her in forgiving Eric. She knew the counseling she received from Samuel and Irene had helped her, and the opportunity for her to continue getting that help was waiting for her. Her most distressing challenge would be dealing with her feelings about Eric wanting someone else in his life.

Bishop Green wanted to help the community and his church congregation seek out and benefit from counseling. For the past several weeks, he had given sermons asking, "What does God's say about the choices we make? What does the Bible say about How to know a true worshipper of God?" After taking a survey one Sunday, Bishop Green learned some of the congregation was not knowledgeable enough about God's Word, the Bible, to handle issues in their lives. They were immensely knowledgeable about secular advice in dealing with the issues in their lives, but they were not as knowledgeable on what God's Word had to say. He needed help with the people who were coming to him for counseling. He knew that Nouthetic Counseling, biblical counseling from the Bible, would help the people greatly. There were not many people he knew who were skilled in Nouthetic Counseling. After he met Rev. Brown and learned that he had experience in this area, he knew this man of God would be a great help to the community.

By the time Denise met Bishop Green and Rev. Brown, relatives and friends were coming for the Thanksgiving feast. Denise left the living room, where Nana and Gramps were welcoming their guests, and went into the kitchen, looking for Aunt Annie Mae. She found her in the kitchen, preparing a dessert for dinner. Denise thought that this would be a good time to talk with her. Denise asked about what she was preparing for dessert. She told her it was a special dessert she learned from Maria and her family, with whom she lived while she was in Mexico working as a missionary and building a church for their congregation. Aunt Annie Mae said she always made the dessert on special occasions. Denise thought out loud, "What so special about today?"

Aunt Annie Mae looked up from her dish and said, "Today is a day I want to share with the special people God has brought into my life. Because I am experiencing a dream that has come true."

Denise asked, "What dream is that?"

Aunt Annie Mae did not look up. She continued to work on her dish and said, "You will find out with the others tonight."

Denise had forgotten what she had wanted to talk to Aunt Annie Mae about. Now she was wondering what Aunt Annie Mae's surprise was. While they were talking, Rev. Brown brought his son, Raymond, in to introduce him to Denise and Aunt Annie Mae.

In his quiet and gentle demeanor, Rev. Brown introduced Raymond. "Ladies, I would like for you to meet my son, Raymond."

Both the ladies said together, "It is nice to meet you."

Aunt Annie Mae asked, "What do you do, Raymond?"

As Raymond finished shaking the ladies' hands, he said, "I am a surgeon for the county hospital here in California."

Before Raymond could finish giving his professional job description, his father interrupted him and proudly added, "The best surgeon in the nation!"

Aunt Annie Mae wanted to know, "What kind of surgeon are you, Raymond?"

"I specialize in plastic surgery." Denise stood listening to the conversation, allowing her aunt to decide its direction. Aunt Annie Mae wanted to learn more about Raymond. "So Raymond, you are in a money-making business?"

Raymond was used to these types of questions. How much do you make in a year? Do you do noses and face-lifts? How much do you charge for butt lifts? "My work at the hospital is not for profit. I help restore people's lives. So working for money is not in the picture. I work with some other doctors who do reconstructive surgery for patients who have anything from birth defects to those whose have been injured in accidents. We work as a team, and we also travel to different parts of the world, helping people who cannot get this kind of help in their countries. We like to think of ourselves as giving people new lives."

Again his father wanted to add, "And do not forget your counseling. How many of these people also need counseling to deal with the changes the injuries have caused in their lives."

Aunt Annie Mae said, "You are just an angel, going about and bringing new life to people who needs it. Good for you. Tell us about the most interesting case you had."

"Well, interesting you should say that. It was a man who—" Then Nana and Gramps came into the kitchen and let them know it was time for dinner.

After dinner Aunt Annie Mae went into the kitchen and brought the dessert out. She told the history to them about the dessert and why she wanted to make it for them. "This is a dessert I have enjoyed making to express my love for the people I am delighted being with. Well, I have something I wanted to give to each of you."

Denise wondered if this was the surprise she had mentioned earlier. Aunt Annie Mae continued, "I wanted you to know God has allowed one of my dreams to come true." She reached in a bag and brought out a beautifully decorated package with a ribbon tied around it. As everyone's eyes focused on the package, they listened very carefully to her every word. "I wanted you to know this is something I have waited a long time for." Then she carefully untied the ribbon and then removed what was inside the package. She held it up so everyone could see. "This is my book that I have finished writing. It is called *A Collection of Untold Stories of the Black Woman.* I have brought it as my gift to you. This is something that I cherish very much. It is a collection of stories I have gathered over the years from African-American and African women, stories of their struggles in life. There are stories about women who became slaves and their families searching for them. There are collections of photographs of people and places I thought were very interesting in telling the different stories. Joseph helped me put the book together. I want to thank you very much for being a part of this experience."

Cousin Henry asked Aunt Annie Mae which story was her favorite. There were so many, but one will always came to her mind. It is the love story of Adanna and Kumasi. Kumasi was a great warrior who was in love with the king's daughter, Adanna, which meant "father's daughter." Kumasi was a fierce warrior and a crowned prince of the Ghanny tribe, and he wanted Adanna to become his bride. One day she went into the jungle to find her prince, who had been gone on a hunting trip to find food for the village. She wanted to surprise him with the things she had made for their new home. She had adorned herself with a floral arrangement that her handmaids had made for her and different blends of fragrant oils. Her father, the king, had told her many times not to go out alone and to never go near the river. In her excitement she forgot the warning. She was captured, placed in chains, brought to America, and made a slave. She would sing to the wind to take her cries to her father and her prince. Every night she sang the same song. She was sold to five different masters. To each one, she bore two children, giving birth to ten children in total, and they were all sold into slavery. Her hope was never broken. She never gave up on her prince, the warrior, finding her. One night she dreamt of her country and her prince. He was calling for her by the river. In her dream she followed the call of her name. It led her to the river, and there was her prince, the great warrior waiting to embrace her. She reached out so that he could embrace her. Her dream would always end there. She would wake feeling empty because she did not have her prince in her arms. Well, one night she heard his voice calling to her. She went down by the river, and there he was waiting for her and …"

Aunt Annie Mae stopped in the middle of her story. Everyone said, "What happened? What happened? What happened to her?"

She said, "You will have to read the book to know what happen."

Little Dorothy, a young six-year-old who had been crying most of the night, was all ears when Aunt Annie Mae was telling the story. She said, "What happened? What happened to her when she went to the river? I want to know what happened. Mommy, make her tell us what happen to the woman."

Aunt Annie Mae went over to Little Dorothy and bent down. She looked Little Dorothy in her eyes and said, "My dear, the book tells it so much better than I could. I am sure your mother will read it to you." When the evening was over, everyone told Nana and Gramps what a great time they had.

CHAPTER 7

WHO IS JOHN DOE?

The next day Aunt Annie Mae and Denise went shopping at the neighborhood market. Once there, they made their way to the produce section. While scrutinizing the grapefruits, Aunt Annie Mae spotted Raymond standing over a bend of Russet potatoes. "Raymond, it is so good to see you again. I did not think I would see you so soon."

Raymond turned to greet the women. "Good morning, ladies. It is good to see you as well."

Aunt Annie Mae thought about how much she would like to finish their conversation from last night. She was always captivated in human-interest stories because she enjoyed hearing about how God had changed someone's life. Raymond was somewhat pleased that someone was interested in his work. "You did not have the opportunity to tell us about the most interesting case you have worked on."

"Thank you for asking about my work. Yes, it was a time we all will never forget. It was September 11, 2001. I was working in New York in the emergency room. Several people were brought in from the Trade Center explosion. I had just finished assisting in a four-hour surgery when a case came in that needed immediate attention. It was a man who was seriously injured. When he was brought into the emergency room, we were not sure he would live. His face was gone."

Denise and Aunt Annie Mae were thinking the same thing. Denise beat Aunt Annie Mae to the question. "So what happened to him?"

But before he could answer the question, his cell phone rang. Once he saw who it was, he apologized and told the ladies he needed to answer the call. Denise and Aunt Annie Mae continued on with their shopping and returned to Nana's when they had finished.

When it was time for Aunt Annie Mae and Joseph to return home, they thanked Nana, Gramps, and Denise for making their stay a memorable one. Aunt Annie Mae encouraged Denise to socialize more. She told her that meeting new people would help her learn new things about herself.

It was late in the afternoon when Denise got home. Nana told her that they would be having guests for dinner. Gramps was outside cooking his famous barbecue chicken over the grill. Denise wanted to know who was coming over for dinner. Before Nana could answer, the doorbell rang, and Nana told Denise to make a salad. She would see who was at the door. Their dinner guests had arrived. Nana told them to make themselves comfortable because dinner would be served shortly. She told them that if they wanted, they could go out on the patio where Gramps was cooking. "Smells delicious," one of the guests said.

Nana told everyone dinner was ready. After Denise finished the salad, she brought it out to the patio. Even though it was November, the temperature was great for an afternoon picnic. The view from the terrace would add an enjoyable ambiance to the meal. To Denise's surprise, Rev. Brown, Raymond, and their friend, David, had arrived. Raymond admired Gramps's chicken and then looked at the salad. He told Denise how good everything looked, including the salad. Denise smiled and said, "Thank you."

When Denise, Raymond, Rev. Brown, and David selected their seats, Gramps and Nana sat in their usual places. Gramps said grace. "We thank You, Lord, for this good food that we are about to receive for the nourishment for our bodies for Christ's namesake." They all agreed by saying amen. After the food was served, they ate and enjoyed some good conversation. Eventually Nana and Denise started to clean the table. Raymond volunteered to help clean up, while his father and Gramps went inside to play chess. David had to answer his cell phone. Denise told Nana to go rest while she and Raymond finished the dishes. Her day had been a busy one, so Nana went upstairs to lie down.

Raymond told Denise again how delicious the meal was and thanked her for the invitation. Denise quickly reminded him that Nana had made the dinner and given the invitation. "Raymond, I didn't think that we would see each other again so soon."

I must agree with you. I did not think we would be talking with each other this soon myself. How are you enjoying your stay?

She said, "Nana and Gramps have made it a joy to be here. They have done everything they could to make my stay a pleasant one. You know, while we were talking during dinner, I remembered the story you were telling us at the Thanksgiving dinner here at Nana's about the most interesting case you ever had."

As he was about to continue the story, he was interrupted once again. David came in to let Raymond know he needed to leave. He needed to respond to the phone call he had received. He thanked Denise again for a very delicious dinner and asked her to thank her grandmother again for him. Then he left.

While Denise and Raymond finished the dishes, Gramps and Rev. Brown played chess, so the two of them decided to go sit on the porch swing and talk. Denise sat on the side of the swing that was next to the living room window, while Raymond sat in a chair and faced Denise. That made it easy for them to see each other as they continued their conversation. It was a good night for conversation too.

He started, "So you wanted to know about the most interesting case I ever had. I am grateful that you are still interested. Well, let me see. I don't know what all I told you, so let me start from the beginning again. Yes, it was several years ago. It was a time we all will never forget. It was September 11, 2001. I was working in New York in the emergency room. Several people were brought in from the Trade Center explosion. I had just finished assisting in a four-hour surgery when a case came in that needed immediate attention. A man at the hospital was seriously injured. When he was brought into the emergency room, we were not sure he would live. His face was gone. He had been shot, and he was losing blood quickly. When we finally got him stable, we were able to learn more about his injuries. He was not in the Trade Center explosion as we had initially thought. He had been shot and badly beaten, and now he was in a coma. We tried to find his family. So we looked up his name from his driver's license in the telephone book. We called his family, informing them that he was at the hospital. They came in right away. We were shocked to find out this was not the man from the driver's license that we found. This was not his family. We did not know how he had gotten the other man's driver's license. So now we had a badly injured man who was in a coma. We did not know who had shot and beaten him nearly to death, and we did not know his identity. Several weeks later he did come out of the coma, but he did not know who he was. He had no memory about himself or what had happen to him.

"We were faced with two challenges. One was saving his life, and the other was learning this man's identity. Because this was an attempted murder, the police had become involved. The police were the ones who would help us learn his identity and who had done this to him. We removed the bullets, but how could we restore his face if we did not know what he looked like or know his identity. Who could we notify to let them know what had happened to him? So while we worked on giving him a face, the police worked on giving him a name.

We also needed to get a team of specialists together to literally put this man back together again. For a moment, just think about all the stories of Humpty Dumpty and all the king's men trying to put Humpy Dumpy back together again, but imagine you didn't know what Humpty Dumpty looked like."

Denise stopped him in the middle of his story. She wanted to know the end of the story before he could finish telling it. "Did he live? Were you able to restore his face?"

Raymond could see the intense look on her face and said, "Well, to make a long story short, yes, he did live, and we were able to restore his face."

"How did you do that when you did not know what he looked like?"

"We used Patty Lane, a specialist in forensic facial reconstruction. She can rebuild the faces of people who have suffered very violent death and been disfigured beyond recognition. We also used Dr. Henry Simpson, a specialist in facial reconstruction of people who are living with facial disfigurement. I cannot tell you what all they did, but God used them to save this man's life. I must admit that this ordeal was very challenging. I can only say that there must have been a purpose for this man. He not only survived this beating, but he got a new face. They were able to reconstruct the bones in his face, and from that, we had some idea what he might look like. The truth is that he was given a whole new face."

"Were the police able to find out about his identity and why someone would do this to him?"

"Unfortunately, the last I heard, they did not. With all the confusion that happened during the World Trade Center, I believe his paperwork could have gotten lost. Most of the police force was working around the clock at ground zero."

"So what happened to him?"

"He was supposed to be sent out to another hospital. He still needed more reconstructive surgery. I do not know where. But I am sure he got the best medical care. That is why this has been a case I will never forget, the case of the mystery man."

At ten o'clock, Raymond's father came to the door and thanked Gramps for the meal and the chess game. Raymond said, "Yes, it has been a great evening. I am sorry if I kept you up too late."

Denise reassured him that he had not.

CHAPTER 8

THE HOSPITAL CONFESSION

After John Doe's third operation—and hopefully the last operation—he was taken to the eighth floor of the crucial ward unit. Nurse Stewart brought him to his room after surgery. He became Charlie Short's roommate. Charlie had the bed by the window, so his new roommate, Joe Doe, got the bed by the wall with no window. When the nurses brought him in, his face was completely covered in bandages, and there were tubes coming from all over his body. He had bandages on his legs and arms. He looked like a mummy. When Charlie saw him, he raised himself up from his bed to get a better look, and the first thing he asked Nurse Stewart was, "What happened to him?"

She took her time to make sure her patient was securely in his bed. She made sure all the monitors were correctly connected and everything worked as it should. Being a patient of Nurse Stewart meant you would get the best of care. Although conversely, as her patient, it is understood you gave her absolutely no problems. Nurse Stewart was always right. No matter the situation, she was right, and the sooner you understood and accepted that, the quicker you would have a good life in the unit.

Then she turned and looked to Charlie with eyes of compassion, and in a tender voice, she said to him, "This is your new roommate. He is a very sick man who has been and will be in a considerable amount of pain." She patiently told him everything he needed to know about his new roommate. "He has had several surgeries on his face because he was badly beaten and shot several times. You will learn that he does not remember who he is, because of the severe beating he received. So we are going to call him Edmond. I know, Mr. Short, you will be a good roommate to him, looking out for him, making sure he gets everything he needs, especially when I am not here. So you and I will take Edmond into our care."

Charlie lay back in his bed to rest and to allow his strength to return. He looked up at Nurse Stewart, and with all his reserved strength, he said he would do that. This really made Charlie feel good and gave him the satisfaction of knowing someone who was in a worse condition than him would need his help. Nurse Stewart knew Charlie would keep his word. When Nurse Stewart left the room, Charlie took a long good look at Edmond and understood his pain. He started to remember the first time he came to the hospital. Then he began to feel the pain pills taking effect.

Edmond had been in and out of consciousness for three days, and he was beginning to moan and groan. This let Charlie know that he was coming to. Charlie began to talk to him. He reassured Edmond that everything would be all right, and he pushed the button for the nurse to come. Charlie told the nurse that Edmond was coming to and was moaning and groaning in pain. The nurse knew that the pain medication was wearing off and that he would need some more, maybe a stronger dose. Charlie wanted to do all he could for his new roommate to help him feel better. He also thought how good it would be having someone to talk to. That would give him something to do to fill the long days in the hospital.

When Edmond became more conscious, his moans and groans became screams. The nurses attended to him. Some male nurses needed to secure his hands so that he didn't removed the tubes from his mouth and appendages. His voice was not very audible. Nevertheless, his screams told everyone that he wanted the pain to stop.

The day finally came when Charlie was able to have a conversation with Edmond. At first they were short conversations. Both men were not strong enough to carry on lengthy conversations. Each day Charlie looked forward to talking to Edmond. He wanted to learn more about him and the real story about his injuries. He had also become a little curious about what Edmond looked like. Every day the doctors would tell him the bandages would come off soon. Finally, that day came, and Edmond was wheeled out of their room. The doctors removed his bandages and told him the surgery was a success. One of the doctors gave him a mirror for him to see himself. All the doctors watched anticipating what his reaction would be. Wondering if he would recognize himself. Edmond took the mirror and looked at his swollen face. He slowly looked from side to side. Then he moved his sore swollen face up and down with much care. Carefully looking at all the details of his features. His expression lets doctors know he did not recognize himself. There were no details he could give the doctor on how he should look. At this time, they realized there would be no reward of recognition despite the tremendous effort of the surgeons to reconstruct his facial features. He accepted their advice and what they had to say to him about how he was healing. His face was healing nicely. They told him they wanted to keep a much closer watch over him because the healing would still take more time.

Charlie would try to remember this day. He and Edmond had dinner together in their room. They both were having a good day. The pain they both experienced became somewhat manageable. It felt good for Charlie to have a good conversation without being interrupted by complications from some new infection.

When he first came to the hospital, he hated the food, the place, and the people. He hated everything. He did not hide how he felt about the hospital staff. He had names for all the staff. He called them everything except children of God. However, time in the hospital had changed his attitude and behavior. He no longer yelled, "Get that $#@ out of here." Now he said, "Thank you," and, "Please."

It was mealtime, and this was the first time they both were awake. Usually, if Edmond was awake, Charlie was not, and when Charlie was awake, Edmond was sleeping. Typically, they were each given sedatives to provide them with tranquil rest that would last through afternoon meals. After Charlie glanced over his meal with a smile, he asked Edmond how his meal was. Edmond was not able to eat solid food yet. Edmond looked at him and affirmably shook his head. When they finished their meals, Charlie asked, "Well, my man, what are you in for? I know that sounds like something you would say to someone in prison, but for a while you will begin to feel as if you are in one. I mean, the pain and just not feeling good or unable to get out of the bed makes you feel as if you are in a prison. First, I know we have not really had the opportunity to formally introduce ourselves. I am Charlie Short, and I am glad to have you for a roommate."

Edmond put down his dinner, a nutritious drink. Because he still had some difficulty with speaking, he slowly said, "Edmond."

Charlie had waited so long to ask him about what had happen to him. "What happened to your face? What did they do to your face?"

Since it was still strenuous for Edmond to speak, he slowly took his hand and pretended to write in his left palm, telling Charlie that he would prefer to write than try to speak. Charlie was more mobile than Edmond, so he looked for some paper and a pen on the table that separated their beds. Communicating this way would take some time, so Charlie would have to wait a little while longer to learn about Edmond.

While Edmond was slowly getting the use of his speech, he and Charlie began to communicate. Facial expressions and laughter were both painful for Edmond, but having Charlie as a roommate, he was encouraged to put forth the effort and not give up. In spite of difficulty, Charlie encouraged Edmond to be persistent. Charlie wanted and needed Edmond's companionship. The more Edmond's condition improved, the more curious Charlie became about this man's identity. This was one of the first relationships he had truly invested in. Because of the time they were spending together, Charlie slowly learned that Edmond had no memory of his past and didn't remember anything about himself. The beating had left him with amnesia. He didn't know what had actually happened to him or who would have hurt him like this. Edmond had much to contend with, whereas Charlie was beginning to see Edmond as more than a roommate.

After the men had their breakfast, the men had a special visitor. With a big smile on his face, Gramps came in with books for the men to read. This was volunteer work that Gramps enjoyed doing. Once or twice a week, Gramps would bring books, newspapers, and magazines for the patients to read, and sometimes, he would rent movies for the patients to watch. He always made sure that the newspapers and magazines were sports-related and that the movies were comedies because he knew that laughter would make the patients feel better and aid them in getting well. He would spend time with some of the male patients who were very sick and did not have family. He would talk with them and give them encouragement in their moments of hopelessness. When he came in, he introduced himself and let the men know that he had visited with them before, but they had been asleep at the time. He told them that he was glad to have an opportunity to finally meet with them. He stayed for a very brief time and wanted to know if he could bring them anything when he returned. Charlie said no, but Edmond jokingly said, "Yes, bring me my memory."

Over the months the men got to know one another. Each of the men looked forward to seeing Gramps because he was their only visitor. Since Edmond had amnesia and Charlie had not said much about his past, seeing Gramps was always a pleasure. Whenever the opportunity presented itself, Gramps used it to witness to them. One day after Gramps had shared Jesus Christ with them and left them with their thoughts, Charlie asked Edmond, "What do you think about some of the things Gramps has told us about Jesus Christ?"

Charlie said, "The last time someone told me about Jesus was when I was growing up. My grandfather told me about Jesus. I believed, but as I got older, I guess I strayed from what I had been taught.

Edmond looked across from his bed and said, "I don't know whether or not I've been told about Jesus." The medication he had taken earlier made him sleepy, so he decided to take a nap. Charlie was taking what Gramps had told them about Christ seriously. It hit him hard that all the people he once associated with, the ones he thought of as friends, had not come to see him. He lay there in the bed, thinking about how much time he had left to live? He was slowly leaving this world and facing eternity. He remembered all the times God tried to get his attention, but he refused to listen. He had not wanted God to have any part of his life. He thought God would take away what he thought was fun, and He would restrict life with boring limitations. He once thought living for God was for losers and that people like Gramps were jerks, but now they were the ones who visited him and gave him hope. He thought about how he had lived his life and all the people he had hurt. The people who were once in his life were all gone now. They were either dead, hiding from the law, or living a life of lies. They just didn't know what made life important and precious. All the same, this was what he had made of life, and it was slowly fading away. He wanted to make a difference. He wanted to make life better for someone.

Edmond was doing better. There was still some swelling in his face. Nevertheless, he could continue his recovery as an outpatient. Unfortunately, this would add to Edmond's dilemma. Where could he go to continue to recover? The hospital would be in need of his bed, and Edmond still wasn't able to completely care for himself. He needed rehab for his arm and leg. Even if he found a place, he would still need help to get to and from the hospital so that he could actually go to rehab.

It had been a month since Gramps had seen Edmond and Charlie. He and Nana were out of town on a much-needed vacation. When he returned, he went to see the men and brought them souvenirs. It was a joyous reunion. When Gramps entered the room, both men's faces lit up the room. Charlie did something he had never done before in his life. When he saw Gramps, he reached out to give Gramps a hug. It was the type of hug you would give someone you loved and had not seen in a long time. More and more Gramps saw a change in Charlie. Where life had made him hard, love was making him gentle. In reality, Edmond and Gramps were his only family. There was no one else. No one called or visited him to see how he was doing. No one touch his hand or his heart with love. When Gramps finished greeting the men, he gave each of them their souvenirs, and he showed them pictures of his wife, Nana and their vacation. Then he wanted to know what was new with them. Charlie told him that he could feel a difference in the new medication that his doctors had given him. Notwithstanding, Edmond's news was bittersweet. He told Gramps about his new dilemma. Gramps listened very carefully and said very little. After lunch the men called it a day, and Gramps went home. Two days later when Gramps returned for a visit, he had good news for Edmond. He would no longer need to worry about where he would live once he was out of the hospital as an outpatient.

Gramps had some friends who would be happy to welcome Edmond into their home. Edmond was not expecting to hear this news. He was beginning to wonder about the things Gramps had shared with him and Charlie about Christ. After Gramps made the offer, Edmond couldn't stop thinking about how incredible and awesome it felt to have this need met. Life for him was getting better. After Gramps left, Charlie and Edmond would have their last talk together as roommates. It seemed as if they had known each other for years. They laughed and talked about their time together. Then Charlie told Edmond that there were things in his life he has regretted. Edmond asked what those things were.

Charlie stared out the window in a daze as if he was watching his thoughts materialize before him. He was reliving that horrible day. Then he said, "There are many, but the one thing I regretted the most was the night that I helped some friends kill a man."

Edmond's eyes grew bigger as he listened and learned about another part of his friend's life. Without thinking, Edmond asked, "Why would you want to kill someone? What did they do that would make you want to kill them? How did you kill him?"

Charlie was quiet for what seemed like a long time. Then he said, "I have long wanted to forget, but my conscience will not allow me to. I wish I could erase that day from my memory. I have been told confession is good for the soul. Maybe that is true. Anyway, it all started with an offer to make some easy money." Then Charlie started to cough, and he had to call for the nurse. Nurse Stewart answered the call. He told her he was having difficulty breathing and wanted something for the pain. Once Nurse Stewart administered the medication, she told Edmond that Charlie needed to rest because the medicine would make him sleepy. Charlie apologized for not being good company, but he said he would try to do better tomorrow. He thought a little rest would help him feel better. Then Charlie closed his eyes. He lay back in his bed and never said another word. The next day when Edmond woke, Charlie had been taken out of the room to another ward. When Edmond inquired about his whereabouts, no one could tell him anything.

CHAPTER 9

EDMOND'S NEW HOME

Gramps opened the door for Edmond so that he could sit in the front seat next to him. When Gramps brought Edmond to his new home, he reassured him he would take him back to the hospital to visit with Charlie. Later he learned that Charlie had requested that no one know about his relocation. This confused Edmond, but he would honor the request.

Edmond was wondering what his new home would be like. Who were the people who lived there, and how long would this place be his home? Then Gramps said, "I hope you like your new home. The people there are great. Why, you couldn't find a better group of people. They will take good care of you. Now, let's see. There's Ronda and Ron Benson. They are from Memphis—southerners. Some of the best people you will ever find. They open their home to people who need help. Usually they help people who have come to their church and need to relocate, such as yourself, or people who have lost their homes. Why, they have helped people who needed protection from domestic abuse and people who are in need of a place to stay for a short period of time. They have opened their home and helped people for ten years. Ronda is a great cook. She and Ron have raised five kids. Now they have ten grandchildren. Would you believe they know all of their kids and grandchildren's names? They can say each child's name without making a mistake. So these are people who are on top of things. So they are able to handle anything that will come up.

"Then there is Mike. He was once better known as Pimp Daddy. He just recently accepted Christ into his life about three weeks ago. Before he accepted Christ, he was a pimp, but when one of his soon-to-be girl's grandmother learned what happened to her, she came looking for him with vengeance in mind. This woman showed no mercy. When Mildred, one of her friends, saw Mike talking to her thirteen-year-old granddaughter, she called her on the phone and told her what she was watching. This woman wasted no time. She did not take the time to contact her husband to let him know what was happening. She took a baseball bat and went into Mike's sanctuary. I have no idea how she was able to get in, but she did. She asked one question, 'Where is Mike?' Once she had that information, she was swinging that bat better than a professional baseball player. Would you believe this man always carried a gun with him no matter where he went? Even into the shower, the bathroom, and to bed. It didn't matter. That gun was always attached to his body. It was like a part of his body. She called him everything except a child of God. She beat him senseless and left the scene. When he was in the hospital, she came to visit him. You could say she encouraged him to change his line of work. She told him if he knew what was good for him, he'd better not file charges against her, and he'd better not come within fifty feet of her granddaughter. If he did, he would surely feel the hand of God on his body. Then she told him he needed to accept Christ into his life or continue to live a life in danger. I do not know what she told him, but it was what he needed to hear to make a change in his life. The love of God will give him the peace he needs for a better life. So these will be the new people in your life. I want you to know that they are good people. Well, Mike is in the process of learning."

When they arrived, the Bensons met their guests in the driveway. They wanted to give Edmond one of their down-home welcomes. When they were inside, Ronda had a home-cooked meal ready for him, and Ron showed him to his room. Edmond would have that part of the house all to himself. His first night there, Ronda baked a special meal to make Edmond feel welcome. It was a southern dinner with black-eyed peas, mustard greens with mashed potatoes, chicken fried steak, corn bread, iced tea, and peach cobbler for dessert. To Ronda's surprise, Edmond offered to help with the dishes, but Ronda would not hear of it, not on his first night there. But it would be good to have his help later while they were all getting to know him. Edmond went to his room to take a look around. It was a cozy room. Ronda had put an assortment of magazines in his bathroom and bedroom. There were books and the newspaper to read too. There were plenty of hangers, but Edmond did not have much in the way of clothing to put in the closet and dresser. The clothes he was wearing were from the hospital's lost and found. As he lay across the bed, he began to think about his life. How did this happen to him? Why did it happen to him? There was one singular question he most wanted to have the answer to. Who was he? Would anyone help him find the answers to these questions? If people did know him, would they know him now? He did not look the same, or did he? He wondered, *What did I do to make someone so angry that the person wanted to hurt me? No, they wanted to kill me.* This thought really began to scare him. What if that person or those persons were still out there and still wanted to do him harm? This was the first time he had thought about this. Well, this was just too much right now, so Edmond decided to go to sleep.

Edmond lived with the Bensons for four weeks. His physical therapy in mending the nerve damage to his leg and arm was improving. The swelling in his face was almost gone. Now that his body was doing better, he thought more and more about finding out his identity. Not knowing his identity would make it difficult for him to get a job. He would need some form of identification.

This experience was teaching Edmond how to pray. He was becoming a strong believer in Christ. Each time he thought about how nice people had been to him, helping him with what he needed and offering him a place to stay so that he could get to the hospital for therapy. Every new person who had come into his life had shown him the love of Christ.

CHAPTER 10

A NEW LIFE

It had been a month since Denise had moved out of her grandparents' home. She enjoyed living with them, but having her own place felt even better. Each time she planned to visit with them, something would come up. She was either sending postcards with her new address to all her friends or talking with friends who had not known about her decision to move. Buying new furniture and other things made her new place feel like home. She did not want anything that she had shared with Eric. This was a new start, and she did not want anything to remind her of her life with him. She had made new friends, and her life was beginning to feel normal again. There had been a few times when she went out on dates. She even started to go to church with her grandparents.

After her move Denise had boxes of things that she no longer needed, mostly Eric's things. When she thought about how to get rid of it all, Nana came to mind. She gave Nana a call and told her about the boxes. Nana told her it was perfect timing. She knew just who could use Eric's things. She told her that Gramps would be over later to get the boxes.

Gramps came over to the Benson's early the next day to see Edmond. Ronda was glad to see him and offered him breakfast. He was grateful for the offer, but he told Ronda that he had already eaten. He explained that he had come over early to bring Edmond some things that he may be able to use. He told Ronda how grateful he was that they were willing to help Edmond. He realized Edmond did not have any clothes. Because Edmond had worn nothing but hospital clothing, he was sure the man would enjoy wearing something with style for a change. Gramps helped

Ronda place the boxes on the kitchen table, and she opened one of the boxes to see what was inside. Then she opened another one ... and another one until all the boxes were opened. There were designer sweaters, shirts, pants, packages of unopened underwear, shoes, socks, ties, aftershave lotions, new razors, and razor blades. Ronda looked up from the boxes and said, "Who got a divorce? From the looks of these boxes, someone had a very bitter divorce."

Gramps asked her why she would say that. Ronda explained that all the clothes were not folded but just thrown into the boxes. "These are expensive clothes, nothing but name brands. To just have them thrown into boxes looks like someone was very upset about something."

Gramps gave a little grin and simply said, "These things belonged to Denise's husband."

Edmond was glad to get the things. He thanked Gramps and took the boxes to his room. It really did not matter to him how the clothes fit. He was just glad to have them. He was getting a little tired of wearing Mike's pimping suits and a pair of gym pants from Ron. The clothes had a good fit compared to what he had been wearing. Maybe with a little more weight, they would fit even better. He could use everything except the razors, but he had plans to use them once his face had completely healed. Since he was starting to grow a beard, the razor would help him keep the beard shaped.

Later he called Gramps to thank him and Nana again for the clothing. Nana offered him a proposition that he could not refuse. Nana explained to him that she and Gramps would be going out of town to do some speaking engagements. There were several communities who wanted her to speak on how to organize a CWHS so that they could organize their own youth activities to keep them out of trouble and off the streets. She needed someone to take care of the office while she and Gramps were away. Her speaking engagements would last for a month, and she wanted to know if Edmond would run the office while they were away. It did not take long for Edmond to think about the offer. He realized that getting a job would be impossible since he did not know his identity, and besides, he needed a way to earn an income. He agreed.

Nana also told him that the position came with the title of CWHS assistant manager and that there was a place for him in the back of the warehouse that had been converted into a condo. There was a bedroom with a small kitchen and a closet for him if he decided to accept the position. Edmond told Nana that he could not thank her enough. He thought to himself, *Maybe all those things that Gramps told him about Jesus Christ were true*. Every one of his needs had been met. He started to think about all the things that had happened to him. His body was healing. He had people who were concerned about him, and help was always there for him. Now he had a new place to live, a new job, and new clothes to wear to his new job. "Now, God, please just help me learn who I am."

After his first day of work, Edmond was tired, but he wanted to organize his closet so it would be easier for him to get dressed in the mornings. He wanted to get to work on time and look his best. As he was going through the boxes Gramps had given him, a small black box trimmed in gold fell from the clothing. Edmond reached down to pick it up. He closely examined the box. Edmond looked inside and found pictures. Most of them had been cut up and torn apart. At the very bottom of the box, there was a beautiful matching black leather book trimmed in gold. The cover of the book was engraved with a dove carrying two hearts joined together with a ribbon. At the end of one of the heart, the words "Love for Eternity" were written. He opened the book and began to read it. It was someone's diary. Some rips suggested that someone had torn some pages out. As he started to read the diary, the phone rang. He stopped and laid the box along with the diary down on his bed. Then he went to answer the phone. It was the wrong number. He wanted to return and read the diary; however, it had been a long day, and he was tired. As he looked at the diary, he thought to himself, *Maybe tomorrow will be a better day to figure out what to do with his newfound treasure. I need to get an early start*. So he put the box and the diary back in one of the empty boxes and went to bed.

The four weeks that Edmond fulfilled the position as assistant manager gave him little time to do or to think about anything else. He wanted to focus on finding out his identity, but time did not allow him the opportunity to do so. He thought it would be better to wait until Gramps and Nana returned to put more time into his search. His skills using the computer were improving, considering he was teaching himself how to use it. Classes would help, but there was no time to learn just yet. He felt good about himself as he taught himself other skills. It made him wonder what other things he could do. He wondered about what he used to do for a living, if he was married with a family, and if he had been a good spouse to his wife and a good father if he had children. What were his interests? The more he accomplished at the center, the more he wondered about what kind of person he was. Was he a loving person who helped other people like Gramps and Nana? He knew that he would find answers with time.

While at the center one morning, Edmond received a call from Nana. She called to see how things were going for him and to see if he needed any help with anything. He reassured her he did not. He enjoyed working there. All the same, it gave him little time for anything else. Nana told him she understood that, but in a few weeks, she reassured him, things would change. It would be the off season then, and things tended to slow down. He thanked Nana again for all she and Gramps had done for him. It was an opportunity to work, which was helping him learn some of his skills. He could not stop thanking her for the clothes. He knew he could never repay them. Nana let him know that working in the center was a big help for them. They had asked him on such short notice. She wanted him to know how much of a help he was to them, but as for the clothing, she told him he could thank the person who gave them to him himself. She gave him Denise's e-mail address. Reaching her by e-mail would be much easier and quicker than calling. They thanked each other again and said their good-byes.

After talking to Nana, Edmond thought it would be a good time to reach out to Denise and thank her for the clothes. The center was the only place where he had access to a computer. When he e-mailed Denise, he told her how much the clothing and the other articles in the boxes meant to him. They came at a time when he needed them the most because he did not have anything to call his own. Everything he needed was there.

Denise was slowly getting her life back. She was enjoying her new job. She was allowing herself to meet new people, and she was making new friends. She missed meeting up with her girlfriends Gwen, Sam, and Amy. Maybe a visit would do her some good. It would be great to see them again and tell them all what had been happening to her. She preferred visiting to e-mailing or calling. They meant a lot to her, and she would rather see the looks on their faces when they saw the new her.

Her new home was starting to look the way she wanted. It was inviting, cozy, and very comfortable. It was just what she needed in her new life, a place to come home to, a new home for a new beginning. Her favorite place was the terrace. She put out a patio table with an umbrella and two chairs on the terrace so she could enjoy her view. Every morning she would have her breakfast out there. The trees that surrounded the area gave her some privacy. Having breakfast out there before she went to work was great therapy too. This became a place where she could sit and think about her life and how it had changed. Today was one of those days. It was the weekend, and she had no plans. So she just wanted to sit and *think*. She made herself a cup of coffee, her favorite, Irish cream, and drank it with one of Nana's blueberry muffins. She thought about some of the things Nana had told her about forgiveness, what she had learned from her counseling sessions, how she needed to forgive Eric for what he had done, and how she needed to forgive herself. Forgiving Eric, she understood, she needed to do that, but when she thought about why she needed to forgive herself, well, that confused her. It really did not matter. She knew deep down in her heart, soul, and mind that doing what Nana told her would be the right thing to do. How she was going to do it was the problem. *How does one forgive?* she wondered. *Do you do it one time or many times?* Out on the terrace, enjoying the view, sipping her cup of Irish cream coffee, and nibbling on Nana's blueberry muffin, she felt the need to stop thinking about everything she needed to do about her past. So she decided to check her e-mail. She went to get her laptop from the kitchen table.

Denise decided to open and read her e-mails before she started on her next project. She saw a new e-mail address. She wondered who had sent her a message, because very few people had her e-mail address. She was always very careful about the people she gave it to. She wondered if she should open it. When she looked closer and saw it was from the CWHS website, she opened it and read the e-mail. It was from Edmond, and he was thanking her for the boxes of clothes. He explained how much they meant to him. She thought to herself, *Something that no longer had value to me has become very important to someone else*. She decided to e-mail him back to tell him that he was welcome.

When Edmond got to work, he always started the day by opening and answering CWHS's e-mails, which often took much of the morning. After an hour of sitting, he needed to get up and walk around. He still needed to do the exercises the therapist gave him to work the muscles in his leg. When he opened the last e-mail, he realized that it was from Denise. It was pleasant to see that Denise had responded to him. Without thinking, he e-mailed her back, "You are welcome."

Before long the two were e-mailing each other regularly. Each morning Edmond looked forward in anticipating getting an email from Denise. It really made his day. The reality was he enjoyed and was delighted in the fact that he was socializing with a woman. This was very new to him and not to mention Denise was the first woman besides Rhonda, whom he had communicated with daily before he moved into his little condo. He realized the two women did not socialized the same. Communicating with Charlie everyday was how he had learned how to socialize, but this was a woman. He was learning that men and women socialized differently. Their interest in socialization made talking challenging. He just wanted to take his time to get to know Denise. He was pleased in knowing that a woman would take a moment to respond to him in such a way that made him wanted to know more about himself to share with her. He tried to be careful what he shared with her about himself. Of course, he was more curious and attentive when she would tell him things about herself.

It seemed as if they both were experiencing life the same way. They were starting new lives. They didn't know many people, and they didn't have the chance to meet other people. However, where she wanted to forget her old life, he was trying to remember his. Nonetheless, the e-mails were becoming an intimate way to meet, and it seemed to work for both of them.

As the time approached for Nana and Gramps to return, Denise wanted to give them a dinner party. She thought that inviting a few friends over to welcome them back would be a great idea. She would hire the same caterer who did the appreciation dinner for the volunteers.

She also thought that it would be good to invite Edmond to come. That way she could meet him. She always felt meeting someone for the first time would be better with other people around. It would not be so overwhelming trying to always think of something to say and wanting to get a good look at the person without him or her knowing.

She e-mailed him to inform him of the date, time, and place. When Edmond got the e-mail, he thought a party was a good idea, but he wanted to take Denise to a really marvelous place. He had so enjoyed her e-mails. As he thought about meeting her for the first time, he found he did not want to talk with her with crowds of people around them. It would take away from the intimacy of meeting for the first time. He wanted to enjoy their meeting without being interrupted at a social event. Then he thought that meeting like this could work in his favor, After all, he couldn't afford to take her to some marvelous place or even drive her there. Not knowing his identity was becoming more of a problem than he thought. He didn't have a driver's license. He wasn't sure if he even remembered how to drive. *What will I tell her about myself? We talked mostly about sports, the news, and church. We did not really talk about ourselves. Now, thinking about it, it may not be good, because not knowing my identity may frighten her away*, he thought. But she gave him the invitation, and he accepted. As the date grew closer, Edmond felt like he might get cold feet. He was starting to think that maybe it was not a good idea for the two to meet, but at the same time he wanted to know what Denise looked and sounded like. *I need to pray about this and let God tell me what to do.*

Denise realized that she had no idea what Edmond looked like. So she e-mailed him later that day to get a description of him. He did not get to read the e-mail until the next day. He e-mailed her back.

> Hello, Denise,
>
> I read your e-mail. Ha-ha. It will be easy to find me in the crowd of people. You will be able to recognize me by my clothes because I will be wearing the clothes you gave to me. But then I need to know the description of you. How will I recognize you? Please e-mail me a picture of yourself so I will be able to recognize you.

CHAPTER 11

THE DIARY

When Gramps and Nana returned from their speaking engagements, Gramps thought it would be good for he and Edmond to go visit Charlie. With his new computer expertise, Edmond was able to do some research, and he found Charlie on Facebook. They went to the gift shop to purchase a few things that they thought he would use and enjoy. When they got to the floor and requested permission to visit with Charlie, the nurse told them that he was no longer in the ward. Gramps inquired as to his whereabouts. The nurse stopped her task, looked up, and informed the gentlemen that Charlie had gone home. They wanted to know if the hospital had an address for him. She informed them that it was the hospital's policy not to give out that information. The two returned to the center to do more research on Charlie's whereabouts. One of the drivers for the center overheard Gramps and Edmond's conversation and let them know he picked up several boxes and furniture at Charlie's address about two weeks ago. They thanked him, got the address, and went over to visit with him. Upon their arrival a lady answered the door. "Yes?"

Gramps let the lady know why they were there. "We are looking for Charlie Short."

"Charlie Short does not live here anymore. He is dead."

Edmond said, "Dead!"

"Yes."

"When did he die?"

"He died about two weeks ago."

Edmond wanted to press harder for proof. "Are you sure? I mean, how do—"

But before he could finish his sentence, the lady responded with a tone in her voice that left no doubt that she knew. "Yes, he is dead. I ought to know. I am his sister. Now, if you gentlemen don't have any more questions ..."

"What did he die of?" Gramps asked.

"He had cancer. When he had reconstructive surgery for his stomach, the doctors found cancer cells in the lining of his stomach that were spreading throughout his body. When the doctors told him that he did not have long to live, he wanted to return home. He returned home to died."

"Did he die alone?"

"No, I was with him. He was at peace with God. He accepted Christ before he died."

Gramps was glad to hear that. He had witnessed to Charlie and prayed that he would accept Christ as his Lord and Savior. "We are sorry to bother you, and thank you."

Gramps told Edmond, "No matter how prepared you think you are for death, you are not." Learning of their friend's death left both men feeling numb. They went home.

It was hard for Edmond not to think about what had happened to Charlie. He cherished the time they had together. Thinking about Charlie's death was making him depressed. Edmond thought that taking a walk would help him feel better. When he returned home, he decided to go to bed, but it was hard for him to go to sleep. When he reached for the clock to see what time it was, it fell on to the floor under the bed. As he reached under the bed to get the clock, he felt something that wasn't the clock. He turned on the nightstand light and looked under the bed. It was a book. He looked closer and realized it was the diary that he had found in the boxes of clothing.

He remembered telling himself that he would read the diary when the time was more convenient. He wasn't able to sleep, as he was already overwhelmed with thoughts about Charlie. Thoughts flooded his mind of the time they had together and how he would never have the opportunity to see him again or to tell him good-bye. Tonight was a good time for him to begin the diary. He opened the pages and started to read.

Dear Diary,

Today is June 10, 1999.

This is the last day of school. I will graduate in a few days. I am so excited. After graduation I will go to New York to spend the summer with my cousin, Lori. For two years we have planned this. We made a list of all the things we want to do.

He turned a few pages and read some more.

Dear Diary,

Today is November 15, 1999.

Today was not a good day. I wrecked my car while on campus. Dad said it can be fixed. I just hope I will not be without my car for very long. Every time I think about my new car being wrecked, it makes me want to scream. It was my graduation gift that my parents surprised me with when I returned home from spending the summer with my cousin in New York.

With part of the page torn away, he read,

Dear Diary,

Today is May

Tonight while my friends Amy, Sam, Gwen and I were leaving the Midnight Club, my car would not start. Then this pleasantly attractive man named Eric Bishop came over to help us. He called his mechanic about my car. The mechanic told him to have the car towed to the shop and that he would take a look at it tomorrow. Then he called for a tow truck and had my car towed to his mechanic's shop to see what was wrong. He then took us all to our apartment. The next day he picked me up and brought me to the shop and made sure the car was operable before I left the shop. He even stayed with me while they were working on it. I found he was very charming, witty, and the most handsome man I had ever met. It was like meeting a knight in shining armor. He was a real hero. He wanted to know if—

Dear Diary,

Today is—

I have found4 the love of my life. Eric, Eric Bishop is the most magnificent, extraordinary, impressive, spectacular man I have ever met. He is everything I want in a man. He is the man I want to marry. He is the man I want to share my life—

Reading the diary took Edmond's mind off of Charlie. It helped him to relax. He thought Eric was a real charmer. It made him feel good to see how nice and caring he was to Denise, while at the same time it grieved him that he had probably broken her heart. At least he figured from all the torn pages. How deeply hurt she had become in their relationship. He had learned from reading the diary that Eric was an opportunist, a man without a conscience who thought of no one but himself. He hoped he was not a man like Eric, a person who would treat someone who loved him with such contempt. There were days when he experienced flashbacks, but it was not happening as frequently as he wanted. He thought he would read a little more tomorrow. With that thought, he went to sleep.

Nana and Gramps thanked Denise for the dinner party and the great job she did in arranging everything. The food and music were great. Nana told Denise she loved the band and said they did a great job. Gramps was enjoying himself. Denise liked that. She wanted to do something for her grandparents. They have always been there for her. She wanted to do something to show her appreciation.

It was getting late, and Edmond still had not come. The dinner was within walking distance from his home. Denise was looking and asking people whether or not he had arrived. Did Edmond get cold feet? When everyone had left, Denise told her grandparents that there was someone she had wanted them to meet. Unfortunately, she was not able to introduce them to him, because he did not come. Gramps said, "I am sorry. Who was this person you wanted us to meet? What is his name?" She told them his name is Edmond. Nana said, "Edmond. When did you meet Edmond?"

"I met him on CWHS's website. He sent me an e-mail to thank me for the boxes of clothes."

Nana told her, "Edmond is the young man who managed the office for me when we were out of town. He such a nice young man. He is the man who lived with the Bensons. He did not have much. You could say he only had the clothes on his back."

"Well, Nana, he was supposed to be here tonight."

Nana was sure that something unexpected had come up.

The next morning Denise got an e-mail from Edmond explaining what had happened to him last night. He was on his way there when two elderly women needed help. He stopped to help them, and it took a little longer than he thought. He asked Denise to please forgive him. He would try to make it up to her. Denise e-mailed him back and told him about the great dinner he had missed. The food was fantastic, and the music was so good that you wanted to just dance all night. Everyone had a great time. She, Nana, and Gramps were sorry he could not make it.

Not knowing his identity was beginning to take a toll on Edmond's mind. Every day he prayed to God to help him learned who he was. With each day that passed without him knowing the truth, it was becoming more difficult for him to live his life.

Nana told Edmond what a great job he did while she was away. She wanted to know if he wanted to continue to work for CWHS. Edmond assured her that he did. He enjoyed working there. Nana told him she was sorry that he did not come to the dinner Denise had given them, but she would love to have him over for dinner tomorrow night. Edmond accepted the invitation.

When Denise came over to Nana's to return her vacuum cleaner, Nana asked if she would like to stay for dinner. That sounded like a great idea to Denise. She didn't want to go home and cook anyway. Besides, there was nothing in her refrigerator or cabinets that she could prepare. So without further thought, she said yes. Denise asked if there was anything she could do to help. "Sure, make a salad and some lemonade, and when you are finished, please set the table."

When Denise was setting the table, she only had place settings for three. Nana quickly informed her that they were having more than three for dinner. "Nana, you never said that there would be more people for dinner. How many? Who will be here for dinner?"

Nana was busy making the coleslaw for the barbecue, so she didn't hear Denise's question. When Denise started to ask again, the doorbell rang. Nana said, "Oh, dear, they are here. Denise, go let them in please."

CHAPTER 12

THE DINNER GUESTS

Rev. Brown and Raymond were on time. They brought a bouquet of flowers and a dessert to show their appreciation for their dinner invitation. Denise welcomed them in and told them that Gramps was in the backyard and Nana was in the kitchen. Raymond handed her the bouquet of flowers. Rev. Brown asked if he could take the dessert into the kitchen. Once in the kitchen, he gave Nana a hug and handed her the dessert. She thanked him and placed it on the kitchen counter near the refrigerator. He told her it was an apple pie. When Gramps opened the door, the smell of his grilled chicken filled the room. It brought smiles to everyone's faces, and he proudly said, "This chicken is finger-licking, mouth-watering, tongue-dropping good!" Nana told him to place the chicken in the oven so that it would keep warm while they wait on the rest of their guests. Then the doorbell rang again. Denise answered the door again. Nana heard her name and came in. As she was welcoming her guest, Gramps called for Denise. She excused herself, while Nana told him to come in. Nana asked Denise to visit with her guests while she and Gramps finished preparing dinner.

Denise told the men to come out on the patio to sit, and she left to get some iced tea for them to drink. When Raymond saw the newly arrived guest, he extended his hand to introduce himself. As Edmond walked closer, he smiled, gave the man a handshake, and said, "Well, hello, Dr. Brown, I cannot tell you how good it is to see you again."

Raymond leaned in a little closer to get a better look and said, "Do I know you?"

"I am Edmond, your mystery man. Remember?"

Raymond could not believe his eyes. He did not recognize him. He said, "It is good to see you are doing better."

"Dr. Brown, it is good to see you as well."

"How many more surgeries have you had?"

Edmond told him that he had lost count. It had taken several to get the bones to mend right.

"How did you recognize me?"

"I remembered your face and the sound of your voice. I know I was doped up a lot, but I mostly remembered the sound of your voice."

"Imagine that."

Then Denise returned with glasses of iced tea and offered them to the men. "Well, I am sorry I did not introduce you to each other, but it looks as if you have done that yourselves. Raymond, it has been a while since I have last seen you and your father. I hope you and your father are doing fine."

Then she turned to look in Edmond's direction. "I am sorry, but I do not know your name. You are?"

Edmond turned to face Denise and said, "I am Edmond."

Denise tilted her head and said, "You are Edmond?" Then Nana came over to make sure her guests were doing okay and to let everyone know dinner was ready.

Denise followed Edmond to the food. "So Edmond, we finally meet. You know, I should have recognized you by the clothes. Ha-ha. Right?"

Edmond agreed. "Right. Ha-ha."

Once everyone was seated and enjoying their meal, Gramps looks across the table and saw everyone talking. He said, "Well, I see everyone has met and is getting to know each other." Raymond told Denise that Edmond was the man he had told her about as his most memorable case, and Gramps reminded her that Edmond was also the man who had received Eric's clothes. Edmond told the group that he was glad to finally meet The Franklin's beautiful granddaughter.

When the dinner was finished and everyone was enjoying the dessert that Rev. Brown brought, Edmond got up and helped Nana clean the table. It gave him the opportunity to get a very good look at Denise. He noticed that Raymond was also enjoying the view. Raymond was explaining to Denise how the church and the county clinic wanted to come together to help soldiers from the Iraq War get back into the community. While Edmond and Nana were doing the dishes, Gramps and Rev. Brown played chess. After he finished the dishes, Edmond joined the conversation between Denise and Raymond. Nana went to watch Gramps and Rev. Brown play chess. At ten o'clock, Edmond's driver, George, came for him. It was not easy for him to leave. He was enjoying the conversation, but most of all he was enjoying getting to know Denise better. While on his way home, George asked him how his evening was. He told him he had really enjoyed himself. As he was talking about his evening, he thought that Denise had to be the owner of the diary. Once he was home, he retrieved the diary from under his bed. He thought that reading it would obviously help him get to know her better. That thought led him to think about himself. He was learning more about Denise than he had learned about himself. Was he married, and if he was, what was his wife like? How long had he been married? did he have children, and if he did, how many? What kind of husband and father was he? Was his family looking for him? What did he do for a living? Where was he from? Still, he was somewhat surprised at how much he had taken an interest in her. His conscience got to him soon. He knew that the diary was personal and that Denise had written it for her eyes only. These were her personal and intimate thoughts that she did not want anyone else to read. Nevertheless, it was too late. That thought came after the fact. He had completed what was left of the book. Most of the pages were torn out or had been marked through with a pen, which made it very difficult to read. He realized that he had likely learned things about her that she would not have told him, and he thought about that line as he prepared for bed. As he lay across the bed, he thought about what the diary had told him about Denise. He had learned how she and her husband, Eric, had met, how he had proposed to her, her favorite flower, her favorite foods, and favorite candy. He also learned about the people who were most important in her life and how she felt about them. She wrote in great detail about her love for Eric, where she wanted to live with him, and the type of home she wanted to live in.

She wrote about the great emotional pain she was in, not knowing about her husband's affair, how she learned about the affair, his death, and the police not finding the person or persons who tried to kill him. She knew that his affair had taken away the time and opportunity to grieve Eric's death. Sleeping pills were the only way she could get to sleep at night. Feeling drowsy, Edmond fluffed the pillows and put them under his head, and the last thought on his mind was Denise.

CHAPTER 13

THE LETTER

The off season had begun, and Edmond found that he had extra time. He was using the extra time to find out how he could learn about his identity. When he was not on the computer, he would use the gym at the center to exercise. One evening while he was at the gym working out, Denise came in with Raymond. They did not see him, because he was on the rowing machine behind the treadmills. They were there talking with Gramps. When Gramps left the room and they were alone, he noticed that Raymond's distance was changing. He was getting closer and closer to her. It looked as if her space was becoming his. The man who was waiting for his turn on the machine came over and reminded Edmond that his time was up. When he got up from the machine and proceeded to the next machine to continue his work out, the couple had already left.

Nana asked Edmond and some of the other volunteers to help put in some new equipment in the gym. After they had finished, he asked Nana how Denise was doing. He explained that she had not e-mailed in weeks and that he had not seen her around the center. Nana told him that Denise was out of town. She had been out of town for a couple of weeks, visiting with friends. He thanked her for the information, and he returned to his office. When he did, a gentleman came up to him and asked if he was Edmond. He acknowledged that he was, and the man handed him an envelope. When he took the envelope and looked at it, he wanted to ask why the man had given to him, but he had already left.

Edmond got up from his chair and looked out the door. He couldn't find anyone out there. He walked around the corner, but no one was there either. He walked back to the office. He sat in his chair and opened the envelope. There, he found a letter. He opened the letter and started to read it.

The information you are looking for about your identity will be found in a locker at the bus station. Find enclosed two keys. Take the train to the bus station. Once there, find locker B362. Use the key that has been clearly marked B362 to unlock the locker, and there you will find a box inside. Inside the box is a bag. Use the other key to open the box. All the information you need about your identity is inside that bag.

There was no name or date on the letter. No letterhead, just a plain sheet of paper with the type-written message.

Edmond sat there and thought, *What is this? Someone's idea of a joke? Maybe it is the answer to my prayers. What must I do?* He prayed out loud, "God, only You know what I must do. Please tell me." He stood up and started to walk around the room, thinking as he walked. He looked at the clock, wondering if there was time to catch the train to go to the bus station. What could he lose if he did go? He put the envelope inside his jacket. He asked his friend George to drive him to the train station. It would be quicker if someone drove him there. Once on the train, he read the instructions again and again and again until he knew every word by memory. He was going to do exactly as the letter told him. He could do nothing but think and pray. Who was the man who had brought this information to him? Who wrote the letter? Why did they write the letter? Why would they not just tell him what he needed to know? He was so focused on his thoughts that he did not hear the pregnant woman ask if the seat next to him was taken. The day was cloudy and cold, but you would never have known it, because Edmond was sweating. He was thanking God for an answer to prayer. He waited a long time for this. Now all his questions about himself were about to be answered. It was about an hour's ride on the train to the bus station. The ride felt like eternity. Every ten minutes the train stopped to let passengers on and off. Each time the conductor announced the stop. Edmond did not hear a word until he heard his stop be called. He could not move. His mind was telling his body to move, but he just sat there. His mind told his feet to move, to run to the door before the train stopped.

Edmond told himself, "You need to be at the door before the train stops. Move!" He could not. Then he felt a gentle touch. He had no idea who touched him, but he was glad. There he was at the door. He didn't know how he got there, but he had. He was not sure if he had walked or if someone had carried him. He was quickly losing track of time. Once the doors opened, he stepped out onto the platform and walked in the direction of the bus station. He stopped and asked the first person he saw, "Is this the way to the bus station?" They reassured him he was going in the right direction. His shoes were beginning to feel like there was lead in them. He finally arrived at the station and went to section where the lockers were located. His eyes were like lasers zooming in on every letter and number. When he entered the room with the lockers, he saw wall-to-wall lockers everywhere. He eventually found the B section and then three hundreds, and then he found it—B362. He went to it. He pulled the envelope from his pocket, and it slowly came out. He tried to put the key in the lock, but his hand was shaking so badly that he could not do it. He needed both of his hands to slide the key into the lock. As tears were running down his face, he turned the key. Nothing happen. He prayed, "Lord, please help me." He tried turning the key again, and the locker unlocked. He slowly opened the door, and he found a black box. Hands still shaking, he managed to take the other key out and open the black box. There was a bag inside just as the letter said there would be. He took it by the handle and removed it from the locker. He closed the door and walked away.

It had started to rain. Edmond waited for the next train. The rain started to come down hard. He waited patiently in the pouring rain. Edmond got on the next train for home. He sat there in his seat, dripping wet. He was not sure if he was soaked from the rain or perspiration. He sat there in his seat, clutching the bag to himself. He could not open the bag. *No*, he thought to himself, *I need to be in a place where I can open this bag with no one around me. I need to be alone to think and understand what I will be looking at.* He finally arrived home. It felt as if he was on the train one minute, and the next minute he found himself sitting in his room, looking at the bag. Edmond spoke out loud to God. "Okay, God, this bag holds information about my past and future. It holds the truth about who I am." For the first time, he closely examined the bag. It was a simple black gym bag. There was a zipper at the top, easy access to his treasure. He opened it and looked inside. Inside there was a letter, a necklace, a pocket watch, and an ID card. He slowly took out the letter to read it.

Dear Edmond,

On September 11, 2001, you had an encounter with three men—Jack Letterman, better known as June-bug, Robert Jackson, nicknamed Tank, and me—and it changed your life. On this night, my friend, June-bug, always seemed to have money to do whatever he wanted. A nine-to-five job he did not have. Despite that, he would always say he was never going to punch the clock or have to drop a dime to the boss. He was always dressed and spoke well. For someone who did not have a desire to go to school, he was a very intelligent and an eloquent speaker. He always amazed us with what he knew and what he could do. Always calm and a lady's man. He never talked about who he worked for or what he did, but we knew that he was into drugs. One thing he did not know much about was paying taxes. He did not try to pretend he knew. He would just say, "One day I am going to learn how that tax thing works." So we knew it had to be drugs that gave him an affluent lifestyle.

One day he asked me and our partner, Tank, if we wanted to make some easy money. I wanted to know what we had to do, but Tank only wanted to know how much it would pay. Tank was just as his name indicated. He was six-foot-five and 350 pounds of muscle, and he had a head that no normal hat would fit. He worked out daily at the YMCA. Now, don't get me wrong. He wasn't a bonehead. He was going to college with a 4.0 GPA, working on a degree in engineering, but having fun always excited him. So June-bug told us to meet him at the airport with our bags packed for two days, and he would tell us what we would be doing then.

When we did, he met us and had airlines tickets to fly to New York. A limousine met us and took us to our hotel. Then we both asked him what we would be doing. Once again he told us he would let us know later. When we got to our room, a complimentary basket was waiting for us, and later a complimentary steak and lobster dinner with wine was brought to our suite. It felt like we were on vacation. We were feeling so good that we forgot why we were there. June-bug had not told us, and that was beginning to make me feel a little uncomfortable.

While we were having dinner, I confronted him. He told us we were there to help him get money someone owed to his boss. The next day we were to meet a man who owed his boss some money, and if he saw three men instead of one, that would make it more persuasive for the man to pay the money. Sounded innocent enough, right? We took a cab to a car rental place, and he rented a car. We went to an address for a condo in Central Park West. It was in a very nice neighborhood. June-bug told me to wait in the car and keep the engine running just in case we had to leave in a hurry.

He and Tank went to the door and rang the doorbell. A man answered the door. They went inside and closed the door behind them. I did not see them again. I waited for what felt like hours. I was beginning to get nervous when three men came out the door. I could see Tank and June-bug were walking fine, but the third man, the one who answered the door, had problems walking. In fact, June-bug and Tank were helping him walk. As I looked closer, he was not walking at all. June-bug and Tank each had an arm, and they were carrying him to the car. His head was lowered. When they got into the car, I could see that the man had been badly beaten. June-bug put an address into the GPS and told me to go there. I asked what happened, but June-bug told me to just drive. When I drove us there, we took the man out of the car, and June-bug began to beat him again. He was a bloody mess.

Then June-bug's cell phone rang, and when he answered it, he had me hold him while Tank continued to beat him. Then he stopped talking on the phone and started to go through the man's pants. He was looking for something. It was the man's wallet. He took his driver's license out and said some very selected words that let you know something was wrong. He told Tank to stop beating the man. He told me to take the man's jewelry and whatever else may have his identity. Blood was everywhere. His shirt was soaked in blood, and blood covered his jewelry, a wedding ring, a necklace, and a gym card in his wallet. Then June-bug took a gun from behind his back and shot the man several times. Then we all got into the car and left the man there. I started to shake, and all I could remember was hearing June-bug telling us we had beaten the wrong man. He told us the phone call let him know we were given the wrong address. I asked why he shot the guy if he knew we had the wrong man. June-bug just said, "To put him out of his misery," and then he removed his jewelry and his wallet to make it difficult to identify him. June-bug kept the man's wallet and told us that he was going after the right man this time. He said he was sorry for the mistake and gave us our airline tickets back home and two thousand dollars each for the night's work. I became sick to my stomach, and I couldn't believe what we had done. I never used the money. I just put the money and the jewelry into a safe deposit box.

Later that week I learned June-bug had not returned from New York, and one of his friends named Hunk knew why. He knew June-bug had gone to New York, and he was the last person who spoke with the guy. He told me June-bug was killed in a car accident the very night we left New York. In fact, he was the man who called June-bug and informed him that he had gone to the wrong address. The authorities thought the man who had died in the car accident was you, but it was June-bug. He still had your wallet with your identification in it. I believe when June-bug reached in his pocket for his gun, he dropped his wallet. June-bug's family did not know what had happened to him until now.

Inside this bag you will find the information you have been looking for about your identity. These are the items that were on you the day you were beaten and left for dead. I know you do not remember anything about the incident. But I hope seeing these things will bring back your memory. I was supposed to take these things and destroy them. Fortunately, I did not do that. Because of what had taken place that night, I could not bring myself to destroy them. I guess you can say that it would be like killing you twice.

I took your things and put them in a safe, and I put the money that was on you in a savings account. I cannot explain why. Except I have felt so guilty for a long time knowing what I did. Yet I am grateful for the opportunity to make this wrong right. God helped me learn about the man I almost killed. It is through His divine guidance I was able to find you. He has kept me alive to accomplish this for His glory. I know He has kept you alive to do the same thing. We both could have been dead by now. I hired a private investigator to find where you were living. I do not know how he did it, but he did. I think that this is another divine intervention. So by the time you read this letter, I will not be here. I ask for your forgiveness. I know this will be hard or maybe impossible to do. I just know forgiveness frees the soul.

There is an envelope in the inside pocket of the bag. This envelope contains the information about the saving account I put your money in with interest, and I have also made you one of my heirs. You will inherit two million dollars. The deed of trust to my home has been put into your name as well. I want to restore the life that I took, your life. I know that there is really nothing I can do to replace all the pain and hurt you and your family have suffered. I pray you will get your memory back, and please do something good and promising with your new life. You see, I am dying of cancer, and I am sure by the time you read this letter, I will be dead. I am not proud of the things I have done in my life, but God has given me a second chance. I want you to know that you have been a true friend to me and a great roommate.

Your friend and roommate,
Charlie Short

Charlie Short, you did this to me! I cannot believe Charlie of all people he did this to me. Eric stood up and walked around the room, processing what he had just learned. He then looked at the things that were in the bag. All the things had blood on them. He look at the ID card to a gym and saw his name and a picture of the man he used to be. He read the name on the card. There was an airline ticket, a watch, and a wedding ring with an inscription inside. The dried blood inside the ring made it difficult to read. He took a good long look at everything and put his head in his hands, and then he started to cry.

He looked at his life. It was just a handful of things that he couldn't relate to. What kind of life had he lived? He was married. He said the name over and over again in his head. As he looked at the things that belonged to him, he felt his life had been frozen in time. Even so, he stopped and thought about what he had said. Then he said, "Bishop, Bishop." He had heard that name before. He said it again, but this time when he said it he remembered. "Bishop, Denise was married to an Eric Bishop." He knew the name. He knew who he was. It did not become real until he heard himself say his name. "I am Eric Bishop, Denise's husband!"

CHAPTER 14

IS IT TRUE?

Edmond went to the mirror to get a good look at himself with the photo that was in the bag. He looked at himself and then the photo. He did this several times. It wasn't just the picture that was different. He was too. No matter how the picture looked, he knew he was not that man anymore. God whispered to him, "You are not the Eric in the picture, the Eric who was married to Denise. That Eric has died. Yet his death has given birth to Edmond. That's who you are now. By God's grace, he is alive. Eric died because of sin, but Edmond lives because of grace."

As he walked around in his little room, he prayed to God for answers. Then he fell to his knees, threw his hands up in the air, and cried out to God. "God, please tell me what to do and how to think. Is this Eric really me? Is this who I was? I am changed God. I am not this Eric Bishop. I do not want to be this Eric. The things Denise wrote in her diary about me are too difficult to accept. I once thought and behaved that way, not anymore. You, God, have changed me. I am a changed man, but what do I do now? Please, God, fix the mess I have made, all the people whose lives I have hurt and destroyed. Oh, God, what have I done? What have I done?" His sobs became even more intense. He sat at the edge of his bed, placed his head in his hands, and cried.

Edmond had spent the whole night praying and sobbing. He heard the alarm go off. It was time for him to get dressed for work. How would he faced Nana, Gramps, not to mention Denise? He whispered her name, closing his eyes to see her in his thoughts. "Denise." He picked up one of the photos from the diary, and he looked at it for a long time.

The alarm went off again. He hit the snooze button to keep the room quiet. He thought that maybe he should just leave and not tell anyone. That would be the easy way out, the coward's way out. He could just let people continue to think he was dead when in reality he was not. He was very much alive, and until now, he hadn't had any memory. Denise was living a lie. She was not a widow. She was still a married woman.

Once he had arrived at work, Nana was waiting to see him. She wanted to know if the new shipment of donations had come in. He decided to keep this new information about his identity to himself … for now. He thought it would be best. It would give him more time to plan how to tell everyone and what he needed to do if he was no longer welcome. He then said a simple prayer, "God, please be with me."

He told Nana that the new shipment had come in. He and some volunteers would separate the articles and prepare them for the sale. He asked how she and Gramps were doing. She told him they were fine. He wanted to know when the last time she had seen Denise was and how she was doing. Nana put the paper she was reading on the desk and looked over her reading glasses in Edmond's direction. "She is doing fine. She will be over tonight for dinner. Would you like to come?"

He did not have to think about the invitation. "Sure, and I will come over to help you. Thank you for the invite." Nana thought that would be a good idea and thanked him for wanting to help. She told him what time to be there. Edmond did not want to come over for the food. He just wanted to see Denise. He arrived at the right time. Nana told him that Gramps would be late, so his help was greatly appreciated. As Nana was giving him instructions about what she needed, he wanted to know how Nana felt about Denise's husband. "Nana, what kind of man was Denise's husband?"

Nana was busy seasoning the broccoli soup. "I did not know much about him. Let me see. The first time I met him was a day before the wedding. Of course, at the wedding we did not get the opportunity to be social. I did not meet him again until six months after they were married. Yes, I think it was six months after they were married."

"Did you like him?"

"I can only go on what Denise has told me about him. I told her when she was planning on marrying him to learn as much as she could about him. I told her that spending too much time and money on a wedding and not enough on the marriage was not a good idea."

"What do you mean spending on the marriage?"

"You have to invest time to know what it means to be married. She should have made sure she was marrying the person God wanted her to marry. Just marrying anyone and thinking that it will work is swimming in dangerous waters. Thinking that *love* will just get you through thing is the wrong way. You know, after the wedding comes the marriage. These days young people do not think about what will make a marriage work. They know what will make a beautiful wedding, but they have no idea how to look for a mate. Just so involved with looks and how much money they want to make. They think they can live like their parents, and they never realized there will be challenges that will either weaken or strengthen the marriage. When the looks and money are gone, then what do you have? Just two old people with no money. All I know it started out good, but when Eric died, she later learned in a very painful way that he was having an affair and that someone wanted to kill him."

"Did she learn who and why someone wanted him killed?"

"No, she did not. She felt she was engaged to one man and married to another man. A man she thought she knew. So it had been very difficult for her to get on with her life. I think she is making some progress."

Nana told Edmond to go to the cabinet to get the dishes and set the table. After he had set the table, he turned to Nana and asked, "How does the table look?" Nana turned to look and immediately told him that he needed another plate setting because there would be five for dinner. As Edmond was placing another plate on the table, he asked, "Who is the other person coming for dinner?"

Nana turned with a smile on her face and said, "Raymond."

Edmond thought to himself, Oh no, that's all I need—competition added to my life of challenges. Oh, are they seeing each other?

Nana was still smiling. "Well, I do not know how serious they are about each other, but she has changed. He has been taking her out, getting her mind off of Eric's death, murder attempt, and affairs. She seems much happier."

Edmond said, "Eric had affairs?"

Nana told him, "Denise is not sure if he had one affair or several. She told me that it did not matter, because it still hurts. It does not matter if you are shot or a hammer falls on your toe. It is still pain. Pain is pain."

Edmond thought to himself that there is a blessing in this somewhere. He would just have to look a little harder. Then he thought, *At least I will be here to keep a watch on Raymond. Denise is still my wife, and Lord, I do not want another man moving in before I can make things right with Denise. Lord, please help me. This is not going to be easy.*

When everything was ready, the doorbell rang. Nana answered the door. It was Raymond with a bottle of wine in one hand and Denise on the other. They were laughing. It seemed to Edmond that they had been having a great time before they arrived there. Everyone greeted one another, and Raymond gave the wine to Edmond to put it on ice for dinner. Raymond wanted to know how Edmond had been doing and if he had learned any more about himself. He told Edmond that he had a friend who could help him. After dinner he would give him the man's contact information. Edmond did not want to know any more about himself, especially from Raymond. He needed to keep telling himself that Raymond was not the enemy, but it sure felt like that sometimes. He told him how great that would be and thanked him. Nana told them all that they would have dinner when Gramps came home. As soon as she said that, Gramps came through the door. Everyone took their places at the table. While the conversation was flowing around the table, Edmond was watching Raymond and Denise like a hawk watching a chicken. He did not know how long he would be able to keep this up, but he was willing to try.

Months had gone by, and Eric has been able to keep what he had learned about himself a secret. He did not feel safe in telling anyone until the day he learned from Raymond that he was planning to take Denise to see his parents. Eric knew what that meant. Things were getting serious. That was all he needed to know.

He called Gramps and asked if he could talk to him and Nana. Gramps told him yes. Edmond told him he would bring lunch. When Edmond came over, Nana had the table set for the lunch. Once they said grace, everyone started with their meal. When the meal was almost finished, Gramps asked Edmond what he wanted to talk about. Edmond looked at them and told them that he had prayed about this and had waited for this moment for a long time. Now he knew the time was right to tell them. Nana interrupted him and said, "To tell us what?"

Edmond took out the letter that Charlie had sent to him and had them read it.

Once they finished reading the letter, he gave them the articles that he had gotten with the letter. They looked at him and then the photo. They looked at him again and looked then the photo and then turned to each other. Nana turned her head to look at Edmond at an angle and said in a soft voice, "Eric?"

Gramps did not say anything. He just sat and looked at him face-to-face. Then Nana said again, "Eric?"

Eric said, "I know that this is a shock to you. It was and still is a shock to me. I did not know who to tell or talk to about this. I know you were not expecting to see me of all people again. I know I did not treat Denise right, but I am not that person anymore. I mean, I have changed. When God brought you back into my life, it changed me. I have asked Christ into my life. I wanted to ask you to forgive me for how I treated Denise."

They were still in shock when Gramps said, "What about Charlie? Have you forgiven Charlie?"

Without hesitation, he said, "Have I forgiven Charlie? How can I not forgive him" I know he was one of the men who were involved in beating me nearly to death, but once I looked at what I had done to Denise, I should have asked him for forgiveness."

Nana asked, "You asked him to forgive you? For what?"

"For being in the wrong place at the right time. If I was not having an affair, I would not have been there for him and the other men to beat me."

"What do you mean at the right time?"

"It was the right time for Christ to enter into my life. I have no intention of returning to that way of life. I do not want to live that way ever again. I just need to know if you will forgive me. I know that there are consequences I will have to face for the way I had lived. I do not know how or when to tell Denise. I cannot think about her taking me back, but I just want her forgiveness."

There was quiet. No one said anything. Gramps and Nana just continued to look at Eric. Eric waited for someone to say something. Then Nana said, "Wow! They did a magnificent job on your nose. You know, you look like Eric, and then you do not look like Eric. You know, I like the new Eric. Yeah, I like the new Eric. I think he looks better. I am sorry. I mean, you look good. What do you think, Gramps?"

Gramps still had not really said anything or expressed himself. Then he said, "So it was Charlie that beat you. Wow, imagine that!" Then he looked at the letter again and turned to Eric and said, "He left you some money. What are you planning to do with all that money? Move to Mexico? I'm just kidding. Well, tell us what you want us to do?"

Nana said, "Eric, Gramps and I forgive you. We are grateful Christ has changed your life. That means a lot. I know it will mean a lot to Denise. On the other hand, as you know, Denise will have to speak for herself."

"I know. I just want you to pray for me. Please, please pray for me."

Gramps asked, "Are we supposed to tell people who you are?"

Eric immediately said, "No, no, not yet. I do not want anyone to know, not until I have told Denise."

Nana said, "When are you planning on doing that?"

"I do not know. I mean, I do not know how. I mean—"

Nana said, "We know what you mean. God will tell you when and how to tell her. Just like He told David when he would be king and Nehemiah how to rebuild the wall around Jerusalem. Like when He told Mary she would become Jesus' mother and how—"

Before Nana could continue with the Bible class, Gramps interrupted her, "Eric, we will pray for you, but tell us, son. What are we to call you?"

"Please continue to call me Edmond. I know it would be very challenging since you now know who I am."

Gramps asked, "Tell us how it feels to know who you are, to be yourself again."

Edmond said, "It will feel good to know, but I still do not know everything. It will be great to have my life back once I have righted my wrongs with God's help, especially with Denise."

CHAPTER 15

THE CHALLENGE

It would be a challenge to tell Denise the truth. Eric's main goal was not to hurt her as he had done before, not intentionally anyway. He knew that Jesus was with him, and he was totally depended on Him not only for his daily needs but in guidance for showing him how to tell Denise the truth. There was a time when keeping the truth to himself would have been the right thing to do. All the same, that would be living a lie. And Denise would be living a lie as well. She would continue to think he was dead when he wasn't. What if she wanted to marry again? He did not want to dwell on that thought. But what if the truth got out?

George wanted to help Eric find his identity. He had worked so hard. Nonetheless, it was beginning to become problematic for Eric. Since he had learned his identity, he did not want everyone else to know. There were times when George was getting too close. Keeping George away from his personal things was very challenging. He had to keep one eye on George to make sure he didn't find out the truth and the other eye on Raymond with Denise. He knew God was in control of his life. Each day he sought God's advice about what he needed to do. He knew that whatever came to him had to go through God first. He had to let his faith grow in God for the strength he needed to accomplish the will of God. What Eric really wanted to know was how Denise would feel when she realized that Edmond was actually her dead husband.

It was time for the church's annual drama feast. In this year's drama, the church's focus was on relationships. The director knew the title would draw people in so that they would attend the production. The title read, "After the Wedding Comes the Marriage and Forgiveness." It was a very big production. The production had become so big that it was held in the civic auditorium. The community came to support the production. It helped to support scholarships for the children who wanted to go to college. After the play Denise and Eric met in the lobby. While walking to her car, Denise and Eric discussed the play. Eric asked, "So Denise, what did you think of the play?"

Denise turned her lip up as if to say it was not up to her expectation. "It was good. But I have seen better."

Eric reminded her that it was not a Hollywood production and the performers were not Hollywood superstars either. "Maybe you could say that if the performers were professionals, but they are not. The main thing you need to think about is the content of the play, its message. What did you think about the message?"

Denise did not have to think much about that. "It was food for thought. I thought it was interesting that today's sermon and this play had the same message—forgiveness. I guess that is something we all need to do. What about yourself? What did you think about the play since you think of yourself as a movie critic?"

"Well, I am not a movie critic. But I know a good message when I hear one, and that was a good message. No, that was a great message. Forgiveness lets the love come in. That is what Jesus did for us sinners. Forgiveness sets you free to love. Do you agree?"

Denise agreed with him. Even so, she was feeling uneasy about where this conversation was going. Eric knew she was feeling uneasy, but he wanted to know. "So Denise, who needs your forgiveness?"

Before she could answer, Raymond drove up. He apologized for not being able to attend the play with her. "I am sorry I was not here to enjoy the play with you. I am sure it was good. How about dinner? I would love to take you to dinner. Anywhere you wish." She told him she would enjoy that. Raymond said she could leave her car there and they would pick it up later. He thanked Eric for walking Denise to her car. He leaned out the window and whispered to Eric, "Edmond, I know you would gladly drive Denise's car to her house, but I know you do not have a license. Thanks for looking out for her."

Once Denise was in the car, they drove off. Eric was left standing there, enraged. "God, did you see that! I do not know how much more I can take of this. Lord, please help me understand what I need to do. I do not have the strength to keep this up."

Eric started to attend the men's Bible study at church. It was just what he needed. Reading and studying God's Word was helping him develop patience and endurance. It gave him hope.

One day he was supposed to meet George at Joe's Café. He caught the bus, so he was able to get there before George. While he waited, Raymond and Denise came in. When they were seated, they saw Eric. Raymond asked him to join them. Reluctantly, he did. The first thing he noticed was that Raymond was getting closer and closer to his wife. He was getting too close for Eric's comfort. He was constantly begging and pleading for God to help him. He had to muffle the urge to punch Raymond in the face. At times it was challenging not to get upset with Raymond. He really had not done anything wrong. After all, he had saved Eric's life. Whether or not Eric liked it, Raymond was the one who was bringing joy, happiness, and fun into Denise's life. Raymond asked, "Edmond, how are you doing?"

"I am doing fine, and yourself?"

"We are doing fine."

Eric got that right away. He said, "We?" He thought, Is he answering for her now?

Raymond asked, "Why are you here? Are you looking for someone?"

Eric looked around the room, and then he looked back at Raymond. "I was waiting for my friend George. He was supposed to meet me here. I was wondering why he wasn't here yet and what could have happened to him." Then the waiter came over and whispered something in Eric's ear. Then Eric told them both that George had called the restaurant to tell him that he was running late.

Denise asked Eric to stay and have dinner with them. Eric could see that this did not sit well with Raymond, but Eric happily accepted the invitation. "Thank you. I did not want to eat alone." The waiter came over and gave everyone a menu. While they were looking at the menu, Eric thought to himself, *Ha-ha. You thought you were going to have her all to yourself. Wrong. Not tonight buddy, not tonight.* While Raymond and Denise were looking at menus, Eric kept his eyes on them. The waiter soon returned to take their order. The waiter took Denise's order first. Then he took Raymond's and finally Eric's. Conversation wasn't as lively now as it had been in the beginning. Raymond felt some pressure to think of something quick. "So Edmond, how are you doing in learning about your identity?"

"I am still praying to God for guidance. I know He will show me what I need to do."

While they were waiting for their meal, Raymond's cell phone rang. He excused himself so that he could answer the call. It was a very short call. "I'm sorry, but I will not be able to stay for dinner. The hospital called, and there is an emergency. So enjoy your dinner." He looked at Denise and said, "I will see you later." He gave her a kiss. Eric thought he needed a seat belt to keep him in his seat. His eyes saw every detail of that kiss, and he did not like it. When Raymond took his lips off Denise's, Eric was very close to having a heart attack. He thought, *That is it! That is it! God, You know I cannot take this anymore. This man and his feelings for* my *wife have got to* end. *This cannot continue.* Raymond left, and their dinner came out shortly after that. Eric was gathering his thoughts so that he could talk to Denise. He still wanted to know whether or not she had forgiven him. "Denise, how is your meal?"

"It is good. What about yours?"

"Good, good. I really enjoyed the last conversation we had."

"Oh, what conversation was that?"

"We were talking about forgiveness. That reminds me. Are you taking the class teaching you how to become a disciple of Christ at church?"

"No."

"Why not?"

"I am thinking about it. Are you in the class?"

"Yes. Gramps was the one who told me about the class. After listening to the sermon Pastor Brian did on forgiveness, I thought I wanted to learn more about how to forgive and how to be forgiven. Have you ever had to forgive someone?"

Denise put her fork down and drank some of her iced tea, which gave her a moment to think. "Well, I think the person I needed to forgive is my husband."

"Have you forgiven him?"

"I am not sure."

"What do you mean?"

Before she could answer, the waiter returned and asked if everything was all right and if there was anything else they needed. They assured him that they were enjoying their meal and that they did not need anything. Denise asked, "Where were we?"

Eric reminded Denise where they were in their conversation. "You said that you were not sure if you had forgiven your husband. What did you mean by that?"

Denise swallowed the food in her mouth and said, "You can say you have forgiven someone, but how do you know if you have really done so? I mean, what do you do? How often do you forgive someone, and for what? Do you forgive them for one thing and not another? That's why I say I am not sure. Nana said forgiveness is giving up your right to hurt those who have hurt you."

"So what do you think of that? Do you think that is how to forgive? Could you do that?"

"Nana said that it takes a lot of energy not to forgive. She said that when you do not forgive, you make yourself a prisoner of your own anger. When you do not forgive, you stay angry, and the person goes on with his or her life. And either way, you are still soaking in your anger. She said forgiveness sets you free."

"Do you believe that?"

"Yea, I think it is true. What about yourself? Is there someone in your life you needed to forgive, and have you forgiven them?"

"That is why I am taking the classes at church. It's helping me understand how Jesus has forgiven me. I think forgiveness removes the weight of not forgiving, and it will give you peace. I think it gives you joy."

"As for my husband, Eric, I think I have forgiven him. I have not thought about him in a long time, and not thinking about him helps me to forgive him. When I thought about him before, I wanted to hurt him for all the terrible things he had done to me. So yes, I think I have forgiven him. Yes, yes, I have forgiven him."

"So if Eric was here right now, what would you do?"

Denise put her fork down and looked at Eric and said, "What kind of question is that? I do not know. He's dead, and I want to leave it at that. I think … maybe I should get Pastor Brian's sermon tapes on forgiveness. I am sure I can learn more about forgiveness and do it the way Jesus says to do it. Perhaps I do not feel the anger I once did." That was good news for Eric. It gave him hope. As they were finishing up their dinner, George came and apologized for being late. He was glad that he had arrived in time to take them both home.

Eric called Gramps and wanted to know if he could talk to him. "Hello, Gramps, I wanted to know if you and Nana will be home today."

Gramps told him, "Sure, we will be here. What's up?"

"I am glad you answered the phone. Gramps, I think it is time to tell Denise. I cannot keep this up much longer. I have to keep one eye on George and the other eye on Raymond, if you know what I mean. I can no longer think of things to tell George. I know he is trying to help me, but how do I tell him I am doing fine without lying to him? Last night was the straw that broke the camel's back.

"Oh, what was that?"

"Seeing Raymond kiss Denise did it for me. I have prayed and asked God to please tell me what to do. I have some idea how she feels about me … or her dead husband. I am trusting God to work things out for me. I just want to know I am doing my part."

"What time do you want to come over, and what do you want me and Nana to do?"

"As soon as Denise can come over. At first I thought we could go out to eat, but I thought that may not be a good idea. I am still not sure how difficult this will be for her. I think being in a place where she would feel comfortable may help. Even if it would be difficult for her there, it still would be a better place. Let's say in two hours. It will be time for her to get off from work soon, and maybe she could come by for dinner. If you and Nana would not mind giving us some time alone, enough time for me to tell her. You do not have to go anywhere. Just stay out of sight because I may need your help if things get out of hand, but I do not think that will happen. Having someone close by who has accepted me as the new Eric means a lot. If she decides not to forgive me, I will have to accept that. If she wants a divorce, I will have to accept that as well. If she forgives me but still wants a divorce, I have to accept this as well. No matter what she decides, I will accept it. Do I really want to, no! What I really want is my wife back, and I am going to do everything God tells me to do to get her back. I do not want to see another man with my wife. I am learning how to love, and I want to give my wife the love God has given me for her."

CHAPTER 16

LEARNING THE TRUTH

When the doorbell rang, Nana answered the door. It was Denise. Nana welcomed her. "Hi, come on in. It is good to see you. How was traffic?"

When Denise came in, she gave Nana a hug and put her things on the living room sofa. "It is good to see you too Nana. Where is Gramps? How did you know I wanted to come to dinner? I sure didn't want to cook, and besides, I have nothing to cook at home. What are we having anyway? I hope it is some of Gramps's barbecue chicken." She followed Nana into the kitchen. "Nana, what can I do? I am ready to eat. I am starving."

Nana turned around and said, "Girl, you are full of questions. Go wash your hands, and you can help me with the salad." The phone rang, and Nana went to answer it. Eric was calling to see if Denise was there. Nana told him the time he should come. After dinner Nana told Denise that she and Gramps needed to go on a short errand and would return shortly. "Edmond needs to come by," she said. "When he comes, please let him in."

As soon as Nana and Gramps left, Eric came. When he rang the doorbell, Denise let him in. "Hello, Edmond, how are you? Nana and Gramps just left. They will be back shortly. Come on in and sit down. We just had dinner. Would you like something to eat?"

"No, thank you."

Denise looked at Eric. "What's wrong, Edmond? You look worried."

"I do?"

"Yes, is there something wrong?"

Eric looked at her, and Denise could see that there was something very wrong. "Edmond, what is wrong?"

"Denise, I need to talk to you."

"You need to talk to me? About what?"

Eric took her by her hand, led her to the sofa, and asked her to sit down. "Denise, I want you to know that I have learned my identity. I have learned who I am."

"You have. That's wonderful." She smiled. "I am so excited to hear that. I know what this has meant to you. Well, tell me who are you." Eric reached into his pocket and pulled out the letter that Charlie had written to him and handed it to Denise. She excitedly took the letter and started to read. When she had finished, she looked at Eric.

"Well, you know what happened to you, but who are you?" He took the articles Charlie had given to him and gave them to her to examine them. After she did, she was in complete shock.

Eventually she said, "No! No! No! It cannot be true. This cannot be true!" As Eric reached out to her, she pulled away. She did not need to look at the picture again to make sure it was him. It was just the fact he was there with the letter, not the mention the articles she had examined. She knew. She covered her eyes with her hands, concealing him from her view. She started to breath heavily, and she started shaking. As she was about to move toward the door, Nana and Gramps came in. At first she did not know they were there. Eric looked at them, and the expression on his face said it all. Denise was not taking this well. She started to cry, saying, "Why! Why! Why are you doing this to me?" When she turned around and saw her grandparents, she fainted. Eric caught her before she hit the floor. He picked her up and carried her to the sofa. Nana went to get some smelling salts from the bathroom. Gramps went to get a wet towel to wipe her face. After Nana used the smelling salts, Denise came to. The first person she saw was Eric. She softly said his name. "Eric. Eric, is it really you?"

Eric had not said a word since he had given the letter to her. He only said, "Are you all right?"

Denise tried to sit up. She did feel a little dizzy, but she quickly revived herself. She looked at her grandparents and said, "Do you know who this is? Did you know?" The expression on their faces told her what she didn't want to believe, but she knew it was true. "How long have you known?" She looked at them, grabbed her things, and then left.

CHAPTER 17

THE DECISION

It had been days since anyone had seen Denise. She did not return her grandparents' or Eric's calls. She did not answer her door. They were not sure if she was home or out of town. They knew that giving her time would help her to face the truth. However, because they didn't know how she was doing, they were becoming concerned. Eric had begun to look for blessings even in the worst of circumstances. As difficult as it was to accept how Denise was taking the news, no one needed to call him Edmond anymore. Now they could call him Eric. He phoned Nana and Gramps to see if they had heard from Denise. They had heard from her actually. He told them that he had been there several times; however, this time he was going over to her place, and he wasn't going to leave until he spoke with her. And that was what he told Denise at her door.

Denise eventually let him in. "Denise, I know finding this out was hard. Please speak to Nana and Gramps. They aren't the one to blame. Denise, I am not asking you to take me back. I'm asking you to forgive me."

Denise finally said, "Was that what the conversation was about at the restaurant? Forgiveness? All this time, you walking around here, pretending, not knowing who you were when you did."

Eric interrupted her. "No, Denise, that's not true. Once I got the letter from Charlie, I was in as much shock as you are. I had a difficult time accepting it. I knew I had to accept it as true. I did not know what to do. I prayed and asked God to tell me how to handle this. I did not want to tell anyone until I had told you. You matter to me the most. I had to tell Nana and Gramps. I wanted to wait for the right time to tell you. Knowing you had forgiven me meant something to me. At first I thought not telling anyone would be the best thing to do."

Denise interrupted him. "So why didn't you do that?"

"Because I …" he started. His thoughts turned to their life together. "Because I did not want you to live a lie. I knew the truth somehow would come out. It always does."

With anger in her voice, she managed to say, "You did not want me to live a lie. Well, how thoughtful of you. How considerate and concerned you are. Now, let me see. Was I not living a lie when you were having an affair? Do you have any idea how many people's lives you have destroyed or hurt? Do you? Don't you know someone tried to kill you?" She looked him over from head to toe. "When you went to New York on your little excursion with what's her name, Paul Parker was shot. The criminals thought they were shooting you. They almost killed him."

Eric was learning things he knew nothing about. He was sure he would learn other things about himself that he didn't want to know. Facing his past and the consequences of his wrongs was not going to be easy. He said, "Denise, I'm sorry for all the pain I have caused you. Will you forgive me? I want to give you some time to think about this."

"I do not need time to think about this. Do you know who had to identify your body, your remains? I did!" She stepped closer to Eric. They stood face-to-face. She wanted to make sure he did not miss anything she was saying. "I was alone in that morgue looking at …"

She stopped to put her hands over her eyes, shielding them from that horrible moment. "All that was left of you were your driver's license and some other things. I can't remember. Do you know how I found out you were having an affair? Has that question ever crossed your mind? Well, let me tell you how I found out about your little affair. After your funeral, in my moment of grieving—and when I say grieving, I want you to know that I took a leave of absence from work. In my state of mind, I was numb, lost." For the first time, Eric saw the pain, the deep emotional trauma she had faced. It was in her eyes. He had read about in her diary, and he had caused it. "That day is etched in my mind. It was the most shocking, painful thing I have ever experienced." She had to stop to collect herself. The pain had become so real. She was reliving it all again to let him know what exactly he had left for her to face alone. She closed her eyes, and it was as if she was seeing the images in her head. "Besides being told you were killed, I want you to know, Eric Joseph Bishop, the day I learned of your affair felt as if you put a gun to my heart and shot me. Just let me tell you how you told me about the affair. That's right. You told me! One day after, I was getting the last of your mail from your post office box. I returned home to find a package that UPS had left at my door. I opened the package and was elated. I found the most beautiful negligee and a very expense bottle of perfume. I thought that this was a present from you expressing your love for me. I thought these very expensive gifts were from you."

Eric was now seeing flashbacks of that day when he made the purchase at the boutique while he was in Las Vegas with Nicole. He wished he could make it all go away, but he could not. At times he didn't even want to forgive himself. "I put on the negligee and the perfume," Denise continued. "The scent of the perfume was totally intoxicating. I went to sleep on your side of the bed. It was the only thing that took away the pain of your death." Eric wanted to leave, just walk away. But he could not. He knew he had to endure Denise's painful memories about what he had done to her.

"The next morning the perfume scent still filled the room. It was the first time I had slept in days. I was so happy." Tears were starting to come down her face. "I let myself think that you thought of me as special. When I found and read the card with her name on it, I cannot tell you what this did to me. Then, if that was not enough, I saw your bank statements. At first I thought I had someone else's mail. Then I looked a little closer, and there as plain as day, Eric Bishop and Nicole Warner. I found myself in a state of rage. Anger I had never felt before in my life. I could not believe what I was reading. There was the five thousand dollars we were arguing over a few days earlier. That was the money we were saving for our dream home, where we were going to raise our family. There it was in a bank account for you and your lover. I was alone, Eric. I was in pain that I cannot begin to describe. You died and left me with the pain of an affair, an empty bank account, a broken heart, and a broken marriage, and nothing in this world can take that pain away. Eric, the affair never gave me the opportunity to grieve your death. You have the nerve to come to my home and ask me to forgive you."

Eric now saw how the expression in her face had changed. The tone of her voice had changed as well. "Eric, you took everything from me. You took my life, and you threw me away as if I had no purpose or value. I was discarded. You stopped loving me for me. You want to talk to me. Let me reassure you that we have nothing to talk about. This was an opportunity I thought I would never have—to be able to stand face-to-face with you and tell you how I feel about you because of the things you have done. As far as I am concerned, you are still dead. I think you'd better leave before I kill you myself. I want you to leave, and I never want to see you again. Now leave!"

Before Eric left, he said, "I will come back one year from today for your answer." She turned and walked onto the terrace. He stood there, watching her as she was leaving. As she stood on the terrace with her back to him, he saw her hair softly blowing in the wind. The wind pushed the dress against her body and revealed her shapely figure. She was still as beautiful as he remembered. He wanted to kiss her on her lips and hold her close to him. She did not turn to look at him as he turned to leave. She remained on the terrace after she heard the door close, too numb to cry.

Denise finally visited her grandparents. She wanted them to know that she was all right. They explained to her that they learned the truth recently as well. They wanted her to know the most important thing was that Eric was alive. He had learned his true identity and had changed. God had been working in his life. He was not the same man now as he was before.

Nana took Denise to the kitchen and made tea. She sat next to her and said, "Denise, it was wrong when you married Eric, because He was not a believer in Christ, and that was out of God's will. It will be wrong for you to divorce him, because that would be out of God's will too." Denise listened to everything her grandparents had to say. When they were finished, she left.

Eric got his things together and told Nana he would return in a year. He did not tell her where he was going. He did not leave any contact information so that they could keep in touch with him. He only told her he would return in a year. He thanked her and Gramps for all they had done. He let them know he could not have survived if it had not been for them. They were there to help him when he needed it the most. He asked them to continue to pray for him and for his faith to continue to grow strong in the Lord. He then gave each of them a hug and left.

CHAPTER 18

MAKING THE WRONG RIGHT

The Parkers were sound asleep when the phone rang. April looked over at Paul to see if the phone had disturbed him. He was still sleeping though, and he continued to sleep soundly. She then looked at the clock to see what time it was. It was two o'clock in the morning. The phone continued to ring. April, still half asleep, looked at the caller ID. It only showed the phone number. April answered the phone in a very drowsy voice. "Hello?"

The voice on the other end said, "Hello. Does Paul Parker lives here?"

April asked, "Who is this?"

The phone caller asked again, "Does Paul Parker lives here? May I please speak to him?"

April reached over to wake Paul up. Paul was snoring, and this made it a little more challenging to wake him. With each call of his name, April had to raise her voice. Finally, she was able to wake him. "Paul, there is someone on the phone who wants to talk with you."

Paul looked at the clock and said, "Who could be calling at this time of night? Do you know who it is?" April told him that she didn't know and that the caller ID wasn't displaying the name of the person calling either. Paul took the phone. "Hello?"

The caller asked, "Is this Paul Parker?"

"Yes, this is Paul Parker. Who is this? Who am I speaking with?"

The caller finally gave the information they wanted to hear. "Paul this is Eric Bishop."

Paul was wide awake now, and the look on his face roused April as well.

"Who is it, Paul? Who is calling?"

Paul turned to her and said, "It's Eric Bishop."

"Eric, Eric Bishop!"

"Paul, this is Eric. I need to see you."

"Eric, Eric Bishop, this cannot be. Eric Bishop is dead. He died in a car accident."

"Yes, I know. Paul, I need to see you."

"Is this a hoax? Because if it is, it's not funny!"

"I can assure you this is not a hoax. May I meet you somewhere?"

April whispered, "What does he want?"

"He wants me to meet with him."

April told him that sounded too dangerous. "Maybe we should call the police and let them handle it."

Paul thought about what he should do and prayed. The tone in the man's voice somehow put him at ease. He gave Eric their address with directions to their home. April did not agree with that. She was upset with Paul's decision to let someone they didn't know come to their home at two o'clock in the morning. She left the bed and went to the closet to get their gun. Paul told her not to do anything foolish. April angrily said, "Not to do anything foolish! What do you call what you just did? You foolishly invite a stranger to our home in the middle of the night, and you don't think that is foolish? Please tell me what is foolish! Getting a gun to protect yourself or telling a stranger who is supposed to be dead to come to your home in the middle of the night?"

Paul tried to calm April down. He told her that he understood how she was feeling and that everything would be okay.

By the time they were up and dressed, the doorbell rang. Paul went to answer the door. He peeked through the peephole. There stood a man he did not recognize. He asked, "Who is there?"

"It is Eric Bishop." Paul slowly answered the door. The porch light was on. The light shined on Eric, but it did not help them recognize him. Paul asked him to come in. Eric entered their home and stayed by the door. April went to stand next to Paul.

Paul said, "Please come in and have a seat." Paul led him into the living room. April was right behind Eric. Once everyone was seated and all the lights were on, the conversation started. Paul said, "You are Eric Bishop? Why are you here and not dead?"

Before Eric started to talk, he noticed that Paul had a gun pointed at him. He decided for April's sake to keep it handy in case they needed it, and maybe it would encourage him to tell the truth. Eric wanted them to know that he meant them no harm. "I apologize for calling you so late. I was not thinking about the time. As I told you, I am Eric Bishop. I know I am supposed to be dead, and in a way, I guess you can say I was." Paul and April sat next to each other, looking at Eric, and they said nothing. Eric continued, "I was not killed in a car accident, but I was beaten and shot and left for dead."

He told them the whole story, and Paul asked, "So why are you here?"

"I recently learned that there was an attempt on my life, and the men shot you, thinking you were me."

April said, "Yes, that is absolutely right. They shot him twice."

Eric said, "I am very sorry about that. That is why I am here. To apologize for what had happen to you."

Paul asked, "Do you know who would want you dead?"

"I think I have some idea. Can you please tell me how my father is doing?"

"Your father is getting better. It really was hard on your father. He left the country for a while."

"Are you still managing the stores?"

"No, your father wanted me to take your place as the buyer since Nicole did not want to."

"What happened to her?"

"She left right after she learned you were dead."

"So who is managing now?"

"Becky. Your father gave Becky's position to her sister, Brenda."

They wanted to know what his plan was. He simply said, "To make right what I have done wrong."

He told them how he had accepted Jesus Christ in his life and how God had been blessing him. Even after all the wrongs he had done, God was helping him to make things right. Paul said, "I am glad to hear that. Having Christ in your life will always make life better, no matter what you are going through. Where is Denise?"

"She lives near her grandparents. I learned about the attempt on my life through her."

April asked, "How is she taking all of this? Are you together?"

"I just told her a few days ago about my identity. As I told you, I just recently learned who I am. Denise did not take it that well. I did not ask her to take me back, but I did ask her to forgive me."

Before April got up and went into the kitchen to make coffee, she said, "I guess she didn't forgive you, right?"

"Right, she has not, but I am praying that she will."

Paul asked Eric where he was staying. He told Paul that he had not gotten a room yet. Paul asked Eric to stay with them until he knew what he was going to do. Then they had breakfast, and Eric got some much-needed sleep. There was one more thing that Eric needed to do to make things right with Paul and April.

"Paul, I do not remember everything, but I remember that the reason I hired you was to be my fall guy."

"Fall guy? What do you mean?"

"When I was at that job fair and came over to talk to you, I had done some research and learned why you went to prison and when you were going to be released. I knew you had not been able to get a job, so I wanted to make you a proposition that would be difficult for you to refuse. All I can remember is you were supposed to take the blame for embezzlement. That was one of the reasons I hired you. I know that there is another, but because of my amnesia, I cannot remember what it was. I cannot remember who you were supposed to have embezzled the money from. I was the one who was embezzling the money, but it was supposed to appear like you were the one who was doing it. I want to know if—"

April walked up to him and looked him in his eyes and said, " What does that mean? Do you have any idea what it has taken us to get our lives back to normal. How long it has taken us to do that. I want you to know I felt horrible and hopeless watching my husband laid up in the hospital not knowing whether or not he would live or die. Watching him struggled for his life. There were times he even struggled to breath. Not to mention what it felt like having someone interrogate you about someone who you love about a crime they did not commit? Being asked questions about our personal life by people who do not know you. Forgive you. I forgive you for coming back into our lives late in the night to tell us you are still alive. Putting our lives in fear once again and wondering whether or not it would be the right thing to do in letting you come here. Thinking that chapter of our life was closed and never to be opened again. Eric, I want you to know that forgiving you is truly the only thing I know I can do." She then looked at Paul and said, "I would like to speak for the both of us. We forgive you." Paul walked over to April and gave her a hug to comfort her in her moment of having to recall all that they had gone thought together.

"That is why I came back. I wanted to ask for your forgiveness. I have come to realize what kind of person I was. The only way I can make things right is through Jesus Christ."

Eric later went to see Detective Wilson, the detective on the case related to the attempt on his life. He knew he had to get this all cleared up to use his identity again. He called Detective Wilson and let him know that he needed to see him and that he had information related to Eric Bishop's shooting. When he went to the police department, an officer gave him directions to Detective Wilson's office. When he got there, the door was open, and the detective told him to come in and take a seat. There was an officer in the room sitting in the back. Eric came in and took a seat as he was told. Detective Wilson remained seated. He immediately wanted to know what information this man had on the case. Eric told him that he was Eric Bishop and handed him Charlie's letter along with the other articles. Detective Wilson looked at him, and the other officer got out of his seat and walked over to Detective Wilson to get a look too. After he read the letter, he let the other officer read it as well. Detective Wilson said, "How do I know that this is not a hoax?"

Eric took all afternoon and part of the evening explaining and answering all their questions. When they were satisfied with his answers, he was free to leave. Before he left, he wanted to know if they had arrested anyone for the shooting. The detective told him that they had. "The only name we had to go on was a Bruce. We learned that it was Bruce Morris. When he did not get the money he felt you owed him, he went to get it from your father. Your old man handled himself quite well."

"What do you mean?"

"When Bruce threatened to killed him, he wrestled Bruce down to the ground and took the gun from him and shot him. Later we arrested him for attempted murder. He is serving ten to fifteen years."

"Where is he serving at?"

The detective told him, "At the Rehab Prison Center." He then told Eric he needed to go to court and fill out forms to get them to declare that he was legally alive. He thanked the detective and the officer, and then he left. It took some time to get all the paperwork completed, but he got it done. Now there was one other person he needed to see.

He got clearance and permission to go visit Bruce. Of course, Bruce was surprised to see him. He told Eric that the world thought he was dead. He wanted to know why he was there. Eric told him he had come to repay the money he owed him … with interest. Bruce could not believe what he was hearing. He wanted to know why Eric was doing that. Eric told him how Christ had changed his life. He owed him the money, and he wanted to return it. Bruce told him to give it to his wife. He gave Eric the address. Bruce wanted to know how serious Eric was about doing right by his word. He did not want to wait for the money to go through the mail. Bruce wanted Eric to give it to his wife directly. He told Eric what he needed to say to his wife to let her know that he had sent him. Bruce said, "So that *Jesus* thing really works? Is that what you are telling me?"

As Eric was leaving, he said, "I'm here, aren't I?"

Before Eric left, Bruce wanted Eric to know one thing. "My man, the word on the street during that time was that a contract was out on you. I wasn't the one who was trying to kill you. I wasn't trying to kill you, only threaten you. The bullets that were put into your friend were not from my gun. Remember: I am here to hurt your father, not you."

This was adding to Eric's pain in dealing with the life he had made. How he had selfishly hurt so many people who loved him. To know someone not only wanted to hurt and kill him, but his father. His father was innocent, but to know he had become a victim who had to violently struggle for his life against someone he did not know. He could have been killed for something he knew nothing about. To think he could have gotten his father killed was taking a toll on Eric. There is much he needed Jesus to forgive him for. This is just one of many.

CHAPTER 19

RETURNED IN A YEAR

After finding out about Eric, Denise needed help understanding what she needed to do. She felt she needed to talk more than she needed answers. She really didn't want to talk to her grandparents about her dilemma. She still felt somewhat betrayed by them.

Having two men in her life was no fun. It made her life too complicated. She wanted one, and she wasn't sure if she wanted the other. She knew that they both wanted her. Maybe she was wrong about both of them wanting her. She was trying to remember what Eric told her. She thought about their conversation. He only wanted her forgiveness. He did not ask her to come back into his life. Did it really matter what he wanted? He had been absent from her life for some time, and what memories did he still have of her, of their relationship together? She felt like packing up her things and leaving again. She could move to another place where no one knew her and start her life all over ... again. Would that really help her solve her problem? Was that the solution? Was this really standing up and facing the dilemma? Or would she rather run away? She wanted to get on with her life, but how could she do that now?

She knew that her relationship with Raymond could not continue the way it had. The truth about Eric still being alive meant that she was still married. She was a married woman. If she continued her relationship with Raymond, would that news get back to Eric? And wouldn't it be wrong to put Raymond in that position? She would be using him to get back at Eric. She didn't want to hurt Raymond,, and she knew using him to get even with Eric would be wrong. Realizing she was still married, she could not get the idea out of her head. It was time for Nana's family reunion, so she figured it was a good time for her to focus on more pleasurable things.

Nana's family reunion took place in Mississippi at her parents' farm every year. They had ten acres of farmland. Every year the reunion seemed to become bigger with new family members participating. Last year approximately three hundred people attended. This year approximately 350 were expected to attend. The reunion was also a celebration of Nana's parents' wedding anniversary. This reunion was a big event that had taken place for more than sixty years, and it lasted for a whole week. Nana and Gramps would go down a week before the scheduled event to help other family members get things ready. Everything was done on the farm. Nana would help with preparing the food, while Gramps would help with getting the grounds ready for the campsites and porta potties. Families came from all over the United States to make this pilgrimage. Everyone knew that they either had to use RVs or fly out, but once on the farm, they needed to be self-sufficient. Some of the family members flew out and rented RVs to stay on the farm, while others drove across the county in their RVs. There were tents, RVs, and campers coving the ten acres.

Denise was coming with her parents. They were flying out, and they would rent an RV once they were there. Denise would soon see family members she had not seen in years. She had not seen some since college, and she had not seen others since she was a little girl. There were some she would meet for the first time. She remembered going to the reunion as a little girl. It was the family's vacation. Her parents would save for the event. They would tell her it was better than a vacation. They weren't going to a place just to sightsee or to an amusement park just to take rides all day. This was an event that happened once a year where she could meet her family and see relatives she had never met before, learning all about her family history.

It had taken many years to organized the anniversary and reunion so that it all ran smoothly. There were things that the women did and things that the men did. This was a time when young girls were taught by the older women how to prepare some of the dishes that had been handed down from one generation to another. Everyone had something to do to make sure the event was a success. Age didn't matter. You could be four or ninety years old. Everyone had something to do. Someone was over the different activities, and all duties were assigned. The menu had always been the same—soul food and dishes that were prepared the same way they had been during slavery. It was a time to learn about family history and traditions. The menu included mustard, turnip, and collard greens, creamed corn, potato salad, fried okra with fried tomatoes, black-eyed peas, corn bread, fried catfish, fried chicken, barbecue ribs, barbecue chickens, pigs roasted in the ground, homemade ice cream, pound cake, apple pie, peach cobbler, a red velvet cake to honor the wedding anniversary, and finally iced tea and lemonade to quench everyone's thirst. The farm provided all the food for the event. There were fruit trees and a vegetable garden that would please and satisfy any gourmet chef. The women prepared some food. The men prepared and cooked the meats. It took several days to set everything up and take everything down once the event was over. The big meal was held on the last day of the reunion. Each family had to have their paperwork in by March to make sure they got the camping spot they wanted. It allowed time for the farm to prepare for the event by August.

Denise made sure her calendar was cleared for the event. When she and her parents arrived, she was supposed to help with registration, make sure each family was accounted for, and give directions if someone called who was coming for the first time and did not know how to get there. She also let the families know where and how to get to their campsites. Her days started early at five o'clock in the morning.

One morning Denise went to have coffee with Nana and Nana's mother, Mommy Grace. Nana, Mommy Grace, and her sisters, Lee Lee and Little Sister, were all up early for their breakfast. Mommy Grace was the oldest of her sisters. She wanted to know what Denise was going to do about her marriage to Eric. She was surprised to learn that they knew about her situation. Lee Lee's real name was Laura Lee, but Lee Lee was her nickname because her siblings could not say Laura Lee when they were little girls. Lee Lee reminded Denise in her deep southern accent that the South was known as a place where talk was cheap and plentiful. People wanted to know all about your business and didn't want to tell you about theirs. "Baby, do not think of it as *your* business. It's all our business, You're family."

Little Sister said in another deep southern accent, "That's right. We is family. Women today do not understand how to get a man, a good man. Women just not taught what to look for. Once women today got problems in marriage, the first thing they taught to do is leave."

Denise wanted to know how Mommy Grace stayed married to her great-grandfather for seventy years. In fact, she was wondering how all the women stayed married for so many years. "So all of you have had only one husband?"

Little Sister proudly said, "That's right. We all have kept our vows before God to one husband."

Mommy Grace added, "Now, baby, we are not saying it was easy. Lord knows it wasn't, but it taught each of us how to trust God in keeping your word."

"Who has been married the longest?"

"I have been married to your great grandfather for seventy years. Lee Lee got married three years after me to her husband, Joe Jr., and Litter Sister got married two years after Lee Lee to her husband, Bobby Joe."

"How did you live together for all these years?"

"Since I have been married the longest, but I would like to speak first. Are you committed to keeping your word? Keeping your word first to God? Knowing He sees everything and He surely knows everything? So you don't think you can hide anything from Him. And love! Do you know how to love when you do not feel like it? What Mommy has always taught us is to be nice no matter how angry you may feel, while Daddy told us how to pick your fights."

"What do you mean? How do you learn how to pick your fights?" Denise asked.

Little Sister said, "I learned you cannot sweat the small stuff, because it is not important. Why fight over something that is not important and has little value."

"Like what?"

"Little things like how he left the toilet seat up or who left the cap off the toothpaste. That's when you try to be nice or polite, always showing *respect*. Men want respect, while women want to be loved."

Mommy Grace wanted to know, "You still have the music box?"

"Yes, ma'am."

"There were times when I could not remember anything but the bad times. So when I got the music box as a wedding gift from my mommy, knowing it had special meaning, I wanted to put it where we both could see it every day to remind us that no matter how bad or hard things got for your great-grandfather and me, we were a gift to each other from God. Just thinking about it still brings chills to me. I remember one time when I had gotten so upset with your great-grandfather. I was cleaning the house, and while I was dusting, I went to open it. The music, that simple little tune, always touches my heart. As I listened to the music, I saw our wedding picture neatly placed in the lid of the box by your great-grandfather. I put the mirror next to the picture so we could always see each other as a gift. Each time I would open that music box, I was reminded that we were gifts. I must admit that it is difficult to stay angry at someone when you know that he's a gift, especially a gift from God."

Lee Lee wanted to know, "Your man, Eric, is doing fine?"

Denise wondered how they knew so much. She did not think Nana had told them all of this. Denise asked, "How did you learn about Eric?"

Mommy Grace said, "Do you know your cousin who married your Aunt Daisy's friend, Lulu's daughter, Maureen? Well, he works for the police department up there in Riverside. No, I think it is Redlands near that city of Highland place. He told me about Eric seeing that detective on his case. Well, anyway, that's how we know about Eric." Denise wasn't going to ask any more questions about how they were learning these things. Besides, she noticed that Nana was not talking as much as her aunts and mother were. Mommy Grace said, "Now, baby, I think that Raymond is a good man, but he is not broken in."

The other women agreed with laughter in their voices. They all said together, "That's right."

Denise asked. "What do you mean?"

Mommy Grace said, "Now, I know Raymond can say all the right words and may even have the right moves, but you have invested time into Eric." The other women agreed again with her. This idea was beyond Denise. She didn't understand what Mommy Grace was trying to tell her.

Little Sister said, "What she is telling you is that Eric has had—and let me put this as gently as possible—Eric has had the lust beaten out of him and at the same time had common sense beaten into him. I do not think Eric will be looking for anyone to fulfill his dreams of pleasure and lust. This man is looking to be a husband. So he is ripe and ready to be molded into the man of your dreams. Well, we should say, the man God wants you to have."

Lee Lee said, "Since Raymond is not broken in, you gotta take the time to help him understand what being a husband is about. These men may speak the language of love, but you need to grasp what language they each are using."

"I cannot fathom what you are talking about. What do you mean about languages of love?"

Mommy Grace stood closer to Denise to make sure she didn't miss a word. She wanted Denise to know that what she needed to say to her was very important. "Child, she means Eric understands and is speaking the language of agape love. *I love you as you are ... unconditionally.* Believe me. This brother has been taught his lesson on this by God. While my man Raymond is speaking the language of eros love. Like the songs about love you hear on the radio. These love songs only talk about a physical love between a man and a woman. It is just pure physical love of attraction. You know, here today and gone tomorrow. Eric is saying, 'I want to get to know you for who you are.' I must admit that it has taken him the hard way to learn how to love you as his wife. But I think he is beginning to understand. Did we ever tell you the story about our auntie Madea?"

Denise had not heard the story. She hadn't even heard of anyone by that name. Nana had never really talked to her about family. Maybe she had and Denise hadn't paid attention, because she did not find it interesting before.

Denise knew where Nana got her wisdom. Growing up around women like these would keep you on the right track. Denise told the women that she didn't know the story of Auntie Madea. Mommy Grace said, "Well, since we don't have all day, I will give you the short story, and later we can tell you the whole story." When these sisters came together, they knew one another so well that they would often finish one another's sentences.

Denise was enjoying this moment. She thought about how the South was filled with colorful stories and the language they used to tell the stories just made them that much more interesting. That charm gave them life. These were stories that had been handed down from one generation to the next. The story was about how their auntie was sold as a slave to pay off a debt. When she met and fell in love with their uncle Buckerman after the birth of their first child, they were separated for ten years. They were only two miles from each other. Buckeman was not allowed to come to see his family or to bring them with him, because of a dispute between the two plantation owners. Sounds sad, but that helped them stay together once the opportunity came for them to be together. They never had the chance to say, 'Don't move my things from where I put them. The chicken was cooked too done. Why don't you clean up after yourself?' Those little things were not going to pull those two apart. Young people today do not know and understand the thinking of God. They just don't fear God. How many people you know get up and move about when it is thundering and lightning out?"

Lee Lee said, "That's right. Mommy always told us to sit down and let God do His business. While the preacher is talking to God, people should be listening and praying as well, but they don't. You will find them talking while the preacher is praying, being rude and disrespectful to God. You are not supposed to be moving when the preacher is talking to God."

Little Sister said, "You know, last week I was on my way to see Cousin Luther when a funeral procession was going by, and do you know people did not get out of the way to allow them to go through? I know the police were there to let people know they were coming, but no one stopped and gave honor to the dead. You know men nowadays do not take off their hats when funerals procession goes by. Many do not remove their hats while they are in church. People just don't fear God anymore."

All the women agreed. Denise felt that she understood what the women were trying to tell her. For one thing, she had not thought about Eric in the way they had told her. It was food for thought. She would think about the time she had already invested in her marriage, especially now that Eric was more prepared to be a husband than he had been before. Of course, she could only keep thinking this way with the strength she gained through prayer.

After the brief history lesson, Denise cherished the time she had spent with her great-aunts and great-grandmother. She promised them that she would keep in touch.

* * *

Eric felt pleased with himself. He had returned to visit with his father and Paul. He went to see how his father was doing and to let his father and Paul know that he was still alive. He needed to apologize to them for putting their lives in danger. He wanted to let Paul know how much he regretted him getting shot on account of him and making him a fall guy, and he also needed to apologize for the confrontation his father had with Bruce. Returning the money to Bruce gave him an opportunity to show how Christ had truly changed his life. Now he had to return to take care of things with Denise.

After Eric had returned to the Redlands community, he wanted to focus on restoring his marriage. He realized Denise had made it absolutely clear to him that she didn't want him back in her life. After reading her diary and listening to the pain in her voice, he knew her pain was something that he couldn't fathom. Besides, he was learning to have hope no matter how things looked. But he was a man on a mission to get his wife and his life back.

He made himself comfortable as he sat in a sandwich shop in the mall. It was a lovely outdoor mall that has lush landscaping so that people could enjoy the scenery as they walked along the distinctively named streets. It had distinguishing architectural buildings with the best and finest selection of stores and restaurants. The sandwich shop was a cozy, homey, and welcoming shop with indoor and outdoor seating. He enjoyed their soup and sandwich combo. He ordered the tomato soup with a ham sandwich and hot tea. It was just what he needed for the cold December day. He came to the mall to buy a computer. As he enjoyed his meal, he watched people going about their days, getting ready for the holidays. All the stores had holiday decorations and holiday music playing on the intercom system, entertaining people as they shopped. All this helped him remember a day when he and his father went shopping for a present for his mother when he was eight years old. The sights, sounds, and smells really made him feel like a kid again. He wanted to share this moment with someone special. As he sat there, thinking to himself, he understood what it was he really wanted. He wanted a family. He knew the last time he and Denise saw each other, they were not on good terms. All the same, he thought with time she would change her mind. He knew the way he had come back into her life had been very disturbing and disruptive, and it had brought back many unresolved feelings, emotions, and memories for her. But he had to have faith that she would forgive him and take him back into her life. He had come to accept that the impossible was possible. Then he thought about how impossible it looked for her to forgive him *and* want him in her life as her husband again. He knew thinking that it was impossible was wrong. God had shown him that all things were possible with Him. He thought about how he was still alive. He knew he should have been dead, but he wasn't. God guided him to someone who had the skills to restore his face and give him the medical care he needed. He showed him a place to live and people who cared about him. He knew God must have a plan for his life.

He thought of his family, Denise, Nana, Gramps, and people like the Bensons who took care of him. He had had nothing but the clothes on his back. God fixed it all. These thoughts left a smile on his face as he thought about God's sense of humor. After all, God had guided him to his roommate in the hospital, one of the people who was involved in his beating, which eventually allowed him to learn his true identity and what had really happened to him. How would he have known where to look? He had no clue before. He knew for sure it was impossible for him and Denise to reconcile, but he knew that nothing was impossible with God.

Eric wanted to give Denise a surprise. He only hoped she would be pleased when she saw it. It had become a labor of love for him. The more he worked on it, the more he was anticipating seeing the excitement on her face when she saw it. He loved her, and he wanted her to know that he love her too, but not with the same love he had given her before. He now knew that was not love. He wanted to give her the love that came from God. That was real love. The more he had thoughts of Denise and him getting together again, the more he knew there was one thing standing in their way. That was Raymond's interest in her. Raymond was standing in his way of getting Denise back, and he was sure that Raymond knew this. He was sure Denise had told him everything that had happened. He felt the only way to deal with this was to confront Raymond, and he needed to confront him now. The sooner, the better.

Eric went to great lengths to find out how Raymond spent his time. He needed to confront Raymond now, but where? He had learned from his father when to pick his fights. One day he called the church where Raymond's father, Rev. Brown, worked and told the secretary that he was an old friend of Raymond and wanted to surprise him by letting him know he was in town. She didn't want to give out that information; however, David was there, and he knew how it always made Raymond's day when old friends came to town and looked him up. So David was more than glad to give the information to him. Eric had learned that Raymond went to a coffee shop on his way to work every morning for coffee and a muffin. He called the hospital where Raymond worked to learn more about his routine. He used the same story that he had used at the church. He listened very carefully to what David was saying so that he knew the person he needed to speak with. The hospital confirmed that he had a routine of going to that coffee shop and to the gym. Eric learned that Raymond often went to the gym on Mondays, Thursdays, and the weekends after work. He thought to himself, *Should I wait until he has his coffee and muffin so that he is more alert, or should I approach him before or after he has worked out? Then he might be more prepared to knock my brains out.*

One morning he waited and watched across the street from the coffee shop where Raymond got his morning coffee, and instead of his ordinary routine, he took his coffee along with a newspaper and sat out on the patio to read. Eric got out of his SUV and went across the street. Once he was standing before Raymond, he said, "We need to talk." Raymond was not prepared to respond. He was surprised to see Eric was back in town. He just sat and looked at Eric. Eric continued to talk,

"I want you to stay away from my wife. Denise is still my wife, and I want you to stay away."

"Denise is a grown woman, and I am sure she can make that decision herself. From what she has told me, she does not want you in her life again. So tell me, Eric. If she returns to you, what do you have to offer her? She trusted you before, and what did you give her? Nothing but a broken heart. You left her emotionally traumatized. Why should she trust you again?"

Raymond stood to his feet. If Eric wanted a challenge, Raymond was going to give him one. Raymond told him, "I am not going to sit back and allow you to do that to her again." Was the fight on? Raymond continued, "She only became confused when you came back."

"If she's confused, it's because you are in her life. Stay away from my wife. Listen, Raymond. I don't have any bones to pick with you. Stay away from my wife. Stay away from Denise."

"Let me remind you that Denise has a mind of her own. She does not need you to think for her or tell her how she should feel." Before Eric turns to leave he looks Raymond straight into his eyes and gave him a firm warning . "Stay away from my wife."

Raymond stood there and thought. What did he have to lose if he didn't heed Eric's warning? He saw the rage in Eric's eyes, and after years in the ER, he had seen firsthand what happened in domestic affairs that had gone wrong. He knew what domestic violence was all about. He had seen what rage could do to a person.

Raymond thought about what had happen and wondered what would be the best thing to do. Should he tell Denise, or should he just remove himself from her life? There was a conference coming up to train ER personnel in more techniques for emergency care. He called her and explained that since Eric was still alive, it probably wasn't a good thing for them to continue their relationship. Still, if things changed, he said she could always call him. He told her that he would be leaving for a training conference. They would keep in touch.

Maybe Denise needed that, no distractions. She needed to hear herself think. She needed to know and understand what she was feeling and why. Maybe she was confused, but trying to convince herself that she no longer loved Eric and she no longer wanted him in her life did not reflect her true feelings. She could not explain why she felt the way she did. She didn't want to admit to herself that she still loved Eric and wanted him to stay in her life. Maybe she was letting go of her past. Maybe she didn't want to be a prisoner of her anger. Maybe she was being set free. Maybe she was forgiving, but why should she allow him back into her life? Why? Had he really changed? Would he truly be faithful to her? Would she be faithful to him? She knew being with Raymond had given her such joy and pleasure. In spite of that, there was something that she could not explain or understand. Something was missing in their relationship. And the relationship she would have with Raymond would be an adulterous one anyway.

Staying busy had always worked for Denise. It did help her think. So she decided to take a class in real estate. She wanted to learn the complex world of real estate, and it did keep her from being at home alone. She eventually became a real estate agent and worked at the museum, but she was still looking for something more meaningful to fill her life. One day one of the agents at the real estate office told her about a program at the hospital that was looking for volunteers to come and hold babies for about an hour for two days a week. Some were sick, and their family didn't live nearby. They were children who needed to be loved. She decided to try it, and if she did not like it, she would quit.

She tried it for about a month, and it made a very powerful impact on her life. She was giving a part of herself. Every week she looked forward to going to the hospital to hold those beautiful babies. She would look into their faces and see how much they enjoyed her holding them. Sometimes when she would come in, she would get a baby who was crying. Once the babies were in her arms, she would rock and sing to them. Their little mouths would yawn, and then they would close their eyes and fall asleep. It felt so good to give a part of herself to someone who needed to be loved. She was giving in the way she wanted and needed to give, and the babies would say thank you with simple smiles on their faces.

There was one baby who needed special care. His name was Aaron. He had many complications after his birth. He needed to be held all the time. So the hospital staff was always glad to see Denise come in. She started to come in on the weekends just for Aaron. Soon her two days a week became every day. She and Aaron were becoming good friends. She wanted to learn more about his family. It was the hospital's policy not to give out that information. Nevertheless, she did learn that Aaron's mother was a sixteen-year-old girl who had been raped. She was experiencing emotional and physical problems from the birth. Denise coming every day really helped the hospital, the mother, and most of all, Aaron. One day when she came, she received a letter from the mother thanking her for taking such good care of her baby in her absence. Denise cherished the letter and wrote back to her to let her know how much she enjoyed doing it.

One day while driving to work, Denise saw the house that she had admired for years when she was a little girl visiting her grandparents—the old Henderson house. It was an old Victorian that had history dating back to the early 1900s. Someone was making repairs on the house. It had been unoccupied for several years. It was in a great location. It had once been a fabulous house. It was a house she had always loved and dreamed of owning. It was the kind of house she wrote about in her diary. Nonetheless, that dream of owning this kind of house was gone. After driving by the house for several weeks, she decided to find out who owned the house and whether or not they would list it and for how much. With some research, she learned who was doing the construction on the house, but they weren't going to put the house on the market. The contractor told her that he would let the owner know that she wanted to see the house when the construction was finished.

One Saturday afternoon Denise was getting dressed to go out when the phone rang. It was Eric calling. He wanted to talk with her. It had been more than a year since she had last heard from him. "Hello, may I speak with Denise?"

She said in a soft voice, "This is she. Who is calling?"

"It's Eric."

"Why are you calling? I didn't think you were coming back. I haven't heard from you in more than a year. What do you want, Eric?"

"It has been a year since we last spoke to each other. Well, I told you I would give you some time to think. I want to know if we can talk."

"Talk? Talk about what? What do we have to talk about?"

"Denise, I told you that I would return in a year. I went by to see Nana and Gramps. I told them the same thing—that within a year I would return. I want to know if this would be a good time for us to talk."

"No, this would not be a good time for me to talk. I have nothing to talk about. I do not have the time for this. Anyway, Eric, someone is at my door. I have to leave."

"Okay, Denise, I will—" Before he could finish talking, the line went dead.

It was late in the afternoon on Sunday. Denise had had a full day. She went to the morning services at church, and afterward, she went to see Aaron. After visiting with Aaron, she came home and decided to take a hot bath and go to bed. As she was finishing her bath, the phone rang. It was Eric again. He wanted to talk. He prayed that this time she would be in a better mood. "Hello, Denise. This is Eric. Is this a good time to talk?"

"Eric, what do you want?"

"I am sorry that the last time we talked was not a good time for you. How was your day?"

"I had a good day, and yours?"

"I had a good day too. How are Nana and Gramps doing?"

She told him that it had been a while since she had last seen them, but she was sure they were doing good.

"I still would like to know if we can talk."

"Today is not a good time. I am very tired, and I am preparing to go to bed. What do you want to talk about anyway, Eric?"

"I have something I want to tell you. How about lunch tomorrow? Can you meet me at—"

Denise interrupted him. "I will meet you at Lou's Café. It is in—"

"I know where it is. Let's say noon?"

She agreed.

The next day Denise went to see Aaron before she went to work. He was not having a good day. The nurses told her he was not eating and he had an ear infection. The medication was not working, and the doctor would have to prescribe something different. She became so involved and concerned with Aaron that she forgot her appointment with a client and her luncheon date with Eric. She called her client and rescheduled, and she told Eric that they would have to make the luncheon another time because something unexpected had come up. Later that day Aaron's condition started to improve with the new medication that had been administered, and Denise was very much relieved. There were times when she would put more time into visiting with Aaron than working at the museum and showing real estate.

The next day Eric called to reschedule their luncheon date. "Hello, Denise. This is Eric. How are you?"

"Hello, Eric. I am fine, and yourself?"

Eric wanted to choose his words carefully. "I am fine. I wanted to know when would be a good time to reschedule our lunch date." He was expecting her to give him a date about two to four weeks away.

"You know—today would be a good day. I have a couple of hours free. Let's meet at the same place we had decided on before." He agreed. He arrived at Lou's Café earlier than the scheduled time. He wanted to make sure he was there on time. Since he had a few minutes, he decided to go to the floral shop to buy Denise a bouquet of flowers. The floral and gift shop was in the hospital next door to the café. As Eric was leaving, he ran into an elderly woman who was trying to push a little boy in a wheelchair to the elevator. Eric offered to help her. She smiled with gratitude. Eric asked her what floor she wanted to go to. It was the third floor. The elderly woman told Eric that they were going to visit with the little boy's cousin, who was in the hospital for a broken leg. Once they were on the floor, Eric asked the elderly woman what the room number was. She told him the room number and pointed in the direction of the room. He walked with them to the little boy's room. The children's ward was down the hall from the nursery. As they walked past the nursery, Eric thought he saw a woman who looked like Denise. Once they were at the little boy's room, the elderly woman and little boy thanked him for his help.

Eric walked back in the direction of the nursery to see if what he suspected was true. As he got closer to the nursery, one of the nurses saw him and asked if she could help him. Eric explained to her that he had just left the children's ward and now he wanted to see the babies. She showed him where he could go to the viewing window to see the babies. She asked him if he knew the name of the baby he wanted to see. He told her that he didn't. She then asked him what the baby's last name was. Eric was becoming uneasy. He just wanted to know if he had seen Denise earlier. As he was searching for something to say that would not raise suspicion in the nurse, one of the nurses behind the security window waved to her to signal that she needed her to return to the nursery. He thanked her, and he stood there for a few minutes, looking at the babies as he was turning to leave. He could not believe what he saw. It was Denise sitting in a rocking chair, rocking a baby. He stood there for a few minutes out of her view. He was amazed. There she was holding a baby as if it was her own. Was this her baby? He knew he had been gone for a year, which was enough time for her to have a baby. Was she holding her baby? Was this hers and Raymond's baby? Neither one had said anything to him about becoming parents. He thought to himself, *Nana and Gramps said nothing to me about Denise becoming a mother*. He remembered why he was there. He knew in a few minutes he would see Denise for lunch, and he quickly got on the elevator. He could not get the thought out of his head. Did Denise have a baby? Who was the father? For the first time his hope to restore his marriage with Denise was weakening.

Denise did not tell Eric that this was the same hospital where she worked as a volunteer. This was just one of many things that he didn't know about her life. She thought it would be a good idea to meet him at Lou's Café because it gave her a few more minutes with Aaron. She did not have to watch the clock or stress about being late.

Eric returned to the café after he purchased a bouquet of flowers and found a table for them to have their lunch. Getting to the cafe early was a good idea. Around lunchtime the café tables were taken quickly. He was able to get a great table with a view of the fish pond. He still had about thirty minutes before it was time for Denise to come. While he was waiting for Denise, he found a newspaper and started to read. When he stopped reading to survey the room, he noticed that the café was starting to fill with patrons, ready to satisfy their appetites with assorted dishes. The café was locally known for their lunch specials, specifically their Cajun catfish prepared with fried okra, cheese, and macaroni. But at the top of the list were the beer-batter pork chops. As Eric was about to finish reading his paper, his mind started playing tricks on him. He wanted to leave, but his feet would not move. He felt like he was glued to his seat. He told himself to relax, that everything would be all right. Perhaps he was wrong. He knew he had not gotten all of his memory back, but how could he be sure? There were some things he remembered, and there were some things he could not recall. He was sure that there were things he did not want to call to mind or reminisce about, and this was one of those things that he was sure he did not want to look back on. Only one thing could make a man feel this way, a woman. It was Nicole. No, maybe it is a woman who looked like her. How could he be sure it was just a woman who looked like Nicole and not actually Nicole? And how did he know that it was Nicole anyway? He thought about that question, and a few things came to his mind. She always had the habit of pulling on her ear when she needed to think about something, and she had a nervous laugh when she did not want to face something or when she was afraid. She always wore a bottle of very expensive perfume, Her Scent Only. He was not sure if he remembered the name, but he did remember the scent.

When she came into the café, she went to the serving window to place an order. He watched intensely as she stood there and thought about what she wanted to order. He watched where she put her hands. As she stood before the counter, looking at the menu that was on the wall behind, she put her right hand to her right ear and started to pull at her earlobe. *No, no*, he thought to himself. *This is not her. Why, anyone could pull at their earlobe.* Then she turned to look for a place to sit while she waited on her order. He could see she was looking in his direction and was starting to walk toward him. With every step she took, he could feel his heart beating faster and louder. It was beginning to beat like someone was pounding a drum, drumming for a drama, leaving you tense and fearful with the knowledge that something was about to happen. The last time he felt that way was when he was learning about his identity on the train. *No, this is worse*, he thought. The gym bag gave him a feeling of euphoria. Being in this seat and watching Nicole walk toward him made him feel like he was having a heart attack and a stroke all at the same time. He could feel the hair on his head, his body, and his beard turn gray. He could feel himself age. He was growing old right there in the café. He had walked in a young man, but he would leave there an old man.

He wondered if she remembered him. *Maybe it's not me she's walking toward.* He turned around to see if someone was sitting behind him. There was. Yes, she was walking toward the people who were sitting behind him. That made him relax a little, but the feeling was short-lived. The closer she came, the harder and louder he could feel his heart beat. He looked up and heard her say, "Is this seat taken?"

The words were stuck in his mouth, his head, and his throat. He could only move his head, but he moved it in the wrong direction. Instead of up and down, it went from right to left. So she took the seat. Then he knew without a doubt. He could smell her perfume. That took away any doubt he could have had about who this woman sitting across from him was. Then a thought hit him really hard. Denise and Nicole would be together in the same place. He thought to himself, *God has a sense of humor. All this drama will take place near a hospital. That means there won't be any time lost if I need medical help.* What was he going to do? What was Nicole doing here of all places? He thought he would never see her again. *Will she recognized me?* He put the newspaper up to his face. Then he remembered he was wearing sunglasses. Great, his face was concealed just like Clark Kent's. He was beginning to feel a little more relaxed. She wouldn't see his eyes. Then he prayed. "God, I need Your strength and wisdom to handle this situation. No man has the strength and wisdom to handle women. What was I thinking before? I thought I could handle two women at the same time.I thought I could have an affair with one, while I was married to the other. That was not only crazy but suicidal."

Once Nicole was seated, she told him she would not be there long. She only wanted to sit down until her order was ready. Then he asked her if she ate here often. She told him no. "I am here with my friends. They talked me into coming to a women's conference. We were told that this is the best restaurant in town for lunch."

Eric found the strength to talk. "You are here for a conference? What kind of conference are you here for?"

"It is one of those religious conferences for women. You know the kind that tells you what is wrong with your life and how Jesus can make it better."

"I take it you don't believe in Jesus Christ."

"It's not that I don't believe in Jesus. I don't think I like the idea of needing someone else to be in control of my life. I am a good person, and I know I have made some mistakes in life. Well, doesn't everyone make mistakes? I mean, I am not killing or hurting other people."

Eric thought seriously about the things Nicole was telling him. He knew for sure some of the mistakes she had made, and he knew what kind of person she was. He knew it was not true that she didn't hurt people. She did. They both did. He thought about the things they had done to hurt Denise. He knew they had killed his marriage by having an affair. So he asked, "What is the conference teaching you? Is it a good thing or a bad thing to have Jesus in your life?"

"What do you mean is it good or bad to have Christ in my life?"

"If it is good to have Christ in your life, why? If it is a bad thing to have Christ in your life, why? What are you going to do with Jesus Christ?"

Nicole looked at Eric as if he could see right through her. Jesus was never an issue before in her life, but now it seemed as if He had become the only issue in her life. She wasn't sure how to answer that question. So she asked him a question. "Do you have Jesus Christ in your life?"

"Yes, I do. I was once lost to sin."

"What did you do that made you lost to sin?" Eric knew that there was only one way to answer her, and he wanted to do it with the love of Christ, the same love that Christ had shown him. "Well, among the other things I have done, I know the worst was having an affair. At the time of my affair, I did not understand how much I was hurting my wife. I did not understand how much she loved me. I was destroying three lives—my wife's life, the other woman's life, and my own life. After I accepted Christ, I saw and understood so much better."

"I understand what you mean. What did you do about the affair?"

"God took care of that for me. I have since learned I do not want that affair or any other things that are outside of God's will for my life. Having Christ in my life has changed my world. I do not know what my existence would be like if He was not there for me. One thing I do know for sure is that having Him in my world has made a difference. What about yourself? What are you going to do with Christ?"

"Well, I am thinking about it. Oh, they just called my number. My order is ready. Well, it was good talking to you. I guess you have helped me understand what I need. Thanks. Enjoy your lunch." Eric prayed that she would accept Christ. He felt that sharing Christ with her gave him a sense of peace. He knew he had done the right thing. He thought that it was strange to witness to Nicole of all people. He thanked God for using him in this way. He knew he would not and could not have done this on his own strength.

Denise arrived on time just as Nicole was leaving. As they passed each other, they smiled. Eric met her with a smile on his face and the beautiful flowers. She had no idea how happy he was to see her. He knew for sure he was going to have a heart attack if those two women recognized each other. He waved to Denise, letting her know where to sit. He handed the flowers to her, and she graciously accepted them. He had changed since the last time they had seen each other. A waitress came over to give them a menu and to take their orders. The waitress took their orders and then left them to talk. Talking to each other was not as easy as he thought it would be, but Eric was going to put all his effort into it. He had become more aware of his feelings toward her. At first he wanted only her forgiveness, but when he truthfully thought about his feelings, he knew he loved her and wanted her back into his life. "Denise, I want to thank you for having lunch with me. I hope all is well with you."

Denise told him that it was. Eric felt that it was a great start in their relationship. After the unexpected shock of having to witness to Nicole, he had completely forgotten about questioning Denise about the baby he had seen her holding earlier. He was just grateful they were together, even if it was for lunch. He wanted to let Denise know how he truly felt when the time was right.

She and Eric would talk off and on. He wanted to learn as much as he could about her life, and he wanted to see her as often as she would allow, which was not often. The memories he had of her when they were together were still fresh in his mind. One Friday afternoon he decided to visit her unexpectedly. Denise was surprised when he came over. She invited him in and asked him to have a seat. When Eric sat, she received a phone call. She excused herself to answer the call. Eric looked around the room. He thought it was tastefully decorated. He stood up and looked at the different pictures on the walls and on her table. These were all the different faces of people who were in her life, and he did not know any of them. There were several pictures of her holding a baby and several other pictures of her with a man on the corner of a small table. He picked up one to get a closer look. It was a picture of Raymond and Denise at a dance, and they were both smiling. He put it back on the table. He wondered who the baby was in the picture. He wondered whether or not it was hers and Raymond's child. There was no picture of him anywhere in the room. It made him realize that it had been almost three years since they had been together as husband and wife. That was a long time. He wondered whether or not Denise's feelings for him had changed. Not finding pictures of him—not even one photograph—was a clue about how she felt about him.

When Denise was finished with the phone call, she saw Eric viewing her pictures. She said, "Enjoying the movie?" He turned to look at her. She was even more beautiful than he last remembered. "Eric, I am surprised to see you. Why are you here?" She sat in the chair across from him.

"How have you been?"

"I have been fine."

Eric told her that he hoped his unexpected visit had not disrupted her day. He told her that he would not stay long. "Denise, as I told you before, I wanted to give you some time to think about forgiving me, but there is something else I wanted to tell you." Denise had a feeling about where this was going, and she was not ready for what he wanted to tell her, so she let him know that the call was from the hospital where she was volunteering and that they needed to see her. Eric wanted her to know that it would not take long for him to talk with her, but she insisted that she could not stay. Realizing that he had come unannounced, he did not press her to allow him the time to talk. He was a man on a mission, and he was determined to accomplish that mission. He thanked her and left.

When Denise arrived at the hospital, the nursery staff informed her that Aaron's mother, Brenda had died from the complications of giving birth to Aaron. She hadn't been able to get postnatal care. The news of her death was devastating. *What will happen to Aaron?* she wondered. *Who will care for him? Will they understand how to care for and love him?* Denise wanted to know if she could hold him and let him know what had happened to his mother. It would be hard to let Aaron go. He had brought freshness into her life. He was teaching her how to live and appreciate life. He gave meaning to her life. She did not want to live without him. When the staff informed her it was time for her to leave, she wanted to know if she could have one of his stuffed animals. They allowed her to keep a small stuffed teddy bear.

The next day Denise received a call from Eric. He wanted her to meet him at an address on Indian Canyon Lane. She was still grieving Aaron's situation, but she agreed to meet with him. When she arrived at the address, she hadn't realized where she was really going. Eric was already there waiting for her. Once she pulled up to the curb, he got out of his SUV and walked over to meet her at her car. She wanted to know why he wanted her to meet him there. He opened the door and helped her out of her car. She looked at him and followed his eyes as he looked at the house. He told her to follow him inside. As they were entering the house, Eric asked, "Do you know anything about this house?"

"How did you get keys to this house? This house is not on the market. This is the Henderson's house. The contractor told me that the owner was not going to sell the house. So how did you get keys to it?" Eric told her that he had friends in high places. Denise told him she had wanted to see the house once the construction was finished. She told him how often she had passed the house wanting to know what the inside looked like.

Eric told her, "Well, now is your chance."

"You still have not told me why we are here." He told her to just enjoy going through the house. He said he would tell her later. She told him how beautiful the house was. The contractor had done a fantastic job restoring the house. When she finished, she looked at him and said, "Okay, why are we here?"

Eric walked a little closer to her and said, "Denise, I have wanted to tell you for a long time about how I feel about you. I know I told you I would return in a year to get your answer about whether or not you could forgive me for all the wrong I have done to you. I know I did not ask you to take me back. I have come to realize that I love you and that I want to be in your life again. Will you take me back?"

"You want me to take you back. Look, Eric, I spoke with Raymond, and I know what you told him. Do you think that I am supposed to just let you come back into my life as if nothing has happened? Is that what you think? No, no, it doesn't work that way. Why would I want to do something like that? Do you remember you left me?"

"I know if you can find it in your heart to forgive me, you can. I know the problem is not forgiving me but trusting me."

Denise responded with, "You got that right!" Eric continued. "I know you will have to learn to trust me again. But can you trust God to help you trust me again? Denise, I am not the same Eric you were once married to. I am a changed man. I am not sorry for what I did."

Denise interrupted him, "You are not sorry. What do you mean you are not sorry?"

Eric continued, "The Bible does not tell me to be sorry for my sins but to repent of my sins. Sorry does not tell me what I need to do. I am sorry for picking the wrong meal at a restaurant, or I am sorry for mistakenly stepping on someone's toes. When I hurt people or sin against God, I need to repent. Repenting tells me I need to change how I think. I needed to change my attitude and behavior."

"What does that have to do with us being in this house?"

Eric came a little closer to her. He took her hands and said, "Denise, I would like for us to start our life together again. In this house. This house is yours. I went away for a year to take care of some unfinished business and to have this house restored for you. It has been a labor of love. I realized the more I worked on the house, the more I thought of you and how much I wanted you. I bought this house with the money Charlie left me. Once I had learned from your diary—"

Denise interrupted him and asked, "What do you mean you read my diary? How and when did you read my diary? How did you get my diary?"

Eric told her, "The clothes you gave me when I was living with the Bensons. It had a jewelry box that had your diary in it. I read it. Reading your diary helped me understand how horribly I had treated you. God gave me the opportunity to learn how to love you by teaching me what a terrible husband I had been. Denise, I want to give to you what I took away from you—your dream to own the house of your dreams."

"It was the house of our dreams. It was to be the house we both wanted." Eric agreed with her. Eric then told her, "Denise, I know it may be hard for you to trust me again, but would you trust God to help us work out our problems? God orchestrated the beating of my life. Do you think I want to go through that again? It has taken only one beating to let me know how much I love you, and it has made me want to be a godly husband to you."

Denise wanted to listen to what Eric had to say, but she couldn't completely focus. She was thinking about Aaron. Eric could see that she looked distracted, so he asked what was wrong. She told him about Aaron. Eric asked, "Is he the baby that is in the pictures on your living room table?"

Eric realized he had been wrong in thinking the baby was Denise's. He was surprised to learn the baby was someone Denise had volunteered to hold and love. This child had become a part of her life. This was a part of her life that he could not have imagined. It was good seeing how Denise had changed, but he was not prepared for what else she had to say.

Denise moved away from Eric and moved deeper into her thoughts. She pulled from her purse Aaron's small stuffed teddy bear. She looked at it, and then she held it close to her chest. "Eric, this little baby has taught me so much about living in the short time he has been in my life. I once thought life was all about me living the way I wanted to live. I did not think about other people. Aaron gave me hope. He made me feel love. He made me give of myself. Something I do not think I had ever done before." Tears were beginning to run down her cheeks. "Now that hope, this love, this life is being taken away from me."

Eric asked her to explain herself. He didn't understand.

"Eric, Aaron's mother died yesterday. That is why I could not stay the other day when you came over. I didn't want Aaron to be alone when he learned about his mother, and I don't want him to leave. I want him. I want to make him mine." Eric turned her around to face him and asked, "Denise, have you thought about adopting him?"

"I afraid to think about that. I want to give him a good life, not a selfish life. Not a life to fulfill my needs, but one that will give him the love his mother would have given him. I know she was only a child herself. This girl, this young lady gave all she had to this little boy. She kept him even though she had been brutally raped. She kept and loved him. She did what she could to give him her all. She has taught me that life is about living for God."

"Denise, you don't have to care for this child alone. You don't have to love this child alone if that is what you are afraid of. I would like to love him with you. I would very much want to experience what you have with Aaron.

"I know how Aaron will feel, needing someone to love him when he needs it the most. Believe me … I know. I have been there myself. Not knowing who I was, badly injured, needing to trust someone to love and care for me, encouraging me to have hope and not to give up on believing in myself. I want to be there to help you give that kind of love to Aaron. I know what it has done for me." Denise told Eric that she was not feeling well. She had had a headache all day, and she needed to go home to lie down. It had been a very stressful day for Denise.

The most stressful and painful part of her day was when she spoke to Raymond earlier. They had discussed their future together. Marriage was something that they both wanted. However, while Aaron was in her plans, he was not in Raymond's. As they discussed what they wanted for their lives, Denise was surprised to learn that Raymond did not want children, especially not the first year of their marriage. He wasn't sure if he wanted children at all. When Denise questioned him about what she should do about Aaron, he asked, "Why not let someone in his family adopt him?" He didn't want to care for someone else's child, and he was not ready to have children of his own. Denise knew she had made it very clear to Raymond how she felt about Aaron. He had become a part of her life, and she wanted to become his mother. She thought about what Eric told her today about wanting a life with her and Aaron. Eric wanted a family. He wanted her to know he had changed, and he was committed to loving her as a godly man. She had never known Eric to talk to her the way he did now. She had to admit to herself that he had changed. He wanted a family with her and Aaron.

CHAPTER 20

SURPRISE, SURPRISE, SURPRISE

All of Eric's memory had not returned to him, so he was always learning new things about himself. The one thing Eric would always cherish in his memory was his family. He and Denise renewed their vows again. Eric was living the life with Denise that he had prayed about. Their adoption of Aaron was one of the first things they did together in celebrating their marriage as husband and wife. This completed their unit as a family. A family that was committed to love each other faithfully. Becoming not only a husband, but a father as well, Eric knew that God had given him another opportunity to use his gifts and talents to fulfill the role as a leader in his family, to lead his family in the way God would have them to go. A leader who needed God's guidance in accomplishing this.

He opened another boutique, and Denise quit her jobs working at the museum and selling real estate to become a full-time mother. They enjoyed taking Aaron over to visit with his grandparents and great-grandparents, and they always told Aaron that two generations of parents loved him. Nana and Gramps enjoyed doing the things great-grandparents did best, showing Aaron off to all their friends. Eric could not imagine life any other way. He was learning how to become a father, and he was enjoying every minute of it. He was also learning how to share his faith with others who did not know Jesus Christ. Life for the Bishop family was filled with God's blessings. Life was good.

Nonetheless, the haunting thought was always in the back of Eric's mind. Who wanted him dead, and why?

One evening Eric called Denise and told her not to make dinner for him. He would have dinner at the boutique. The night he was inspecting and selecting the new shipment of clothes for an upcoming fashion show. Denise said that she could bring him dinner so that he didn't have to eat alone. Besides, she had some important news she wanted to share with him. While they were still talking on the phone, Denise asked Eric what he was doing. He explained that the shipment of clothing for the fashion show had come in earlier that day, and he said that he was going over the manifest, doing the paperwork. Eric was distracted while he was talking to Denise, and some unexpected guest came in for a visit. Denise could hear the conversation, but it was not clear.

"Eric, it has taken some time, but this day has finally come."

Eric looked up from his paperwork and saw the figure of a man standing in the shadow of the doorway. He softly said, "Who is there? What do you want?"

The person didn't say anything, just stood there. Eric stood up from his seat and started to walk toward the figure to get a better look. As Denise was listening, she spoke softly into the phone, "Eric, Eric, what is wrong? Who is with you?"

Eric continued to speak, asking the same question over and over again. "Who are you? May I help you?"

The shadowy figure said, "Sure, you can help me. I have been waiting for that help for several years now. Now, I may be wrong, but I have been waiting for your help for three years."

Eric continued to approach the person. "Who are you?"

The person continued to stay in the shadow, keeping his identity concealed. Eric's heart began to race, and then he remembered that he had nothing to protect himself with. He quickly cased the area closest to him, looking for something, anything to use as a weapon.

"Do you think I was going to let this go, Eric? You owe me, and you are going to pay."

Eric said, "Owe you what?" He walked closer to the person, and then their eyes met. Eric immediately recognized the person. Then he remembered. Just as he was saying the person's name, he was shot twice—once in the head and once in the chest. His life flashed before his eyes as he fell to the floor.

When Denise heard the shots, she screamed for Eric. "Eric? Eric!" There was no answer. She quickly grabbed her cell phone and called the police and requested an ambulance at the boutique's address. She then called her next-door neighbor and asked her to babysit Aaron. She grabbed her purse, phone, and keys.

She drove straight to the boutique. The ambulance and the police were already there. The boutique's front was roped off with yellow tape. When she tried to get through, the police stopped her. In a frantic state of panic, she told the police she was the one who had called them, and she wanted to know what had happened to her husband. Then the EMTs brought Eric out on a stretcher. He was unconscious. Denise nearly lost it. She insisted on going in the ambulance with her husband. The police wanted to know if she knew anything. As Eric was wheeled into the ambulance, Denise told them that he was talking to someone. She believed he knew him or her. She could not understand what he was saying before he was shot, but she was sure he knew the person, because he'd called him or her by name. But she wasn't able to hear that name.

The ambulance called to the hospital and told them that they were transporting a gunshot victim. They called in his vitals and informed the hospital they were trying to stabilize his blood pressure because it was dropping. When the ambulance arrived, the doctors were waiting for Eric. He was immediately taken to the emergency room. Denise wanted to go in too. She did not want to leave his side. She had to make sure nothing else bad would happen to him. But the nurse insisted she wait in the waiting room. She said that the doctors would do all they could to save his life. While she was waiting, she tried to reach her grandparents, but she remembered that they were out of the country with her parents. They were on a missionary trip to Kenya to help a sister church build a school. Denise was completely lost. What would she do now? Her parents and grandparents had always been there for her during crises, and now they weren't. Nana was her prayer warrior. Nana knew what to say when she prayed to God. She knew how to talk to God. Her parents knew how to pray. They were all too far away for her to call them. Who was she going to call to pray with her? Who would be there for her now?

So the only thing she could do was leave a message and hope they would return the call if they could. While Denise was trying to think of what she needed to do and how to pray, an officer came over to speak with her. He had a pad and pen with him, and he wanted to ask her about what she knew about the shooting. "Are you the victim's wife? The one who was shot at the Unique Boutique?"

"Yes, I am."

"What is your name?"

"My name is Denise Bishop, and Eric Bishop is my husband."

"How old is your husband?"

"He is thirty-eight years old."

"Do you know who owns the boutique?"

"Yes, my husband, Eric Bishop does."

"How long has he been the owner of the boutique?"

"A year."

"Were you at the boutique when your husband was shot?"

"No, I was not."

"Do you know who called the police?"

"Yes, I did."

"Can you tell me what happened?"

"While we were talking on the phone, someone came into the room and started to talk to Eric. I could not hear what the other person was saying, but I know Eric knew who did this."

"How do you know that?"

"Because I heard Eric say their name, but I could not understand what he said. The name was not clear."

"Do you have any idea what was said?"

"I am so sorry. I could only hear some of Eric's part of the conversation, and that was not clear. It could have been the reception he was getting." The situation was overwhelming for Denise, and she spoke with fear and panic in her voice.

"Thank you, Mrs. Bishop. We will keep in touch."

She said a very simple prayer. "God please, please do not take Eric from us. Please, God, let Eric be all right. Please, God, let him live." Nothing else came to her mind. She stayed at the hospital all night. It wasn't until the next day that Denise got more information about Eric's condition.

Dr. Winters, one of the doctors who had performed the surgery, came to talk to Denise. He held out his hand to shake hers. "Mrs. Bishop, good morning. I am Dr. Winters. I am one of the doctors on the team that worked on your husband."

Tired and exhausted, Denise tried to be attentive. Her mind recorded the doctor's every word. "Yes, Dr. Winters, please tell me about my husband's condition. Will he be all right?" The doctor found a place where they both could sit. He explained that Eric was shot at close range. They were able to remove the bullets, but they still needed to see if there was any brain damage. Right now he was still recovering from the surgery. "Mrs. Bishop, I do not know how your husband did it, but he survived the surgery, although, Mrs. Bishop, we do not know if he will survive."

"You said he survived the surgery. What do you mean he may not survive? Survive what? What are you telling me? He may not live. Is that what you are telling me? Eric could die?"

"Well, we think he may not live. If he does, there's a chance that there will be significant brain damage. I am sorry, Mrs. Bishop. We did all we could." Before the doctor left, Denise asked if she could go to see Eric. The doctor told her she could soon. The nurse would let her know when exactly.

Denise soon learned which bed Eric was in. She walked slowly over to see him. He was hooked up to several monitors, and he was connected to many tubes. He did not look alive, but the monitor connected to his heart showed that he was. She walked over to his bed and kissed him on one of his cheeks. She held his fingers because both of his hands had IV needles in them. She said a simple prayer, "Thank You, God, for saving his life. You have brought him through this surgery. Thank You." The nurse came over and told her that she could only stay for a short time, but she could come back later.

She stood over Eric and told him that she loved him and pleaded with him to get well. "Please, Eric, you must come home to Aaron and me. We need you. Please, please get better." She got a little closer to make sure he could hear her. "Eric, you must get better. I had plans to tell you last tonight that we are going to have a baby. Eric, I am pregnant. Please, Eric, don't die."

She left the hospital and went home. Her energy was completely depleted. Being totally exhausted, she could not fall asleep. As she lay there thinking about the events of the day, she also thought, *God, please help me. I do not know what to do.* Denise began to realize that she did not really have a relationship with God. She asked herself if God would hear her prayer. *Would He listen to what she had to say?* What had she done for His son, Jesus Christ? She asked herself if she knew a Bible verse. None came to her mind. She reached into her nightstand and found her Bible, the one that her parents had given her on her thirteenth birthday. She opened it and started to read until she went to sleep. She was awakened by Aaron's crying.

It was now the afternoon. She thanked her neighbor for caring for him. She didn't have much to tell everyone about the shooting. After the neighbor left, she bathed and fed Aaron. Her mind was focused on how she was going to manage to care for Aaron and Eric. She so wished her parents and grandparents were there to help her. She felt all alone. While Aaron ate his lunch, she turned on the TV so that he could watch his favorite show, *Veggie Tales*. As she was changing the station, she saw the news report about the shooting. She put her head in her hands as she listened to the report and said, "Oh no, now what?"

The phone rang, and Denise answered it. "Hello?"

The caller said, "Hello, Denise, this is Ellen from church. It has been a while since you have been in the women's group. We heard what happened to your husband, and we wanted to see if there was anything we could do to help you. We want you to know that we are praying for Eric to get better and for you and Aaron. If you need someone to keep little Aaron for you while you go visit with Eric, please let us know. We are here for you as the body of Christ." Denise was so surprised to receive the call.

A few minutes later, the phone rang again. CWHS was calling to see what she needed, and they assured her that they would get her message about Eric to Nana and Gramps. They told her that they knew it would be difficult to reach them where they were. Denise did not know what to say. She wasn't alone after all. She knew that it was Jesus reaching out to touch her life. It was Christ using other people to help her. As she was doing the dishes, the doorbell rang. Four women from the church had come over to help her. They asked her what she needed help with. She didn't know what to say. Alice told her she would take care of Aaron while she visited with Eric. Rachel told Denise that she would cook dinner, and Barbara and Laura said they would clean the house for her. They told her that Eric would need her, and she needed to focus on helping him get better. All the women were married with families of their own, and they were there to help her however they could. The only thing that Denise could say was, "Thank you."

When her guests left, the doorbell rang again. When she answered it, she realized it was the FBI.

CHAPTER 21

ARE THERE ANSWERS TO THE QUESTIONS?

When Denise answered the door, there were two men dressed in suits standing before her. One of the men showed her his badge and introduced himself and his partner. "Hello, are you Mrs. Denise Bishop, Eric Joseph Bishop's wife?"

"Yes, I am."

"I am Agent Baker, and this is Agent Cash. We are with the—"

Denise looked closely at the badge and finished the sentence. "You are with the FBI?"

"Yes, ma'am." Denise went numb. She was exhausted and drained. She hadn't had any time to rest. It seemed like one incident after another came up. Her life felt like a roller coaster. Once she heard the men were agents from the FBI, it was difficult to think. What would the FBI want with her of all people?

"May we come in?" She invited them in and showed them where to sit. She told the men that she had just put her son to bed, so they had time to talk. She offered them coffee, but she did not want anything to distract her focus. Agent Cash would ask the questions, while Agent Baker took notes.

"Mrs. Bishop, how long has your husband been the proprietor of the Unique Boutique?"

"He has owned the boutique for approximately a year. What is this all about? Why are you here? What do you want with my husband?"

"Just answer the questions, Mrs. Bishop."

"How long has he been declared legally alive?"

"For a year."

"Do you know Paul Parker?"

"Yes, he once worked for my husband as a manager. Why are you asking questions about Paul? Is he all right? Is he involved in the shooting?

"When did your husband regain his memory?"

Denise was becoming even more concerned because they knew things that she hadn't told them.

"About two years ago. Please tell me what this is all about. I don't want to answer any more questions until I know what this is all about."

"Mrs. Bishop, your husband was working as an informant for the FBI ten years ago."

"An informant! Why would he do that? I don't understand. I knew nothing about this. Eric was an informant for the FB?"

"Mrs. Bishop, a year before you married Eric, he was involved in a scheme to traffic illegal immigrants from China to the United States to start a sweatshop in New York for his clothing stores. To make sure the scheme worked, he hired Paul to be the front man."

"What do you mean the front man?"

"If anything went wrong, the first person the police would suspect would have been Paul."

"Why, why would the police have been suspicious of Paul?"

"Because Paul has a criminal record."

"Paul Parker is a criminal?"

"He is a reformed criminal. Nonetheless, Paul didn't want to be involved in this type of activity. I guess, you can say, Paul was really looking for a nine-to-five with no overtime. When Eric approached Paul with the idea of managing this part of the business, keeping all the paperwork the way Eric wanted it done. Which would be keeping fraudulent records. One set of books that would appear legal. Showing the business was doing good and legit business, conforming to the law and not doing any illegal activity or attempting to deceive the law. Another set of books were for Eric's records, showing how much business he and Ling Lee were doing. They were to show how much money they would make without having to pay taxes. One set that was legal, which would keep the Feds happy, and the other would keep Eric and Ling happy. Paul let him know that he did not want any parts of this, and he was even thinking about quitting."

"Paul didn't quit. Why?"

"Because Eric's father liked Paul's work. And if he had quit, Eric would have to explain why, and it would have made the old man suspicious."

"How did you know this?"

"We had an undercover agent working in the shop that informed us what was happening. So we confronted Eric about his intentions and gave him an opportunity to work for his government with the understanding that if he did not, he could be facing many years behind bars."

"Eric never gave me any indication that this was going on. It is hard for me to concede Eric being involved in smuggling people!"

"Mrs. Bishop, there is a good chance that Eric does not remember that he was involved in helping us capture one of the most dangerous persons on the FBI's most wanted list."

Denise stood up and put her head in her hands. She shook her head. She couldn't understand what she was hearing. Just the same, she collected herself. She needed to hear what else they had to say.

"Eric was told to continue with the setup he had made with Ling Lee."

"Who is Ling Lee?"

"He is a man Eric met through a mutual friend. He is interested in political affairs, dealing with foreign trade. Eric thought becoming an ambassador for the garment district would put him in a position to keep his father's boutique as one of the most fashionable and well-stocked boutique here and abroad, while he obtained clienteles in different foreign countries. The plan was to hide the immigrants in a container along with the shipment of clothing. Once the shipment arrived at a designated location, the people would be taken to a shop where they would live and work making garments with their name-brand labels and selling them at marked-up prices as wholesale to different department stores. The profit and cost would be split between them. While Eric supplied the work, Ling Lee supplied the workers."

"How long did Eric do this?"

"Their strategy did not work as they had initially planned. They never got an opportunity to test it. The reason Eric went to New York was to learn why he had not heard from Lee." As Agent Cash was saying this, he looked at the ground. She knew the other reason for Eric's visit to New York—being with Nicole. He did this out of respect for Denise. "Eric did not get the message that there was going to be a sting."

"A sting. What—"

"A shakedown."

"A shakedown? What?"

"The FBI was going to arrest all the people who were involved in the criminal activity. When we thought Eric was dead, we closed the files on the case involving him."

"Why did Eric not get your message that there was going to be a sting or a shakedown?"

"We learned that Eric was having problems with his cell phone malfunctioning, so we gave him one so that he could have direct contact with us. Unfortunately, when he got to New York, he went to the place of contact where he was instructed to go. He was given the paperwork he would need for customs and the contact phone, but he was mistakenly given the wrong phone, which meant he did not get the message about the sting. We wanted to contact him so Ling Lee wouldn't think that he was a part of the sting. It wasn't until Eric went to see Bruce that Lee learned he was still alive. Lee thought that maybe Eric had snitched, double-crossing him."

"Bruce was in prison."

"That is correct. Word got back to Lee though, and he wanted revenge."

"Eric has a family. How can you kill someone with a family? Why, why would you want to do that?"

"It does not matter whether or not he has a family."

"So this Ling Lee is in custody? He's in jail, right?"

"No, but he will be apprehended. All means of leaving this country are under surveillance. There is really nowhere for him to go without us knowing. All the most likely places for him to hide are also under surveillance. He will be apprehended."

"Well, I don't want this man anywhere near my husband. Who else called the police when Eric was shot? I know I called when I heard the shots, but apparently someone else tried to save his life? The police were there before I arrived, and we don't live far from the boutique. Who was the other person who called, and do you know who shot Eric?"

"Yes, ma'am, we do. Lee's girlfriend, Gloria, was our other informant. She made sure that Lee would be where we could capture him during the shakedown, but instead he changed his plans. When he did, he called Eric on his phone, which had malfunctioned. That meant Eric got no one's messages. He didn't get our message about the sting, and he did not get Lee's message that there was a changed in his plan. He was sending his right-hand man, Tony Underwood, to meet Eric at a new location, and Eric was supposed to bring the money due to Ling for his first shipment of workers. When the sting occurred, everyone was there except Ling and Eric. Ling got away, thinking Eric double-crossed him. No one knew what happen to Eric until days later when it was reported that he was killed in a car accident.

Gloria came to see Eric the night that he was shot to warn him about Lee coming to see him. When she got there, she went to use the restroom. She heard the shooting and went to see what had happen. She saw Lee running out of Eric's office. She went into the office and found Eric on the floor in a puddle of blood. She was the other person who called the police and an ambulance. She is the other person who saved Eric's life."

"I am grateful she also wanted to save Eric's life. Please let her know that for me. So if you know Eric was not part of this, why are you here?"

Agent Cash approached Denise and firmly said, "We may need you to testify for Eric and tell us what he has been doing since he has regained his memory."

"What will happen if I do not want to do that? This sounds very dangerous. I am a mother with a family to care for. Remember: Eric is in the hospital, fighting for his life. There must be some other means by which you can do this. What will happen to Gloria if she testifies?"

"She will have to go into protective custody."

"Protective custody! I don't want that for my family. Will that happen to my family if I testify?"

"We think we have enough evidence placing Lee at the scene of the crime and speaking to his intent. We don't know if your husband will be able to identify Lee as the shooter, because of his injuries. But Gloria will be able to do that, and that is why she will have to go into protective custody. We just need you to confirm what we already know." They thanked her for her time and gave her their card. If they needed her, they would give her a call.

When the FBI agents left, Denise went to her bedroom, lay down, and cried out to God.

On the way to the hospital, Denise talked to Jesus, thanking Him for all He was doing for her. She could not imagine this. People were so willing to help, and she didn't have to ask them. They came to her. This was the first time in her life that she really reached out to God. She remembered the time when the authorities told her Eric was dead. She drowned her sorrows in cheap wine, but that didn't take her pain away. It only made it worst, but now she is praying. This was so new, and yet she wasn't as fearful as she thought she would be. Learning more about Eric's past was still shocking, but she told Jesus to help her deal with it. It was his past. The life they had now was the life that she wanted. It was the life they both wanted. Talking to Christ was new to her, but she wanted to learn more about Him. She wanted to know why He would do this for her. Once she reached the hospital, she said a simple prayer, "God, please help Eric get better. Please bring him home to Aaron and me." She knew the prayer had come from her heart, and she knew that God had heard it.

When she got to the ward in the ICU, she asked the nurses how he was doing. The nurse stated, "There has been no change in his condition. He is still comatose."

She went over to his bed. Even though he lay there connected to tubes, monitors all around him, she knew God would let him live. She sat next to him, held his hand, and thanked God for her answered prayer. She felt in her heart that God had been waiting for her. For a long time, she had been angry with God. She prayed and asked God to forgive her. While He had tried to love her, she had been rejecting Him and His love.

Two days later Denise heard from her parents and grandparents. They had received the news about Eric and held a prayer vigil for him. They were on their way home, and they would be there in a few days. She had received so many cards and calls. Seeing how people were reaching out to her helped develop her faith and made her want to learn more about Christ.

When her parents and grandparents returned, they went immediately to the hospital. Eric's condition had not improved. Denise gave them the update about what had happened and the police investigation. She told Nana how the women at the church and from CWHS came to help her, especially with Aaron.

They wanted to know how she was doing. She looked into her mother's eyes and told her she was three weeks pregnant. She smiled and gave Denise a big hug. Then they each took turns giving her hugs and kisses. Nana asked, "Does Eric know?"

"No, Nana, I never got the opportunity to tell him. I was speaking to him when this happened. He was working late at the boutique, preparing for a fashion show. So I decided to call and let him know I was bringing dinner to him so that he wouldn't have to eat alone, and then I could give him the news."

"Denise, if you and Aaron had been there, you could have been shot as well."

"Oh, Nana, I hadn't thought of that, and I do not want to think that could have happened."

Her father asked, "Do the police know who shot Eric?"

"Yes, Dad, they do, and so does the FBI."

"The FBI! Why would the FBI be involved in the shooting?"

"It was the FBI who came to our home to—"

"The FBI came to see you?"

"Yes, the FBI told me that Eric was an informant."

"An informant!" Gramps said.

"Yes, an informant."

"Why was he an informant?"

"He was helping the FBI capture someone on the most wanted list, a man named Ling Lee. There is so much to tell you about this, but I am just tired, so I will give you all the details later."

Gramps wanted to know where Aaron was.

"The ladies from Nana's church came over to help take care of him. I don't know what I would do if they hadn't. I am so glad you all are here, and I know Eric would be too."

Her father was looking out of the window in the waiting room when he said, "So what you are saying is that Eric was an informant and the FBI has the person who shot Eric?"

"No, Dad, they know who shot Eric, but they do not have him in custody yet. And they want me to testify about what Eric has been doing since he has got his memory back."

Denise's mother expressed concern. "I don't like the sound of this, especially with you being pregnant."

Then Nana added, "And the doctors do not know if Eric is going to live, and if he does, there is a good chance he will have brain damage."

"Yes, what am I going to do, Nana?"

"We are going to pray and trust God. The FBI or police may not have the person who shot Eric in custody. Eric may not know you are going to have a baby. The doctors may not know if Eric is going to live, and if he does live, there is a good chance he may have brain damage. God knows everything though. He knows where this Ling Lee is, and He will show the FBI where he is hiding so that he cannot do any more harm to Eric. Because the power of life and death is in His hands." She held Denise close to her and softly said, "Listen. If God wanted Eric dead, he would have died. He would have died the night he was shot during the surgery or even now. But he is not dead. He is still alive. God has a plan for his life. So do not lose hope or faith. Remember: life and death is only in His hands, and no one can snatch you out of His mighty hands."

They decided to go to the hospital cafeteria for lunch. Denise got a call on her cell phone. She answered it because she thought the hospital could be calling to let her know if there had been a change in Eric's condition. Unfortunately, it was not. In fact, it was her old girlfriend Amy calling to give her the good news. She wanted Denise to come to Las Vegas for her wedding. Denise expressed her excitement about Amy's wedding, but she told her it was not a good time to talk. Denise said she would call her later and explain.

Nana told her to consider attending the wedding.

"Nana, I cannot go to this wedding, not now, not with Eric in the hospital, and we do not know if he will live or die. And what about Aaron and the baby and—"

Nana stopped her in middle of her sentence. "That is why we are here." They all agreed. "What are you going to do? What can you do that we cannot do?"

"How can I leave my family during a time like this?"

"I am not telling you to leave your family, but as this is another crossroad in your life, this would be a wonderful time to witness how God is loving, caring, and providing for you through this critical time. That is why God has us here for you. God is in control, not you. Your faith in God will allow you to trust Him to take care of your family and you. What will worry do for you? You don't want to carry the baby under all this stress. God is taking care of Eric, and He is taking care of Aaron. He has provided professional people who have the knowledge and training to tend to Eric, people who love you, and the police and the FBI will find who did this. I know it will not be easy, and I think I speak for all of us when I say that we want you to go."

Denise was willing to trust God. Eric would live to learn she was pregnant, and the police and the FBI would capture Ling Lee. She knew that there might be other things Eric may have been involved in. Her faith in Christ would prepare her for that. In the meantime, she would take Nana's advice and walk in faith.

CHAPTER 22

THE WEDDING PLANS

Almost four months has passed since the shooting. His condition remained the same. He was stuck in a comatose state. Even so, Denise's condition was changing daily. She was almost five months into her pregnancy, and she has begun to feel the baby move. Every day she let Eric feel how big her stomach was growing. While she took care of Eric, her mother and grandmother watched Aaron. The women from church continued to help out, providing meals and doing some housekeeping. Her father and grandfather used what knowledge they had to keep the boutique open, but they were very grateful when Paul gave them some pointers. It made a world of difference. In Eric's absence the boutique was providing an income for his family.

Denise knew people were there helping her out of their love for Christ, and she was receiving it out of her love for Christ, moving out of her comfort zone. Since the shooting, each morning Denise would go to the hospital to visit with him. They would start their day together by having a daily devotion. She would tell him all the latest news about Aaron, how he was growing, and how their new baby was growing inside of her. She told him how Aaron was adjusting to the news that he would have a new brother or sister. She would place his hand over her stomach so that he could feel how the baby was growing. She wasn't experiencing morning sickness as often now. In fact, her morning sickness has stopped. She wanted him to know everything that was happening in their lives. "Good morning, my love," she would say. "How did you rest last night? I missed you so much as always. The baby is growing, and he or she has started to kick. I don't want to take a sonogram or an ultrasound of the baby. I told Dr. Hope I want to wait for you to be there so that we both can learn together what the sex of our child is. Can you believe it? We are having a baby together. We are so blessed. We decided to adopt together, and now God has decided we should have a baby together. We have so much to be thankful for. Aaron is so excited that he will have a little brother or little sister to play with. We still have to choose a name for the baby.

"Let's see. Today's devotion is from Proverbs 3:1–12. It deals with trusting God while in trials. The author gave a poem for thought. I will read it to you, Eric.

Trust
I will trust in the Lord no matter
what the day may bring.
He is my faithful Lord and King.
There are times when I struggle with
what I may think is best.
When I trust God, He is always faithful,
even when I put Him to the test.
Guide me, O Lord, when the way
is dark and I cannot see
what may be before me.
Please give me hope so I may cope with today's events.
I may not know why, but I do know
that they are Heaven sent.

"Trust is allowing God to take control of not
only your life but each day's events.

This is just what we needed to hear. Let's pray, my love. God, thank You for Your faithfulness and Your love for us. We are grateful for our blessings today. Lord Jesus, it is in Your name that we pray." When Denise was saying, "Amen," Eric joined her. Denise looked up at Eric, completely speechless. She softly said, "Eric, Eric." Then she quickly reached over him and pressed the button to call the nurse to come to Eric's room. "Come, come quickly now!" Denise didn't want to leave him.

The nurse came in with a concerned look on her face. "What's the matter?"

"Look! It is Eric. He, he, he spoke. He spoke!"

"What did he say?"

"He said amen."

The nurse came over to examine Eric. She quickly left the room and called for the doctor. Denise called her parents. They were not home, so she tried to call her grandparents. Fortunately, her parents were there. She was able to tell them both that Eric had spoken. Nana told her that they would be right over.

"Eric, Eric, my love, please speak to me. I love you."

Eric slowly and softly said, "I love you."

Their prayers had finally been answered. Eric had regain consciousness. He was no longer in a coma. Eric was on the road to recovery. The doctors did psychological tests that examined his brain function. All the tests showed no signs of brain damage. He would need some therapy for recovery though. Everyone praised God for His faithfulness, mercy, love, and peace. This could only be the work of God. Eric and Denise knew that God definitely had a plan for their lives.

When Eric returned home, there was so much catching up to do. He was going to become a father for the second time. He enjoyed Denise being pregnant, and he loved being at home with his family. Surrounding himself with people who loved him was the only medicine he needed. Eric's recovery was the main concern. Their focus shifted from who was responsible to helping him to recover.

Each day Denise would tell her unborn baby how much it was loved.

She had grown to enjoy and cherish the moments she had with Aaron in how she would tell him how much he was loved. Nevertheless, that daily practice of holding him close to her chest as she sing in his ear how she loved him would be disrupted while she would be away visiting with her girlfriends in Vegas.

Denise had an early doctor's appointment for the end of her second trimester. Eric was so excited to be a part of the pregnancy. He was a little fatigued from all that was involved in the visit. He knew he had to take it slow while he recuperated from the shooting, but this was an experience he didn't want to miss. Denise thought she would take Aaron to the park while Eric got some much-needed rest. The house was quiet, and Eric lay on the sofa to relax as he drifted off to sleep. He was awakened by a knock at the door. He thought Denise had left her keys again, so he opened the door. He expected to see an expression on her face that said, "Sorry. I did it again. I forgot my keys." As Eric was opening the door, he said, "Don't tell me. You forgot your keys again." But it wasn't Denise at the door. It was Bruce.

"Are you going to let me in, or are you just going to stand there?"

"Why are you here?"

"How can I tell you that out here? Can I come in first so that I can tell you?"

"Um ... come on in."

"Thanks." As Bruce came in, he nodded his head up and down, approving of Eric's lifestyle. "You've done all right for yourself."

Eric showed him where his guest could sit. "So why are you here?"

"Well, since you came to see me while I was in prison, I have not stopped thinking about that."

"What do you mean? I don't understand what you are talking about."

"When you came to see me. Look, I want what you have. I want what you have in Jesus. I know people come to the prison to witness to us, but what I saw in you, I knew I wanted that. I knew I had to have it. You coming to see me when you didn't have to, especially with me in prison, I thought Jesus must be real, very real and very powerful in your life. So I came here for you to tell me how I can get that. How do I get Jesus the way you have Him? I am tired of living like this."

Eric was dumbfounded. He didn't know what surprised him the most, Bruce coming to his home or Bruce wanting to accept Jesus Christ. It did not matter. Either way, he was going to be amazed. "How did you know where I lived?"

"I have my connections, but someone owed me a favor, so I am collecting."

"Well, sure I will be happy to lead you to Christ. Well, if you want Christ in your life, then you know you are a sinner."

"Well, yeah, I don't need anyone to tell me that."

"Do you know that God has a plan for your life?"

"No, not really. I am glad to know that. As you know, my plan has not worked."

"Do you understand what Jesus has done for you when He died on the cross?"

Bruce put his head in his hands. He thought about the things he has done. He didn't want them to be part of his life any longer.

"Yes, I understand what Jesus did on the cross for me, and I want to ask God for forgiveness." Eric stood by the fireplace. He then walked over to Bruce and told him to repeat the Sinner's Prayer. "Dear Lord Jesus, I know I am a sinner, and I ask for Your forgiveness. I believe You died for my sins and rose from the dead. I trust You and want You as my Lord and Savior. Guide my life and help me to do Your will. In Your name, amen."

"That's it? I have Jesus. That was all I needed to do?"

"Well, yeah, God knows your heart. Now you need to get to know God's heart by reading, studying, and applying His Word to your life. Do you have a Bible?"

"No." Eric picked up the Bible on his coffee table and gave it to Bruce. "Here. Take this one."

"Okay, thanks, thanks a lot. Now what do I do?"

"Well, you may want to tell someone what you have done."

"What do you mean?"

"Tell someone you have accepted Christ."

"I will do just that. I will tell my wife. She will be shock … in a good way, of course. Then what?"

"Do you have a church where you can go?"

"Yeah, I will go with my wife. I know she will be so surprised and pleased. I cannot thank you enough. This has meant so much to me."

"You are welcome. I have been more than happy to do it." Eric thought about how God had used him in ways he could not begin to imagine. Eric reminded Bruce to repent each time he sinned. They gave each other a brotherly hug, and then Bruce left. As he was driving home, the traffic on the freeway had come to a standstill. He called his wife and told her what he had done. When he told her about the Bible, he realized he had left it at Eric's. He let his wife know that after he retrieved the Bible, he would return home.

While Eric was thanking God for the experience of witnessing to Bruce, the doorbell rang. He answered it, thinking that Bruce had return for his Bible. When he opened the door, he saw that it wasn't Bruce. He couldn't believe who was standing there at the front door of his home, his sanctuary, his place of refuge and shelter. He thought he was going to have a heart attack. Ling Lee stood there, looking at him. Eric was not strong enough to fight him back from the door as he forced his way in. "The last time I saw you, I thought I left you for dead. I think you are like a cat. A cat that has nine lives. No more! Today you will die."

"Ling Lee, why are you trying to kill me? Why do you want me dead? What have I done to you?"

"No one double-crosses me and lives. No one."

"What do you mean double-crossed you?"

"Don't stand there and act like you don't know what I am talking about! I do not care if you do not understand. But understand this. You will die today. Today you will die."

"Okay, okay, if I am to die, just let me know why. What did I do? You said I double-crossed you. How did I double-cross you? How? All I know is that you have been trying to kill me. Why?"

"You took my money."

"I took your money. What money? Look, for the past three years, I had no memory of my past. I had amnesia. What money of yours did I take?"

"You were supposed to meet Tony at—"

"Tony, I never knew I was supposed to meet Tony. If I remembered correctly, I was to meet you at … I don't remember where."

"I called you and left a message for you to call me."

"Listen, I never got your message. When I was found, I didn't have a phone on me. If I had had a phone on me, it would have been a great help in saving me a lot of time. I had lost my memory. I didn't know who I was."

"That does not matter to me. You didn't do what you were supposed to. You will die."

When Bruce returned to Eric's, he noticed Ling Lee's driver standing outside the house, observing, surveilling for any suspicious activities or any suspicious people who would come to the house. Another man was standing near the rear of the house, doing the same thing. Bruce called the police and told them a crime was in progress, so he advised them not to use sirens. Bruce knew Eric needed help, and they couldn't wait for the police. He knew Ling Lee was a very dangerous person, especially if he thought he had been double-crossed. He prayed and asked God for help. How could he get into the house without the guards knowing? He saw that the next-door neighbor had left his lawn mower out by the garage. He took the lawn mower and pretended to be the gardener. He smeared dirt on his face and clothes. He pulled his cap down over his face and put the earbuds for his iPod in his ear and pretended that he was singing. Then he turned on the mower and start cutting the grass. When he came near the front of the house, the man motioned for him to leave. Bruce continued to cut the grass, pretending he couldn't hear or see him, and then he maneuvered the lawn mower to the back of the house. The man followed. Bruce was trying to buy some time until the police come. The man approached Bruce and motioned for him to stop. He pretended as if the mower was malfunctioning. Bruce motioned to the man, trying to tell him that he could not hear him and that he was having a problem with the mower. Then both men came over to Bruce to tell him to turn off the mower and leave. He continued to tinker with the mower until he turned it off. Just as he was leaving, the police broke through the front door. All three men were apprehended. Bruce came inside, gave Eric a hug, and asked if he was all right. Eric reassured him.

"Man, I am so glad I came back when I did. I was talking to my wife and realized I had left my Bible here." He walked over to the table, where he had laid the Bible. "I know it was God who sent me back here. Thank You, Lord, for saving us." When Bruce saw the police put Ling Lee and the men who were with him in the police car, he went over and showed them the Bible and told them, "You see this Bible. You need Christ in your life. I know. He will make a difference like you can never imagine. Wait until I go home and tell my wife what happened to me today. Jesus is using me! Man, I got a chance to witness!" He and Eric gave each other another hug, and Bruce took his Bible and went home, rejoicing in Christ.

Eric's memory was slowing returning as he regained his health and strength. Each time he was able to recall something, he thanked Jesus with the prayer that there was nothing else left for him to recall. He knew he had once lived as a self-centered, self-seeking opportunist. Each day he looked for ways to express his love to his family. He knew there would come a day when their children would leave and start lives and families of their own. His relationship with Denise was the most important thing to him. It was a relationship for a lifetime. He did everything he could to express that sentiment to her. No matter how insignificant or trivial her requests sometimes seemed, he wanted to fulfill them with love.

As Eric was regaining strength, he and Denise worked on getting the nursery ready for their new baby. Even Aaron at times would make a contribution. Denise often would tell her unborn baby how much they were loved.

After her last doctor visit, Denise finalized her plans to go to Las Vegas to attend Amy's wedding. Being away from her family would not be easy. However, she knew she needed this time to get some much needed rest, which would enable her to a better wife and mother. Once Denise passed through security, she had time to rest and wait for her flight to depart. When she was on the plane and sitting in her window seat, she waited for the plane to take off. When the plane was in the air, she sat back in her seat, looked out the window, and thought as she rubbed her stomach. It was comforting to know how God loved her.

* * *

Amy, Gwen, and Sam met her at the airport. They were so glad to see her. Gwen said, "We missed you so much. Denise, you are pregnant! How many months along are you?

"Five months," Denise said. Amy said, "You must tell us everything that has been happening to you, and how are your Nana and Gramps?"

Denise told them that Nana and Gramps were doing fine, but she didn't come out to talk about herself. She wanted to hear all about Amy's fiancée. But they insisted that Denise tell them her story. On Denise's first night there, they stayed up all night, talking. She told them about how Eric was doing and how much he had changed from the time when they had first gotten married. She shared how God had saved his life twice. She filled them in how God had changed her life with him too. They had adopted Aaron, and she was also expecting a baby. She told them how happy she was being a wife and mother. Everyone was so excited.

The next day they went out for breakfast. Denise asked Amy about her fiancée. "What is his name, and how did you meet? How long have you known each other, and how did he pop the question?"

"Well, his name is Robert Webb. We met at a casino in California while we were playing blackjack. We have known each other for a month. He invited me to go to a wedding with him in Vegas, and later he asked me to marry him in an e-mail." Denise couldn't believe her ears. Amy was so happy and excited about getting married.

Amy told Denise that she was glad that she was there in time to help her with the details for the wedding. "Denise, you did such a wonderful job on your wedding, and we know that with your help I will have a great wedding too."

"How many people will be attending?"

"I sent out 150 invitations for the wedding and for the reception."

When Denise learned how much they were spending on the wedding, she asked, "Have you and Robert gone to see a marriage counselor for pre-martial counseling?"

"A marriage counselor! Why do we need to see a marriage counselor? Robert and I love each other. We do not have any problems. Why do you think we need to see a marriage counselor? We were made for each other."

"You are marrying in a week, how much time have the two of you talked about your marriage?"

Gwen said, "What do you mean?"

"Do you want children? If so, how many? Where are you going to live, and what household chores will be done by whom to keep your home organized? Most of all, what church will you attend? If you attend church, will you worship Christ together to learn how to live for Him? Does he believe in Jesus Christ? Do both of you believe this way?"

Gwen and Amy looked at each other as if they did not understand why Denise was saying all those things. Sam said, "Those things are not important right now. She is planning her wedding! The marriage comes later. Denise, no disrespect, but you sound like your grandmother, Nana. Come on. Let's have some fun. Let's have a good time. Here, we want to show you pictures that will give you a glimpse of Amy's wedding dress and the cake."

Sam went to the photo gallery in her phone. She showed them a slideshow of the wedding dress from different angles and the bridesmaid dresses. "Now, see, here is the picture of the beautiful dress she purchased for only ten thousand dollars. An original of Mac Lou O'Brien's, which is one of a kind. Would you believe the flowers for her bouquets are being flown in from Brazil?"

Gwen took out pictures of the wedding cake. "Look, Denise, this is the cake she got. It is an original, created and designed especially for her by one of the top pastry chef in Vegas."

Amy said, "Don't forget to show her the dress I picked for the reception. It is an original as well. I feel just like a celebrity. Money was not an object. No expense was spared."

After they showed her everything, they all said in unison," Denise what do you think? Denise replied simply, "Amy will have a very beautiful and unique wedding. I am sure it will be a day she will always remember. Like Nana said, 'After the wedding comes the marriage … then later, forgiveness.'"

The End.